# Her Dom's Lesson

*Dominic Powers Series, Book 2*

By

A.D. JUSTICE

Missy -

Second chance love is sometimes the sweetest domination!

Lots of love!

ADJustice
xoxo

Missy -

Second chance love is sometimes the sweetest romance!

Lots of Love!

Kathie xoxo

**HER DOM'S LESSON**





Cover design by Kari Ayasha with Cover to Cover Designs.

Front and back images under license from bigstockphoto.com.



ISBN-13: 978-1502458971
ISBN-10: 1502458977

## Books by A.D. Justice

***Steele Security Series***

*Wicked Games (Book 1)*

*Wicked Ties (Book 2)*

*Wicked Intentions (Book 3, Date TBD)*

*Wicked Shadow (Book 4, Date TBD)*

***The Crazy Series***

*Crazy Maybe (Book 1)*

*Crazy Baby (Book 2, Coming early 2015)*

*Crazy Love (Book 3, Date TBD)*

*Crazy Over You (Book 4, Date TBD)*

***Dominic Powers Series***

*Her Dom (Book 1)*

*Her Dom's Lesson (Book 2)*

# Acknowledgements

I want to take a minute to personally thank those who specifically helped with this book.

- First and foremost, I want to thank my Lord and Savior for His continued grace and love.
- My husband and my two "boys", for believing in me and supporting my endeavors, my long nights, and the days I missed time spending with them. I love you with all my heart!
- My friends who stuck by me, through thick and thin: A.M. Madden, Michelle Dare, Tabitha Stokes, Tricia Daniels, J.M. Witt, Skye Turner, Ren Alexander, T.H. Snyder, Chelle Bliss and Kathy Coopmans. I love every one of you!
- My cover designer, Kari Ayasha, who created this gorgeous cover.
- Every member of my Street Team, who tirelessly promotes my books and recommends them to their friends. I love my Wicked Devils!
- My beta readers: Cheryl F., Dana G., Jasmine C., Shannon H., Christine H., Kimberly K., A.M. Madden, and Michelle Dare.
- Every single blogger who supports authors just for the love of the books. You are all rock stars in my book!
- An extra special THANK YOU goes to my PA, Tabitha Charisse. I LOVE YOU! Thank you for cracking the whip, keeping me going, encouraging me, and reading, and re-reading the same passages over and over again. MUAH!!!

# Chapter One

I'm sitting outside his house again, just like I've done almost every night for the past two weeks. It's been eight weeks since I've seen him, talked to him, felt him, or tasted him. It's fucking killing me. All of this is killing me but I feel like I have no way out. I'm in an invisible cell, there are bars all around me, and I'm completely trapped. I feel like I'm suffocating and he is my very breath. Every day, I feel my strength chipping away. One piece at a time, I'm unraveling.

Sudden movement at his lakeside mansion catches my eye and brings me out of my self-loathing pity party. The huge, ornate double front door is standing wide open and in the center of that double door is my Dom. His hair is slightly messy and he's sexy as ever. His blue button down shirt is untucked and he looks is a little disheveled. His feet are bare and he has a glass of his favorite bourbon in his hand. His eyes scan the area but I don't think he sees me.

The air is completely sucked out of my car and out of my lungs. *OH MY GOD. OH MY GOD.* A woman sashays up beside him, wraps her arm around his waist, and leans up to kiss his lips before she walks down the front steps. He leans against the doorjamb and watches her get in her car and drive off. They wave at each other and I watch, unable to tear my eyes away, as he smiles at her.

I recognize that smile instantly and my heart constricts further. *That* smile used to be for me.

My. God.

My heart has just shattered into a million pieces. *Has he replaced me already?*

He continues to watch her car until it disappears into the horizon. All of a sudden, his head jerks in my direction and, even though I originally thought I was in a safe spot, I now know that he's fully aware that I'm here. I feel his eyes on me, the heat radiating off of his muscular body, and the tension is building to unbelievable levels inside my car even though he hasn't moved from his spot. He straightens his body and I can tell from his stance that his eyes are narrowed in anger – at me.

His arm flies up in the air in my direction as his index finger points at me. With a crook of his finger, he demands that I come to him. Heaving a heavy sigh, resigned to the lashing I am about to receive, I put my car in gear and drive the short distance to his lake house, stopping in the circular drive at his front door. Exiting the car on shaky legs, I'm suddenly scared to death of what he'll say. At this point, I would gladly take any physical pain over the mental anguish I've been in. Nothing he could physically do to me would hurt as badly as what he could order me to do.

Such as, leave and never come back.

He is my Dom no matter what has happened. He owns me – heart, body, and mind. If he orders something of me, I will comply regardless of what it is or what it costs me. I know this and this is the very thing that scares me to death. I say silent prayers all the way up the steps to his expansive front porch. He hasn't moved from the doorway but I can feel his eyes burning into me.

I can't raise my eyes to meet his. I mean I physically can't do it. I feel the weight of his stare, I feel the depth of his pain…the pain I caused him…and I know the inner turmoil he is experiencing. He's my Dom and I know him inside and out. I know he still feels it, too. But now he doesn't trust me and without trust…well, I can't let my thoughts go there just yet. It's too painful and I'm too weak to face it just yet.

I stop in front of him and keep my head bowed in hopes that my reverence and submission will earn me at least a little favor with him. The cold, indifferent tone of his voice dashes my hopes and I fight to keep the tears from flowing. Again. All I've done while I've been alone is cry. Sob. Scream. Let my anguish out. Anguish that I am responsible for causing.

"Why. The. Fuck. Are. You. Stalking. Me," he spits out one word at a time at me with such venom, such hatred, it causes my heart to skip a beat before it speeds up to an unnatural pace. I can't pass out now – at least he is *talking* to me, even if it's not what I want to hear.

"Dom, I..." the fear of how he'll react to the truth worries me and I'm not sure I can finish the sentence. Until...

"I asked you a question and I expect an answer." His demand interrupts my thoughts and the submissive in me must meet his expectations.

"Dom, I miss you," my voice is so very soft and fearful. His laugh has no humor in it. It's sarcastic, cold, and mocks me, just as I deserve. "Please don't send me away," I beg.

He steps to the side and from my peripheral vision, I see him extend his hand inside the house, inviting me in. My heart leaps – will my Dom forgive me? Will he take me in and let me tell him everything? *Oh, please, please, let that be the case.*

I enter the room and take ten steps and then stop, just as I've been trained to do in the past. The clicking of the double doors closing sounds behind me but I wait. My Dom walks to the bar in the far corner of the room, removes the stopper in the decanter, pours a drink, replaces the stopper – and then nothing. There are no other sounds – not him taking a drink, not him walking across the room to me, nothing but deathly silence.

My whole body jumps and I can't contain the shrill sound of my startled scream when the crystal tumbler flies by me, crashes into the wall, and splinters into a million pieces just a few feet away. I involuntarily recoil and step back a few steps, until I bump into an immovable wall of muscle. My body instantly reacts, knowing its master. Even though my mind knows my presence here isn't welcome, I can't help but melt into him.

His mouth is suddenly close to my ear. The sweet smell of the bourbon mixed with my Dom warms my skin and causes tingles to rush down my body when he speaks. His baritone voice is lowered in a low, sultry whisper, causing every part of my female anatomy to respond simultaneously and puts me on the verge of combustion.

"You shouldn't be here, Sophia," he croons in my ear before switching to the other side. "What is it you want from me?" He moves my hair from my shoulder, pulling it over to one side and exposing my neck and ear. "What is it your body craves, Sophia?"

I involuntarily moan and arch my neck. My head is tilted back on his chest, which I now realize is bare. *When did he take his shirt off?* His warmth seeps through me and makes me want him even more. He's waiting for my answer and I'm so worked up, I can barely think of how to formulate an answer that won't get me kicked out on my ass.

"Dom, I've missed you. My body craves only you, Dom," I respond honestly. I've lain in bed wide-awake for hours on end, feeling like I'm losing my mind with missing him so badly. It's no less than I deserve, but I am silently begging him to not send me away.

"It's Tuesday," he whispers and I feel his lips against my ear. "You're wearing a short skirt and high heels for me, aren't you?"

"Yes," I answer breathlessly, knowing that every Tuesday, Thursday, and Saturday, I've worn a similar outfit simply because he once requested it of me.

"I wonder, Sophia, if you've met my *entire* command about your outfit," his voice hypnotizes me. His touch brands me once again but his hands haven't touched me except for moving my hair out of the way.

Before I can answer him, I feel his fingers hitching my skirt up one millimeter at a time. The tortuously slow pace is killing me and I'm ready to tear all of my clothes off for him. But, I know that will actually only delay things. This is the way my Dom likes to do things and I love what he does to me.

When he's finally pulled it up far enough, I shiver uncontrollably as his hand reaches between my legs from behind. His finger finds my heated core and gently strokes me back and forth. His mouth is again at my ear and I instinctively lean my head to the side, giving him all the access he wants. His mouth pushes against my ear at the same time his finger thrusts inside of me. He strokes me eagerly as his whispers become louder, "No panties, Sophia. You followed my orders well, my girl. And you're so wet for me – before I've even touched you. I wonder, has my sub missed her Dom?"

His tempo quickly increases and he adds another finger, stretching and filling me. His movements become rougher, exactly as he knows I love it, and I want to squirm. I want to ride out this feeling and I want to give him all the pleasure I can possibly give. But, my Dom has told me before that I'm to remain still until he tells me to move – so that I don't resist the pleasure he's giving me. He pushes me to limits I didn't know I could take and gives me more pleasure than any woman has a right to ask for.

"Yes, Dom, so much," is all I can manage to verbalize. I've missed him more than I could ever explain. More than he could ever know.

The tightening and pressure building inside me is tremendous. Dom has a strict rule about me reaching climax before he tells me it's okay to do so, but I'm seriously considering taking the punishment and just letting it go right now. It has been so long since I've felt his touch that I'm about to burst into flames. My ability to fight it is waning and it's about to happen with or without my consent.

My body is suddenly cold and bare. The warmth of his bare chest is gone. The sweet, warm breath of his whispers has disappeared. His hands are no longer on me, bringing me to the most exquisite pleasure I've ever felt. I'm standing alone in the middle of the room, as if I'm a statue on display, and he has completely retreated from me. The sound of the stopper and decanter are all I hear before the liquid is poured. I hear him swallow one shot. Two shots. Three shots.

Then, he's suddenly behind me again, but he's not touching me. His voice is cold and distant again. He mocks and ridicules me with his next words.

"Do you really think you can just show up here and I'd just take you in? Give you what you want?" His voice becomes more forceful, "Give you pleasure–only for you to fuck me over again? You're out of your fucking mind. Get. Out. Of. My. Fucking. House."

Straightening my skirt, I turn to leave, as he demands. I still can't make eye contact with him.

His blue eyes are probably blazing through me and I can't bear to look at them and see the hurt, the anger, and the hatred toward me. He doesn't understand it–any of it. He doesn't know yet why I had to do what I did and now I'm afraid he will never let me tell him.

Before I reach the door, his parting words shred me to pieces and I don't know if I'll ever recover from them.

"I am not your Dom," he enunciates each word clearly and forcefully, leaving no room for doubt. The sobs wrack my body before I even take the first step out of his home.

*God help me. What have I done?*

*Eight Weeks Earlier*

I'm in my office working on contract negotiation replies but I can't keep my mind focused on what's in front of me. The stress of this whole mess is going to be the death of me. *Death*. That thought alone makes me shudder as the scene of the house fire tortures me, set on an endless loop to repeat in my mind. I drop my face into my hands and fight back the anxiety that threatens to overwhelm me.

Dom was almost killed and I know that was the sole purpose of the fire. I don't believe it was intended for me since I wasn't even supposed to be at his house on Sunday nights. Dom insisted that I stay with him all weekend after we'd been apart during his business trip. The truth is, I wanted to stay with him and never leave, but I knew it would cause trouble in one way or another.

As if my thoughts could conjure the devil himself, my phone rings and my whole body cringes when I hear his voice on the other end.

"Sophia Vasco," his tone is mocking, "are you ready to do your Master's bidding?"

"You are *not* my Master and I've told you for *weeks* that I'm not helping you any more," I spit out at him through gritted teeth.

"Don't talk to me like that, you little bitch," his disgruntled voice yells at me. "I own you and you will do what I fucking tell you to do, when I fucking tell you to do it. You know that man that's been fucking you? Yeah, I got plans for him. I will ruin him one way or another. And you *will* do your part."

Dom has the sexiest Southern drawl I have ever heard. The timbre of his voice changes depending on what he has in mind, but it always soothes, excites, and owns me. Dominic's voice sends shivers down my spine and chill bumps across my skin without even trying. Harrison's drawl and ignorance, on the other hand, only serve to irritate me, grind on my nerves, and evoke feelings of deep resentment.

That is exactly what's happening right now.

"Harrison," I feel the vein in my neck throbbing with my anger, "Leave. Him. Alone. You are wrong about him and I'm not having this conversation with you again."

"Well, well. He's fucked you real good, hasn't he? I bet he's had you every way 'til Sunday, but he's even managed to mind-fuck you, too. How 'bout I give him a call and tell him what you've really been up to? How'd that be?" Harrison laughs as if he's just said the funniest thing ever heard.

I'm not laughing.

"Why don't I save you the trouble and tell him myself?" I throw my free hand up in the air as I ask, gesturing wildly at his crude comments. The fear building in the back of my throat threatens to choke me because the one thing I've feared the most is that Harrison would do just that. I'm scared that he will tell Dom before I get a chance to explain.

I hang up on Harrison, leaving him to wonder if I will really do it or not. It's in this moment that I decide, without a doubt, that I have to tell Dom. He deserves to know the game that's being played, and my part in it, before the next stunt kills him. This scares me more than anything I've ever done - more than running into that burning building, more than what is at stake if I double-cross Harrison, and more than what anyone else will think of me.

If I lose Dom, I don't know if I can recover from it. He has become everything I thought no one would ever be. He is good, kind, and loving. He cared about me, and my safety, before he even really knew me. He moved me out of that awful apartment in the gang territory without a second thought. He's taken me in, shown patience and understanding, and has given more love than anyone I've ever known.

Rising from my desk on shaky legs, I slowly walk down the corridor toward his office. Realizing it's now or never, I have to tell him everything before Harrison calls him first. Knowing that bastard, he would do it just to spite me. As I approach, I hear Tucker and Shadow talking with Dominic but someone steps into the office with them before I reach his door.

It's Cheryl, our corporate lawyer, and suddenly a terrible dread settles over me. Grabbing the wall to keep from falling, I take unsteady steps, painstakingly slow, but I know that this is bad. Something tells me it involves Harrison and that's why he called me at work. I silently pray with every step I take, *Please let it be about something else.* I chant this over and over as I approach his door, but there's no doubt in my mind that it's about me.

As I reach the door, I hear Cheryl describing a sexual harassment lawsuit against Dominic. Her voice is direct as she explains, "This is very serious, Dominic. Those papers name all the employees who have seen and heard inappropriate comments and behavior from you toward Miss Vasco."

The air has just been sucked out of my lungs and I'm incapable of taking another breath. So this is Harrison's next attempt to destroy Dominic, but it also destroys my relationship with him in the process. I haven't given him enough credit at all. Even if he speaks as though he's ignorant, he is apparently very clever when it comes to sticking a knife in someone's back.

Cheryl takes a step into Dominic's office and suddenly I'm in the limelight. All eyes are burning through me, like I'm a rodent to be destroyed and removed from their sight. Dominic gets up from his desk, his muscular body moving toward me with confidence and purpose. His normally warm blue eyes have taken on an icy glare. I try to speak to him as he approaches the doorway, but his murderous look slaps me across the face and renders me mute.

Then he slams the door in my face and I know, without a doubt, Harrison has beaten me to the punch. I've done too little too late. I should've told Dominic a long time ago but it never felt like the right time. In hindsight, there really isn't a good time to tell someone that you were sent there to help destroy him. To make him fall for you so that it would be easier to betray him. To pretend to be his submissive only to prove that he's not really a Dom.

But he is–he's *my* Dom.

I can't catch my breath and I immediately begin hyperventilating. Dana knows what's happening since she heard Cheryl's report, but she comes to my aid anyway. She helps me sit down and talks calmly and soothingly to me until I'm able to focus my vision and control my breathing again. When I look at her, I expect to see hatred and disapproval, but instead I see sympathy and understanding.

"You will have to give him some time, Sophia. He won't be capable of listening to any explanation you have right now," Dana says, as if she knows everything. "In time, he'll hear you out. After that, you'll have to respect his decision, regardless of what it is."

All I can do is nod in agreement. She's right–there's no way he'll listen to me right now. With the cold, angry look he just gave me, there's really no way he'll listen to my side of the story *any time* soon.

# Chapter Two

The worst day of my life happened nearly three weeks ago today. It was my own private D-Day, *Dom-Day*, when I lost my Dom. I haven't seen him since he slammed his office door shut in my face. He is forever etched in my mind and my heart. His muscular build, mixed with his stunningly handsome face, haunts me in my dreams. His blue eyes darken with lust and lighten with laughter. The tattoos that adorn his chest and arm are made of intricate patterns, colors, and shapes. His sexy, smug smile and loving murmurs echo in my mind. My god, my chest physically hurts from the loss I feel.

Cheryl moved my office to another floor so I haven't even been able to *accidentally* run into him. I overheard a couple of the department heads talking earlier and they said he had taken an extended vacation after all he's been through, with the wreck and then the house fire.

They didn't know I was standing there, eavesdropping, trying to garner any possible morsel of information about him. Thankfully, they didn't say anything about his absence being my fault. The gag order is apparently working very well since most of the employees haven't treated me any differently. There are obviously a few who know and I feel their judging, penetrating stares even when they smile and try to act normal.

"No, Dominic had a two-week Caribbean vacation planned. He's back from vacation now," Darren says into the phone. "He's not in the office, Rich. He's on location in Tennessee this week and will be back next week."

My heart is racing and I feel faint. Grabbing onto the doorframe, I steady myself and listen to Darren in this one-sided conversation. "No, Rich, I don't think he will agree to another week away in San Diego so soon. What can I do for you?"

Knowing that Darren will be on the phone for a while with Rich, I retreat back to the solitude of my new office. Sitting in my office alone has become somewhat of a new pastime for me. I still handle all of my work and as much of Dom's work as I can without stirring suspicion, but nothing fully takes my mind off my man. The same thoughts are constantly flowing through my mind and they're driving me insane. Dropping my head into my hands, I squeeze my eyes shut and try to block them out, but just like every other time, it doesn't work.

*Is it really over between us?*

*Did he stop loving me?*

*Will I never touch his face again?*

*What will I do if I've lost him forever?*

"Sophia, did you hear me?" a male voice booms from my door.

Quickly jerking my head up, I realize it probably appeared as if I was asleep on the job and I slump down into my chair even more. "No, Darren, I'm sorry. My head is killing me. What did you say?"

His eyes soften and his voice changes to reflect his empathy for me, and my obvious pain.

"I'm sorry, Sophia. I didn't mean to shout and make it worse."

"You didn't," I reply warmly. "What can I do for you, Darren?"

"Rich Daltry with *D-Force Games* called. That man is impossible. I don't know how Dominic deals with him," Darren rambles. "Anyway, can you pull this contract and double check the language we included regarding last minute changes?"

"Sure, Darren. I'm certain of what was included, but I'll double check it anyway and get it right back to you."

"No rush," Darren laughs. "Let him stew until tomorrow. I'm not calling him back today."

Giving Darren a small smile and nod before he leaves, I can't help but compare him to my Dom. Where Darren wants nothing to do with the negotiation and the argumentative side of this business, Dominic thrives on it and readily accepts the challenge. The differences in their personalities couldn't be more apparent, but they do complement each other very well. Just the mere thought of Dom in contract negotiations brings back memories of our trip to San Diego, when everything between us started.

The pain is so intense that it feels like my chest will split in two. I raise my hand to cover my chest like that will help ease the pain in some way. My desperation is at the breaking point and my hand reaches for the phone receiver. It's become a physical need and a compulsion–I have to hear his voice just one more time. It's been so long and it's killing me.

I can't say goodbye. No matter how wrong I've been in all of this. I can't let him go without fighting with everything in me. Dominic is everything I've always wanted, nothing I've ever had, and the very man I never believed existed. No man in my life has ever been so good, so kind, and so loving to me. He gave me all of him and I took it. I just took it from him and I hurt him, I hurt myself, and I lost the only man I will ever love.

Quickly dialing his cell phone number before I lose my nerve, I listen as it rings and pray that he answers, that he doesn't answer, that it goes to voicemail, or that he just walks into my office and takes me away from all of this. My mind is so screwed up, I can't think straight when it comes to him. The only thing I can focus on is work and that's because I want him to be proud of me again.

"Dominic Powers," his rich voice answers.

Caught in my inner turmoil, I forgot the phone was even still ringing. He's really there – he answered my call. Then I realize that the only number that would've shown on his caller ID is the main exchange at DPS. He wouldn't have any way of knowing it was me calling, and of course he would take a call from his own company's phone number.

"Hello? Anyone there?" he asks, his voice slightly agitated at having to ask twice.

Frantically trying to think of any reason to speak to him, my mind comes up completely blank. I have no valid reason for calling him, nothing that wouldn't be completely transparent in my intentions. Then it hits me, I *need* to be completely transparent with him now. He needs to know how I feel and I need him to hear me out completely.

Before I can speak, he sighs heavily, "Sophia? Is that you?"

"Dominic, I need to talk to you," I finally squeak out.

"Is this about work?" he asks, but his voice doesn't hold any hatred or disgust. That fact alone gives me hope.

"Not exactly. I just need one chance to talk to you and tell you everything. I miss you so much, Dominic," I blurt out before I can stop myself.

"Miss Vasco. We are colleagues. That's all," he replies, his tone says there is no room for argument. He's made up his mind and there's nothing I can do to change it.

"To be effective colleagues, there are some things that we need to discuss," I rephrase my original message. Trying a different tactic may work, but in all honesty, all I'm feeling right now is desperation.

"I will consult my attorney and get her guidance on the matter," he replies dryly, shredding my heart all over again. "She may agree to it if she's present."

"Anything, Dominic," I agree. "Whatever you say, I will do."

There is complete silence for a full thirteen seconds. It is the longest thirteen seconds of my life. The only way I know he hasn't hung up on me is because I can still hear the background noise. My fingers grip the phone receiver tightly, holding on for dear life and praying this is my life preserver, saving me before I sink into the black water below.

"I wouldn't count on it, Miss Vasco," Dominic finally says. "Goodbye."

The line goes dead and I wish I were dead along with it. I have nothing now.

Spending the rest of the day reviewing every word of the *D-Force Games* contract, I am confident in the soundness of the language. Rich Daltry is panicking and grasping for straws, but I copy the necessary sections, highlight the appropriate wording, and leave the paperwork on Darren's desk. He's already gone for the day, as are most of the others, but I just can't bring myself to leave yet.

Sitting alone in the executive condo is just not my idea of fun. I'm hiding from my life by working as much as possible. But, my life is the very man who owns this business and being here doesn't help me forget him. There's no way I can win. The pull to go to Dominic's office is too strong for me to resist. Silently, I approach his door and turn the handle. It's unlocked and dark inside, so I flip on the lights.

His large, oak desk sits proudly in his office and it mocks me. So many memories of my Dom and me on that desk flood my mind and my heart. Tears escape my eyes even though I thought there was no way I could cry ever again. Wrapping my arms around me, I hug myself tightly and just let the tears roll and fall where they may. Sitting in his chair, I can still smell his manly Armani cologne and I curl up in a ball.

It's well past dark before I leave the office building. That's fine with me since it gives me less time alone in the condo before I come back to work tomorrow. Making the drive back on autopilot, I'm pulling into my parking spot before I even realize I left the office parking lot. No radio, no music, nothing to distract me from this pain.

Just as I reach my condo door, my cell phone starts ringing. My only hope is that it's Dominic calling me back to tell me he'll hear me out. I dig my phone out of my purse in a hurried frenzy and my heart drops when I see the name on my display.

*Harrison.*

At first, I decide to ignore it but I know Harrison. He'll just keep calling and calling until I answer. I'd rather get it over with now and have the rest of the night to be left alone. Hitting the green button, my voice is hollow as I answer.

"What do you want?"

"That's no way to speak to your Sir, Sophia. You will be punished for that," he threatens.

I don't care. But, I don't respond and give him the satisfaction of threatening me again.

"So, where's Dominic?" Harrison asks, drawing out my Dom's name in a mocking tone.

"What do want with him, Harrison? I've already told you that I'm not helping you with anything ever again. I'm done. Find someone else to threaten."

"Oh, no, little girl, that's not how it works. You signed the contract so you belong to me. I am your Sir," Harrison taunts.

"I've learned a thing or two about submissive contracts, Harrison, and that one is not a real contract," I challenge him. "You are not a real Sir. You are not my Dom. Don't call me again."

"You think your precious Dominic is just perfect, don't you? I bet he fed you some bullshit line about my sister committing suicide, didn't he? Said the police found a note. He's *lying*, Sophia. He killed her and he'll kill you, too, as soon as he gets the chance."

This is the story that Harrison has told me since I met him. It's never changed from this version. Harrison is convinced that Dominic killed Carol Ann and he had convinced me of that at one point in time. He's wanted revenge on Dominic for his sister's death. But, Dominic says that Carol Ann committed suicide by jumping from their twenty-third floor balcony. Could Dominic really have killed her? I can't believe that. Ever.

"I read the suicide note, Harrison. It wasn't a bullshit line," I reply, but my words lack conviction.

"Did the note say that she was committing suicide, Sophia? Did she write the words? Did she even say goodbye? She didn't leave a note for our parents or for me! Do you know how hard that's been on us for the past year and a half? We know she didn't do it on purpose! We know *he* is to blame. But he covered it up with his money and his connections," Harrison continues to try to persuade me.

"I have proof that he did it, Sophia. I'm taking it to the police and he'll be arrested when he gets back from his little trip. He will finally go down for what he did to my sister!" Harrison yells.

"What proof?" I ask, sitting up straight and suddenly interested in what he has to say.

"Like I'd tell you so you can run and tell him," he sneers. "You need to come over and see it for yourself. Make up your own mind. But, you'll see,

Sophia. You'll see that I've been telling the truth the whole time."

"I'm not coming over to your house, Harrison," I refuse.

"Okay. End up dead like Carol Ann, then. Who do you want me to notify to come identify *your* body?"

Sighing my resignation, "Fine, Harrison. I will come by and see your so-called proof. Then I'm leaving and you will leave me alone."

"Whatever," he replies with contempt. "Just be here tomorrow night at nine o'clock after I get off from work."

"I mean it, Harrison. After this, you have to leave me alone."

"Yeah, you said that," he snaps before hanging up on me.

I've been on autopilot at work again today. My mind knows I have to find a way out of this funk, but there's nothing to make me happy. I somehow make it through the hum-drum day that has become my existence and I'm on my way back to my condo before I remember that I'm supposed to go to Harrison's house tonight. Groaning in frustration and exasperation, my mind wages an inner war on whether I should go. At the last minute, I decide to get it over with and hold him to his word to never bother me again.

He calls for me to enter when I knock on his door and I walk through the darkened house to find him. "Harrison?" I call out into the blackness.

"In here," his muffled voice calls from the bedroom.

I approach cautiously, obviously not trusting him as far as I can throw him. When I enter his room, I feel his arms encircle me from behind, the awful stench of his breath flows across my cheek as his puts his mouth close to my ear.

"It's about time you got here, little girl," he scoffs. "You've kept me waiting long enough."

The stale stench of cigarettes and whiskey permeate his breath and I have to consciously stop my gag reflex from taking over. Twisting and turning, I try my damnedest to break free from his grip but he just keeps squeezing tighter. The panic starts welling up deep inside my chest. I know what's coming next. He's going to tie me up and do whatever he wants to me. The very thought of him touching me makes me sick to my stomach.

"Don't you worry, sweetheart," he jeers. "Ol' Harrison has plenty for you. I need to finish up with her first," he inclines his head towards the bed.

In the darkness, I can just barely make out a figure lying on the bed. My stomach roils and I have to consciously fight back the urge to vomit. There's another woman in his bed. She's tied up and has a ball-gag in her mouth. I can't see her face very well since my eyes haven't adjusted to the dim light yet, but from her frequent sniffles, I know she's crying.

Harrison suddenly jerks me up in the air and I wildly kick my legs, trying to come into contact with any important part of his anatomy. He's so strong, and I'm so weak from not eating, that I'm no match for him at all. He deposits me into a chair that's directly in front of the bed and he slaps me hard across the face. It temporarily stuns me as he straps me in so tightly that I can't move at all. The taste of coppery blood fills my mouth, and uncaring where I am, I spit it out in the floor of Harrison's bedroom.

This earns me a slap across the other side of my face.

"You stupid bitch!" he yells. "You'll clean that up before we're done here."

He climbs back over the silent form on lying on the bed and I hear her whimper as he settles in between her legs. "Sophia gets to watch us, baby. She knows she has to share me. I'm too much man for one woman to handle."

As I think back over all these encounters he's made me watch when he brought other women home to fuck them, it makes me sick all over again. Harrison said this is how it was supposed to be. But now I know better. I know that my Dom would never do this to me. He explained to me how it should be, he showed me what real love is, and he promised I'd never have to share him and he'd never share me.

The only thing that's running through my mind now is how I can get out of this house before Harrison finishes with her and starts with me. He removes her ball-gag and she begins moaning in pleasure. Bored, I look around the room and let my eyes adjust to the darkness more. Leaning my head back, I close my eyes and feign indifference as I work relentlessly at freeing my hands.

My wrists are raw from the constant rubbing of the insides of the restraints, but I've managed to get one hand free. Harrison's grunts are gaining in volume and tempo, so I know he's close to finishing this round and I don't have much time. Tugging and pulling on the other restraint, I finally free my other hand and bend to unfasten the ones around my ankles as quickly as possible.

Harrison rolls over off the other woman and folds his arm across his eyes. Within a few seconds, he's snoring and she's out like a light, giving me time to get free and escape from the house before he wakes up. Moving silently through the house, I open the front door just as I hear Harrison yelling for me. Running in a dead heat, I think I'm in the clear as I reach my car when I'm suddenly yanked backward by my hair.

"You're not going anywhere, bitch!" he growls in my ear. "It's your turn, sweetheart."

I scream at the top of my lungs and he twirls me around, backhanding me across the face and knocking me to the ground. There is only blackness and bright starbursts in my vision field now. Sluggishly trying to move, I feel like I'm watching a slow motion film where I'm the main character. I feel a hard thud and realize I'm knocked back to the ground as he continues to hit me and his hand wraps around my throat. Suddenly, Harrison is lying on top of me, tearing at my clothes with one hand while squeezing my throat with the other.

When I think back to all the abuse I've endured at this man's hands, all under the guise of being a Sir who loves me and was training me, I feel more than foolish, stupid, and naive. I don't even know where to begin to start fixing this mess now, but I know I don't have the strength to fight him off any longer. I'm dizzy from all the blows to the head.

I'm fatigued from lack of food and I just don't care any more.

I've dealt with all that I can take.

Harrison's screams fill the night and I struggle to open my swollen eyes. I have no idea what's happening now. All I know is I'm confused, dazed, and heartbroken. A familiar voice calls to me, low and soothing, telling me to hold on and that help is on the way.

I must be hallucinating or dreaming. I know that voice, but I know it can't really be his.

# Chapter Three

A large hand grips mine when I try to move. The familiar male voice whispers to me, "Be still, Sophia. I'll be right back." I feel him move away from my side, but that's the only indication that he's moved away from me. His footsteps are silent and stealthy. He's clearly in his element in the dark of the night.

I'm lying on something very uncomfortable and it's sticking into my back. Although I'm not sure I can sit up, I know I need to get out of here before Harrison comes after me again. I hear tires screeching and then sirens in the distance, but everything's so jumbled, nothing really makes sense to me. Somewhere in my mind, I know I need to run as far away from here as possible. My body just doesn't seem to want to cooperate with me.

"Be still, Sophia. The ambulance is almost here," he says as I feel him at my side again. "Harrison got away. But, don't you worry, I'll find him."

Struggling to open my eyes, it feels like they're both covered with something heavy and sticky. I manage to force one eye open and I search for the owner of the comforting voice. My vision is fuzzy and there's not much light, but I immediately recognize the shape of his body. The timbre of his voice suddenly clicks in my head. But, it still doesn't make sense.

"Tucker?" My voice barely squeaks. My throat is so raw and sore when I try to speak.

"I'm here, Sophia," he replies, his voice thick with concern. For Tucker to sound concerned, I know I must look pretty awful.

"How?" I whisper.

"Don't talk right now, Sophia. The ambulance and police are pulling up. We can talk later. We need to get you to the hospital."

Tucker rises to meet the paramedics and deputies as they pull up at Harrison's house. Whatever I landed on is still sticking in my back and I try to roll over again, but I should've known that Tucker's hawk vision wouldn't have strayed from watching me. Before I can even push up from the hard ground, he's back at my side and the medics are rushing over with the gurney.

"Where do you think you're going?" Tucker asks in his take-no-prisoners tone.

"Fell on something," I whisper in an attempt to explain my predicament.

"They're about to pick you up, Sophia. Just wait one more minute."

Since I don't really have a choice right now, and I'm unable to do it on my own anyway, I do as he instructs. They check me out thoroughly before rolling me over and slipping the backboard underneath me. After I'm securely fastened to it, I'm lifted on to the gurney and thrust into the back of the ambulance.

"I will meet you at the hospital, Sophia. I'm following right behind you in my truck," Tucker calls out from the back door of the ambulance.

"Girl," I urgently whisper.

"What girl?" the medic asks, clearly perplexed but also concerned.

"Inside," I manage to respond before one medic rushes out of the back of the ambulance.

The cop stops him, "I have to clear the house first. Wait here." He unsnaps his gun from its holster and moves quickly toward the house. After a few minutes, the cop returns to the front door and yells for the paramedic to come with him. Tucker sternly instructs the second paramedic to stay with me as he also runs toward the house. A few minutes later, I hear a call come across the radio requesting a second ambulance for this address, telling me they found the girl that Harrison left inside.

I exhale a sigh of relief. I'm so thankful for the help and care I'm receiving. This gurney isn't the most comfortable, but it's so much better than the hard, rocky ground where Tucker found me. I know there'll be questions for me later–from the cops and the paramedics. But the ones from Tucker are the ones I dread the most. These are my last thoughts as I allow the darkness behind my eyelids to overtake me.

The hissing of the oxygen flowing is the first sound I hear as I wake from the best sleep I've had in weeks. The mask over my face immediately makes me feel claustrophobic and I clumsily fumble to rip it off my face. A large, warm hand gently wraps around mine and stills my movements.

"Sophia," Tucker says softly, "let me."

Gladly lowering my hand, I let Tucker pull the mask down my face to my neck. I can still feel the oxygen flowing, and knowing Tucker, this is his way of compromising with me. The chair scraping across the floor is my notice that he's moved his chair closer to my bed.

"Where?" I whisper and immediately wince. My throat is raw and my neck muscles are sore, even the slight movement from trying to talk is extremely painful.

"You're in Baylor Medical Center, Sophia. You're very lucky. We came in last night and you've been in here for about eighteen hours now. You've had an MRI, a CT scan, and X-rays, but the good news is there's no permanent damage. You have a lot of soft tissue damage– like bruising and swelling –that will take time to heal, but no brain bleeds or anything permanent," he quickly explains and I try to grasp what he is telling me.

No permanent damage is the general gist of his message and I'm happy with that for now.

"Your voice will take a couple of weeks to get back to normal. Harrison was choking you and the pain you feel is from the swelling inside. The doctor said you have to keep from talking as much as possible or it'll delay your healing."

I nod and gloomily think that I have no one to talk to anyway, so that really doesn't matter. The thought of Harrison getting to me when I can't scream for help fills me with fear, though. Trying to open my eyes is another feat that feels impossible.

My lids feel like they're weighted down with cement blocks and, again, I only manage to open one eye.

"Your eyes are really swollen, Sophia. You have some pretty bad shiners. That's why you're having such a hard time opening your eyes. Once the swelling goes down, your vision will be back to normal," Tucker explains in a way that's much more gentle than I'm accustomed to hearing from the big brute. This fact alone tells me that I must look even worse than I feel.

"When?" I ask, trying to keep my questions to single words and just hope that he understands my intent. Tucker doesn't disappoint me.

"When will you go home?" he asks to clarify and I nod my head. "That's up to the doctor. She really didn't give me a lot of information since I'm not family. I didn't know who to call for you," he says, almost apologetically.

I just slowly– and carefully –shake my head from side to side to tell him there's no one to call. There's no one to care about me. No one will come running to my side to make sure I'm still alive.

"Just rest now, Sophia. You're safe," Tucker reassures me.

My eyes are closed but my mind is racing. Everything has spiraled out of control and I'm not sure it can even be contained now. Harrison has royally screwed me over and I've allowed it. I helped it. Every day, I had an opportunity to put an end to this whole charade and I didn't take it. To that end, I have to take responsibility for my actions and accept that I've lost the love of my life.

The door to my hospital room opens, creating a distinctive clicking and creaking noise that I recognize without even opening my eye. There's no point in looking to see who it is. My family doesn't know, and wouldn't care, that I'm in here. My Dom has severed all personal ties with me, so I know it's not him. If it happened to be Harrison, I know that Tucker would protect me. Most likely, it's hospital personnel making their rounds.

"Miss Vasco," an authoritative female voice calls my name. "I'm Dr. Fallon and I've been overseeing your care since you were brought in last night."

I force my good eye open and give her a nod of understanding. Moving to sit up straighter is painful, but I know from experience it'll only get worse if I don't start moving now. Tucker rises from his seat and raises the head of my bed as I readjust my position to face the doctor.

"Would you mind excusing us?" Dr. Fallon asks Tucker directly.

"Not at all," Tucker responds. "I'll be right outside, Sophia. No need to worry."

"Thank you," my voice croaks as I momentarily forget I can't speak.

Dr. Fallon notices and promises, "Your voice will return in time. It's best that you not strain it until then. Use low whispers when you must talk. I'll try to phrase most of my questions as a '*yes or no*' to make it easier on you."

I nod and give her a small smile since anything else is too painful right now. In watching her confidence and poise, it occurs to me that I've spent way too much of my life being a victim to someone else. Not all of it was my fault, but somewhere along the way, a pattern has emerged and I don't like it at all. It's way past time for me to be strong, stand on my own two feet, and face the future with my chin held high.

Dr. Fallon takes the seat Tucker vacated and reviews the information in my chart before speaking. "Your eyes look a little more swollen today, but that's normal. The swelling will start subsiding now and your vision will return. Your MRI and CT scans were all normal, so there's no permanent damage. You probably feel like you've been run over by a car, though," she finishes with a smile.

I nod and whisper, "Yes!"

"On a scale of one to ten, with ten being the worst, what's your pain level today?"

"Four or five," I whisper. My injuries hurt, no doubt, but it's not the worst pain I've ever felt.

"Miss Vasco, I haven't prescribed you any strong pain medications because your blood work indicates you're pregnant. Were you aware of this?"

I'm stunned speechless. Even if I were able to talk, scream, or yell, there's no way I could. I shake my head, not in response to her question, but in response to my own inner turmoil. Did I just hear her correctly? *I'm pregnant?*

*What. The. Fuck?*

"I take it you didn't know yet," Dr. Fallon presumes. Correctly.

When I look at her, my bottom jaw is still on the floor, my heart is beating erratically, and my head just slowly moves from side to side of it's own accord. My hands draw together in my lap, my fingers wringing each other relentlessly as I try to calm my heart.

"When was your last period? How many weeks ago? You can hold up fingers if you need to," she instructs.

"Calendar?" I whisper and she hands me her phone after pulling up the calendar app on it. I scroll back through the dates, counting back and trying to remember when it was. I point to the week and realize it was just over six weeks ago, right before the time when my whole life fell apart.

Holding my throat for support, I whisper to her, "Lighter than usual."

"Are you on the pill?"

"No. Implant," I whisper and point to my arm. My short answers will have to work for now or I'll have to start writing out the answers. My anxiety is making my throat constrict even more than before and even whispering is becoming more difficult.

The knowing look on her face concerns me. "Are you sure the implant didn't come out on its own? Did you doctor specifically feel for it and tell you it was in place?"

I think back and try to remember the specifics of that day. "No," I whisper. He simply gave me an injection to deaden the area, made a small incision to insert it, and walked out of the room when he was finished. He didn't touch my incision site after he inserted the implant.

She examines my arm, feeling around the area where it should be. She manipulates my arm into different positions as she continues her examination. Her face gives nothing away but I think I've been holding my breath the entire time. What is she going to tell me?

"There's no implant in your arm, Sophia," Dr. Fallon explains. "The implant is small and has to be placed in a specific location for the best benefits. Your doctor should have felt of the site immediately afterward and ensured it had been inserted correctly. I don't feel it anywhere in your arm, which leads me to believe it was either never fully inserted or it fell out immediately after the procedure."

Sitting in stunned silence, the only recurring thought I have is that Dom will never believe me. He'll think I lied about the whole thing just to trap him with a pregnancy. My anxiety is increasing by the moment.

Dr. Fallon makes some notations in my chart before returning her gaze to me. "Based on this information, you are somewhere between four to eight weeks pregnant, but I'm leaning more to the six-week timeframe. That's probably why your menstrual cycle was lighter than usual during that time. Your obstetrician will be able to pinpoint a more exact time with an ultrasound.

"As far as everything else, you're very fortunate that it's soft tissue damage only. That takes a while to heal, too, but you'll fully heal without a problem. You won't feel like working for the next couple of weeks so I'll give you a doctor's excuse. Is there anything else you need?"

*Yes, but you can't help me with that, doc.*

Shaking my head *'no,'* I whisper, "Thank you."

"It'll take a little while for the discharge papers to be finished. Do you have a ride home?" she asks and then looks at the door to my room.

"Don't tell him!" I whisper urgently to her as my swollen eyes dart between her and the door.

"I won't, and I'll tell the nurses to make sure to keep it quiet, too, when they review your discharge instructions," she assures me as she walks to the door. Stopping, she faces me, suddenly suspicious, "Did *he* do this to you?"

I aggressively shake my head from side to side and instantly regret it. "No. Saved me."

Her demeanor softens as she considers my words. "He's a good man, then. He'll understand when you're ready to tell him."

I don't have it in me to explain why Tucker isn't the baby's father or why he can't find out that I'm pregnant yet. This situation just became so much more fucked up, so much harder to deal with, and so much more important to me in the span of two little words.

*You're pregnant.*

I'm pregnant.

I may actually hyperventilate now.

Tucker appears at the door with a bag that he didn't have with him before he left my room. I look at the bag and back up at him quizzically. Without saying a word, he knows what I'm asking him.

"Dana came by and brought you a change of clothes. She said she brought some pajamas that would be 'suitable for the hospital,' whatever the hell that means," Tucker scrunches up his brow as he looks down at the bag in his hand. "She said there are some other things in here that you need, too. What did the doctor say?"

"Home," I whisper my one-word answer to him. I'm going back to the condo, with a baby growing inside me, and no way to tell the father.

"Now?" he asks, surprise laces his tone and facial features. That's an unusual reaction for Tucker, the normally calm, cool, and collected former military man.

I nod and hold out my hand for the bag. Tucker steps outside the door and closes it behind him so I can get dressed. Dana has impeccable taste in clothes and has sent the best possible pajama set for the hospital. The fabric blend of the light green set makes it flow freely against my skin. The nurse walks in just in time to remove my IV catheter and help me put my shirt on. She reviews the discharge information while Tucker is still in the hall, so I don't have to worry about him hearing anything about making an OB/GYN appointment.

"Who will be responsible for driving you home today?" the nurse asks a standard protocol question. It should be easy to answer and is for most everyone else. When I don't attempt to answer, she looks up at me and I shrug my shoulders. She quickly walks to the door and calls Tucker back inside. "Will you be taking Miss Vasco home today?" she asks him pointedly.

"Yes," he responds and looks up at me for verification. Smiling at him in appreciation, I nod at him and move to stand up. Dana has also included matching house shoes with my clothes and the nurse helps steady me as I slide my feet in one at a time.

"Have a seat while I get the wheelchair, Miss Vasco," she instructs. Turning to Tucker, she says, "Pull your vehicle up to the front door, under the awning. We'll meet you there in a jiffy."

Tucker obviously doesn't want to leave me unattended even for a minute. He looks conflicted for a moment but he finally relents when I motion with my hands to shoo him away. "I'm okay," I whisper to him.

He stands in the doorway until he sees the nurse returning with the wheelchair. "Here she comes. I don't like leaving you, Sophia. But, it's either here in your room or outside the hospital. I'd rather it be here if it has to be at all. Don't leave without the nurse," he levels me with his gaze.

"Okay," I respond. After he leaves, I realize that my hand had instinctively covered my stomach while he was talking. His concern for my safety was evident in his voice and actions. My innate concern for my baby resulted in my unconscious effort to protect him.

It was never my intention to become pregnant. When I tell Dom, he'll automatically think I've tried to trap him. He will doubt that it's his baby. Knowing these things is one thing. When it actually happens, when he actually accuses me of it and turns me and our baby away, will be another thing. *That* will be the worst pain I've ever felt in my life. That will be my twenty on a scale of one to ten.

*Holy shit. I'm pregnant!*

# Chapter Four

"That looks like him now," the nurse says as Tucker pulls up to the front door of the hospital where we are already waiting for him.

I chanced a glance in the mirror before we left my room to smooth my bed hair down. The angry purple, black, and red bruises and swelling startled me. Knowing it must have been bad simply by the way Tucker reacted to seeing me, I tried to prepare myself. When I actually saw it for myself, it made me feel sick. I ran quickly my fingers through my hair and pulled it around my face to hide as much as possible.

Thankfully, it's a slow time of day, so there aren't many people coming and going at the moment. Tucker jumps out and jogs around to open my door for me. "All set?" he asks and I all I can do is nod in reply.

Even after everything that's happened, he's still the consummate professional. I would never know he despised me if I didn't know how loyal he is to Dominic. He helps me into the cab of the truck and I gingerly put my seatbelt on.

When Tucker takes his place in the driver's seat, I croak out, "Car?"

"I had your car picked up and taken back to your condo. It's fine and there whenever you're ready for it," Tucker replies in pure business mode.

"Thanks," I whisper and Tucker gives me a single nod response. He's not accustomed to being thanked for doing his job, but I feel like he's gone above and beyond the call of duty in the last couple of days.

As he drives, thoughts of Dominic flood my mind. My only link to him is sitting next to me and I can't speak. Literally – I have no voice to ask about Dominic. *Where is he? Is he doing okay? Does he miss me? Will he ever hear me out and let me explain everything?* I know I deceived him and that was one of his hard limits. Hard limits are established so that they are never breached. Trust is absolutely non-negotiable in this relationship, but he taught me that trust has to be shared between us. It was never meant to be a one-way street.

I have to know if forgiveness is also part of this relationship.

I can't take it any longer and the need for answers completely overcomes me. "Dominic?" My eyes plead with Tucker when his head jerks in my direction. His eyes leave the road for a second as he scrutinizes me. I tilt my head to the side and reach to touch his arm. My hope is the contact will remind him of the times that I wasn't the enemy.

"He's still out of town. He doesn't know about this, Sophia," Tucker tries to give an ambiguous answer, but it's crystal clear to me.

Dominic doesn't know because Tucker was only told to follow me, check my whereabouts, and determine if there was anything he could use against me. Dominic doesn't want to know anything personal about me. He only wants to know of anything that could possibly help him with this lawsuit. The fact that my former Sir just beat the shit out of me wouldn't have any direct bearing, except to add fuel to the fire of not trusting me.

Leaning my head back on the headrest, I release a deep sigh, hoping it conveys everything that I can't say–even if I wanted to. But, I won't put Tucker on the spot or make him feel like he's in the middle in any way. Not that there's any contest as far as loyalties go, but I think he feels a sense of responsibility for me in my current state.

"How long will you be out of work?" Tucker asks, back to strictly business. He glances over at me and I hold up two fingers.

"Two weeks?" he asks to clarify and I nod my head. "Okay, Dana has delivered your laptop to your condo along with all the files on your desk. If you need anything else from the office, just email her and she can send the courier to deliver it to you. You obviously won't be able to take any calls, so Dana will distribute a statement to let people know your only mode of contact will be email. When you feel up to it, you'll be able to work from your condo."

For anyone else, working from home would be a dream come true. For me, it feels like an unfortunate set of circumstances that'll prevent me from seeing Dominic even longer. Catching Tucker's eye, I incline my head toward him, silently conveying my gratitude for everything. I can only hope the he understands as he watches me intently.

"Sophia," he says, his voice pained. "I don't -," and he stops speaking. He's frustrated and I instantly know he wants an explanation for everything that has come to light in the last few weeks. "I don't understand what happened. Or, I guess I should say why it happened."

He ponders his statement for a few seconds before amending it again. "No, I don't understand *what or why*, to be honest with you," he sounds more pissed off now. "Why would you do this to Dominic? He was good to you. He took care of you. He *loved* you, Sophia."

Hearing that word used in past tense shreds me inside.

He sighs loudly, "I thought you loved him, too. You fooled all of us."

I vehemently shake my head from side to side. "No!" I try to yell but my voice doesn't cooperate and I immediately grab my throat in pain. But, it's not that pain that I care about at the moment. "I love him!" I try to tell him.

"Don't talk anymore. I shouldn't have said anything, especially knowing you're not supposed to talk. It just really bothers me."

Grabbing his arm, I squeeze it until he looks at me. I mouth the words to him again, "I love him!"

Tucker turns into the front drive of the condo and puts the truck in park. He sits silent for a minute as he considers the phrasing of the bomb he's about to drop on me. "If you loved him, you wouldn't have used him like that, Sophia. You wouldn't have kept another man hidden just so you could file a sexual harassment lawsuit against him and demand a lot of money to keep it out of court and the media."

My eyebrows draw inward and my mouth drops open. "What?" I strain to speak, my vocal chords growing increasingly more sensitive by the second. "No!" I don't want his money, or to hurt him, or to take him to court. I don't understand what all is happening. All I know is that Harrison is behind it, pulling the strings, and orchestrating the whole charade from behind the scenes.

"Let's get you inside so you can rest. You've had a rough twenty-four hours. Maybe you should reconsider your relationship with Harrison Dictman," Tucker says with barely masked condescension in his tone.

I want to scream, deny every allegation, and explain what started this whole mess, but no one is listening. No one can hear me over all the noise this situation has created. Tucker exits the truck and comes around to help me out. He grabs what few possessions I have with me and escorts me up to the condo.

Once inside my unit, he says, "I think it would be best if we just say you have some personal medical issues to attend to, if anyone persists in asking for you. Otherwise, when you feel able, you can do everything through email."

I nod in agreement. What else can I do anyway? After Tucker leaves, I pull out my hospital discharge papers and consult the over the counter pain medications I can safely take during pregnancy. The nurse also wrote that gargling with warm salt water might help soothe my throat, so that is my first order of business. Not being able to talk is the fucking pits.

After sleeping with a frozen gel pack over my eyes all night, the swelling is considerably better this morning. The bruising is still just as ugly, but there's nothing I can do but let time and vitamin C heal it. Since I can't talk enough to call anyone, I decide to drive to my doctor's office to make an appointment.

Arriving just as the doors are unlocked, I approach the receptionist's desk. Her smile quickly fades as she takes in my injuries. I give her a rueful smile and, after the best round of charades ever played, I have successfully conveyed my situation and what I need. A few clicks on her computer and a few seconds later, her smile spreads across her face.

"We had a cancellation call late yesterday afternoon and that spot hasn't been filled. I can get you in with Dr. Tabitha Perry right now. Do you feel up to doing it now?"

Nodding eagerly, I can't hide my excitement. I'm so ready to be checked out and hope to get some reassurance that the baby wasn't injured. Before bed last night, I wrote out several questions for the doctor to answer for me. In hindsight, I probably should've done the same for the poor receptionist, too. She hands me a stack full of paperwork to complete and I take my seat in the waiting room. Taking a blank sheet of paper with me, I jot down the pertinent details of my injuries since I know I'll be asked about them more than once.

As I'm filling in the blanks in the patient chart paperwork, a thought pops into my head from nowhere and I have a moment of panic. *Is Tucker still following me? Does he know I'm here?* Shaking my head to clear the thoughts, it occurs to me that there's no doubt he is patiently waiting outside. Just because I'm in my OB/GYN's office doesn't automatically mean he would know I'm pregnant.

Still, I'm sure he is uber-diligent and thorough with his research of me now that I've betrayed Dominic. These thoughts continue to haunt me as I finish all the paperwork and turn it in to Shelly, the receptionist. I'm lost in my own thoughts of how Tucker feels betrayed by me, but he also must think *he* let Dominic down. That somehow he didn't do his job and protect Dominic from me. When all this started, I never considered all the implications of my actions. My tunnel vision blinded me, keeping me from seeing the truth, and I made the worst decision of my life.

"Sophia Vasco," the nurse calls from the doorway.

Standing, I walk toward her and, as expected, she looks at me with dire concern. "What happened to you?" she exclaims, her voice thick with concern.

Handing her the detailed note I wrote, her eyes quickly scan the details and her head occasionally nods as she takes the information in. When she finishes reading, she looks up and smiles at me.

"No talking, huh?"

Pursing my lips to show my frustration with it, I shake my head from side to side in response.

"I had laryngitis once that lasted for a month! I know a little of how frustrating it is to not be able to speak," she sympathizes. "No worries. We'll take good care of you."

I'm escorted to the lab area to have blood drawn and the lab technician hands me a cup and shows me to the bathroom. Once I'm in the patient room, the nurse regurgitates everything for the doctor. After enduring the usual pelvic examination, and a lot of note taking by Dr. Perry, she helps me to sit up on the exam table. Reaching over to pull my list of questions out of my purse, I hand her the paper as she sits in her chair beside me.

"What have we here?" she says warmly. After silently reading through the questions, she smiles at me when she says, "You're very thorough."

Returning her smile, I nod and shrug my shoulders. I mouth the words, "It's my job to be."

"Your first question is if the assault could have hurt the baby. Did he hit or kick you in the abdomen at any time?"

I shake my head '*no*.'

"All of your injuries were sustained on your face and head?"

I nod '*yes*.'

"Then, it is highly unlikely that your baby would be affected. It's smaller than a pea right now, enclosed in an embryonic sac that is filled with fluid. The sac is inside your uterus, which is protected by layers of fat, muscle, and skin.

"We can do a transvaginal ultrasound to look, if that would make you feel better. But, I have to warn you that at this early stage it is *very likely* we would only see the sac. Ultrasounds are typically performed with an overly full bladder to give us a better picture of the internal contents," she explains. "If you want an ultrasound, I just want you to know that the lack of seeing a baby or a heartbeat does *not* mean there's anything wrong. Understand?"

"Yes," I mouth.

"Do you want to have an ultrasound today?"

"Yes," I mouth and nod to make sure she understands.

Picking up the phone, she dials an extension and orders the ultrasound technician to prepare the ultrasound room for me. Sighing, I'm both relieved and anxious. Keeping her warning in mind isn't as easy as it sounds. If there is no baby, and no heartbeat, I'll worry constantly.

"For your next question regarding medications to help the swelling and bruising heal faster, we recommend avoiding any over the counter medications if at all possible. You can take ibuprofen occasionally, or acetaminophen more regularly, if needed. Never aspirin. But if you can do without them, I would recommend that. Are you in a lot of pain?"

Shaking my head '*no*,' I point to my throat and shrug one shoulder.

"Your throat hurts the worst?" she asks to clarify and I nod. She suggests the salt-water solution to gargle and the throat lozenges with extra vitamin C.

"And, the last question is about your number of weeks gestation. We may not be able to get an accurate measurement until your next ultrasound. Your notes say you had the implant in your arm but it's not found now?" she clarifies and I nod. She conducts much the same examination as Dr. Fallon did but comes up with the same results.

"With your light period roughly six weeks ago, followed by an apparent failure of your implanted birth control, it's safe to say you are most likely between the six and eight week mark. Split it down the middle and say seven weeks," she smiles. "Ready for that ultrasound now?"

*Am I?*

Tentatively, I nod and Dr. Perry opens a door inside my examination room. It adjoins the ultrasound room, allowing me to avoid the busy hallway. Once I'm comfortably resting on the examination table, the ultrasound technician explains each step of the procedure to me. She's so nice and didn't even flinch when she saw me. My suspicion is that the others have already filled her in on my injuries.

"My name is Melissa. If you have any questions, just get my attention and I'll be glad to answer them for you. Sound good?"

Taking a deep breath, I nod and she begins the ultrasound. My silent prayers become a chant inside my head. *Please let my baby be okay.*

"Look at this, would you?" she says excitedly and turns the monitor screen more toward me.

The 3D image is crystal clear – even I can read it. There's a tiny baby inside me and his heart is clearly beating. My mouth drops open and tears spring to my eyes. Unconsciously, my hand reaches out to the screen to touch my baby. He appears to be healthy to me. Unable to tear my eyes from the screen, I whisper, "Okay?"

"Everything looks fine right now, Miss Vasco. You appear to be about eight weeks pregnant," Melissa explains. Using the keyboard, she takes various measurements and explains a lot of medical jargon. The underlying message is that she doesn't see any abnormalities, the baby has a good heartbeat, and I am approximately eight weeks pregnant. Melissa prints several pictures for my file and duplicates for me to take home.

*My little miracle baby.*

After I'm dressed, the doctor returns with a prescription for my prenatal vitamins and a bag full of various pregnancy-related items. This gift bag makes everything seem so much more official and real.

And scary.

After a stop at the pharmacy to get my prescription filled, my energy is zapped and I can't wait to get back to the condo for a nap. I forgot to ask the doctor about morning sickness so I will just look it up online later today. The project planner in me wants to make lists and check off the items as I complete each task. It's so ingrained in me now from the years of school, an internship, and on the job.

As I'm driving to the condo, I catch a glimpse of Tucker's truck a few cars behind me. This isn't by chance. If he wanted to remain unseen, I would never know he was back there. I have to talk to Dominic. He has to hear me out and let me explain everything that's happened and why. He needs to know about the baby. I don't want him to find this out from anyone else – not even Tucker.

When I pull into the parking garage, Tucker pulls in and then parks beside me. I quickly stuff my pregnancy gift bag into my oversized purse and grab the prescription bag off the front seat. Tucker opens my door for me and I climb out of the car with a confused look on my face.

"We haven't been able to find Harrison. Have you heard from him?" Tucker asks. So, this is his 'hello' now.

Giving him a disgusted look, I shake my head but never move my eyes from his.

"I have some things to do so I won't be around anymore." He's trying to be indifferent, but I hear the concern in his voice. He's been pulled off watching my every move, which also means he won't be there to protect me if Harrison shows up. "I just thought you should know."

My heart is breaking because I know this directive came from Dominic. Tucker must have talked to him and Dominic pulled him off watching me. Was that intentional so that Harrison has a better shot at me? The worry must be evident on my face because Tucker's hard stare softens.

"Sophia," he says, exasperated and unsure of how to proceed.

"Fine," I whisper. *Fine* that he's off my detail. *Fine* that I'm alone. I. Am *Fine*. Or, at least, I will be eventually. The look I leave him with before walking off to the elevator tells him everything I can't verbalize.

*I let you down–but you're letting me down, too. Guess we're even now.*

His frustration is obvious and we both know his hands are tied. He knows I'm not out of danger but he's following orders. He's loyal to Dominic and I'm the traitor. But I didn't deserve what Harrison did to me and Tucker saved me. It's all so very fucked up and I'm way too tired to deal with this shit right now. I leave him to wallow in his own annoyance. My bed is calling my name.

After a long and restful nap, I awake to my stomach rumbling. Realizing I skipped breakfast, I rise and make a soup and sandwich for a late lunch. With Tucker not following me, I have an opportunity to go to Dominic's lake house and try to talk to him without him having advance knowledge that I'm coming. As I'm in the bathroom freshening up, the first wave of nausea slams into me like a freight train. Maybe I should look into "morning" sickness sooner rather than later.

My heart is pounding as I pull into his driveway. Nervously, I walk up to the large, double door and ring the doorbell. The chimes sound throughout the house but there are no other sounds coming from inside. Table lamps illuminate various spots throughout the house, but it doesn't appear that anyone is actually here. I try the bell once more, just because I can't bear to leave without seeing him, but to no avail.

Over the next two weeks, my days are spent working from the condo and my evenings are spent watching for my Dom to appear out of thin air. With saltine crackers and Sprite to help settle my stomach, I wait for any sign of him. My body has mended. The bruises have faded away to the point that only a few are still barely visible. My voice has returned to its normal tone and pitch. The only thing left to heal is my heart that is still shattered.

My daily routine has been unchanged over the past two weeks – working and waiting for Dominic. With the exception of today, when I finally feel well enough to go shopping in the middle of the day and run smack into Kayla Powers, Dominic's mother.

# Chapter Five

***Dominic***

"Follow her. I want to know her every move," I bark into the phone at Tucker.

"You got it, boss," he replies before we hang up.

Shadow is in the car with me but he doesn't say anything. I haven't exactly been the best company since all this shit went down with Sophia. I still can't believe what all the facts are showing me. The nagging feeling that a vital piece of the puzzle is missing lingers and that makes it hard to concentrate on anything else. Being back in Tennessee this week doesn't help either.

The best of my programmers are at the facility now and are working their magic. The install has had the expected glitches but we've planned carefully for this entire project. I've found myself wishing, more than once, that Sophia were here with me to manage the project milestones and deliverables. We've been here three days this week and I've had to take over the conversations too many times.

Today will be another long fucking day. Another long fucking week.

Somehow, we make it through the first step of the installation without me killing Jason, our current project manager. He has none of Sophia's best qualities and it thoroughly pisses me off that he makes me think of her at all. Shadow and I climb into the back of our car just as my phone starts ringing.

"Powers," I answer.

"Boss," Tucker says tentatively and I'm on instant alert.

"What is it, Tucker?"

"Dominic," he only uses my name when he is reminding me to keep my shit together. "She's on her way to Harrison's house."

"Cut her loose, Tucker. That's all I need to know," I instruct him and quickly hang up.

"Son of a bitch!" I yell for probably the hundredth time this week. Our driver doesn't even flinch at my outbursts anymore.

"Problems at home?" Shadow asks, as he arches one eyebrow and one side of his mouth quirks upwards. If I didn't know better, I'd swear there was a hint of sarcasm in his voice.

"What would give you that idea?"

"Just a hunch," he says with a nonchalant shrug.

"She's on her way to Harrison's house right now," I growl.

"You knew that could happen," Shadow chides.

"Yeah, I knew. It's just hard to accept that she saved my life and then did all this shit to me." I lean my head back and close my eyes. I'm so fucking pissed off right now I could take someone's head off. Like *Harry Dick-man's* head.

"Look, I'm not trying to get involved in your personal life. But, I saw her when she realized you were still inside that burning house. That was no act, my friend. She was frantic and she didn't stop to think about her own safety for a second. I know people, man. There's more to this story."

"Have you found out anything else about her and Harrison? What they're up to?"

Shadow turns his head away from me and looks out the window. "I'm working on a couple of leads. I'll know something certain soon."

This guy is the master of vagueness.

"What the hell does that mean, exactly? How are you working on a couple of leads if you're with me all the time?" My voice deepens as I challenge him.

"I'm a man of many talents, Dominic. One of my best talents is knowing when to relay information," then he turns his head and looks me in the eye, "and when not to."

"*What-the-fuck-ever.* I'm done. Stick a fucking fork in me–I am *done.* In fact, I've been considering some secrets of my own. I'm going to make them both fucking pay for this. I'm going to thoroughly enjoy watching them squirm."

"Remember, '*he who seeks vengeance should dig two graves.*'"

Looking Shadow dead in the eye, I reply. "You're right. Thanks for the words of wisdom. One grave for Harrison. One grave for Sophia. Got it."

Shadow chuckles lightly and shakes his head. "Whatever you say."

"You know something I don't?" I ask incredulously.

Shadow's smirk is honestly the only answer I need, but I continue to stare him down and wait for a verbal response. "I know plenty, Mr. Powers. Like I said, I know when the show my cards and when to play them close to the vest. This is how I operate and it's not negotiable. There's a reason you hired the best. Take my advice and it'll be fine. I will update you as soon as it's time to update you."

"You're right in that I hired Steele Security because of the agency's reputation. But this is *my* life and if you have information, I deserve to know it," I demand.

Shadow turns his huge frame to face me in a covertly aggressive manner. His voice deepens, the corners of his eyes narrow, and his gaze hardens. "I have contacts working on this case that you wouldn't dare even *look at*, Mr. Powers. The information they get comes in small bursts and then we have to piece it together to get the full picture. Our intel says your life is still in danger," he pauses for effect, and I am instantly filled with dread. "The most recent chatter says *Sophia's* life may be in danger and *she* is possibly the primary target at this point. So maybe you should get to digging that grave a little faster."

"You just let me pull Tucker off of following her knowing that?" I bellow.

"My job is to protect you and yours. She's not yours anymore, now is she?" he asks pointedly.

"That doesn't mean I want her to be hurt or killed!"

"This is exactly why I don't share information until I'm absolutely certain it's time. Now you'll second-guess your every decision, trying to determine what's best for everyone else. You're already distracted. You didn't even notice that we've been sitting in the hotel parking lot for the last five minutes. Leave the security concerns to me and you focus on running your business," Shadow demands.

He's right–I wasn't paying attention to anything else. I know I won't be able to get this veiled threat against Sophia out of my mind now. Jumping out of the car, I call Tucker's phone. It rings several times and goes to voicemail. After several more attempts, my aggravation has increased one thousand fold.

"Tucker!" I yell into his voicemail. "Call me as soon as you get this message."

Pacing back and forth in my hotel room, I oscillate between worry and anger. I'm worried that something has already happened to her and I'm angry that I care about it at all. She sided with my fucking enemy. She helped to try to bring me down. Then, she filed a sexual harassment lawsuit against me and has been demanding an extraordinary amount of money to keep it out of court and out of the press.

Cheryl, my lawyer, has reminded Sophia's lawyer many times that there is a motion filed for a gag order. We both know that won't mean shit if it goes to court, though. It'll be a media circus and every aspect of my life will be torn apart for the world to make snap judgments. I have no doubt that my whole lifestyle will be called into question and used against me by those who don't have a clue of what a real Dominant/submissive relationship even looks like. I'll be portrayed as an overbearing, heavy-handed man who uses my position and authority to abuse women.

On the off chance that Christine, my housekeeper, has heard from Tucker, I quickly call her. "Christine, have you seen or heard from Tucker? I can't get him on the phone."

"No, I'm sorry, Mr. Powers, I haven't been to the lake house since you told me to stay away. I haven't heard from him. Should I go to the house and check?" she asks, her voice filled with concern.

"No, I'm sure he's fine. I'll try him again later. Thank you, Christine." We say our goodbyes and I sit heavily on the bed. When everything became so dangerous, I told her to stay away from the lake house. I didn't want her to become collateral damage in anyone's attempt to get to me.

Shadow and I have dinner together, but in my distracted state, I'm not very good at keeping up my end of a conversation tonight. Tucker still hasn't returned my call and that has never happened. Never.

"Would you stop worrying? This is exactly why I didn't tell you anything. Tucker is a professional and he's fine. He's just busy and he'll call you when he can. He knows you're with me and that you're safe. Whatever he has on his hands is his priority right now," Shadow scolds.

"Have you talked to him?" I ask.

"Have I *told* you that I've talked to him?" Shadow retorts.

The waiter approaches and I order bourbon on the rocks to help me relax and take the edge off. There's nothing I can do from here anyway. Two more days of installation hell and I can turn the rest of the project over to my team to handle from here on out.

On the way to the worksite the next morning, I don't mention anything about Tucker not calling me back. Shadow isn't concerned about his whereabouts so I drop it for now. Tucker and I will have a major conversation when I get home. There's nothing I can do with my cellphone locked up in the security office all day anyway.

Friday afternoon is finally here and we are on our way back to the Knoxville airport where my private jet is waiting. My cellphone's ringtone breaks the silence of our ride. Glancing at the screen to decide if it's a call I want to take or not, I can't hit the green button fast enough when I see the name.

"Tucker! Where the fuck have you been?" my voice booms through the car.

"Dominic," Tucker tentatively says and every muscle in my body freezes as I wait for him to continue. "It's Sophia. Do you want to know?"

Do I want to know about Sophia? That's a loaded question if I've ever heard one.

"Tell me," I state and ready myself for the worst.

"I've been with her for pretty much the last twenty-four hours. This is the first chance I've had to call you back. I followed her to Harrison's house night before last, like I told you. Right after we hung up, she came running out of his house and he was close behind her.

"By the time I got to them, he had already beaten her up pretty badly. He was hitting her, tearing at her clothes, and choking her, but I knocked him off of her. He took off on foot just before the police arrived. He had another girl tied to the bed inside the house. That girl had been drugged, most likely with ecstasy or maybe even ruffies.

"The ambulance took Sofia to the hospital and they kept her for a twenty-three hour observation. There's no permanent damage, but she has a lot of facial swelling and bruising. She's not supposed to talk for the next week or two while her throat heals. I dropped her off at her condo yesterday."

Rage. Fury. Anger. Wrath. There is no word to describe the intensity of my feelings toward Harrison. His depravity knows no limits. The very fact that he calls himself a Dom is an insult to me.

This is all the reason I need to track his ass down, beat him to a bloody pulp, and remind him what it's like to tangle with someone his own size.

"How was she when you left her?" Part of me needs to know. I don't know what I plan to do with the information.

Tucker sighs heavily and I hear his frustration in it. "She was sad, Dominic. *Very* sad. I went back this morning to tell her I had some things to do so I wouldn't be around. There's no doubt she saw right through me, though. You should know, she told me she loves you. Damn near completely lost her voice trying to tell me."

"Then *why* the fuck is she suing me for sexual harassment and why the fuck is she demanding so much money to hide everything that happened between us?" I shout.

"She looked surprised when I asked her about that, man. I don't know what to tell you."

Drawing my fingers and thumb across my jawline until they meet in the middle, I consider his words. "Stay on her, Tucker. I've felt like there's something missing all along. I don't know what it is, but make sure she stays safe."

"Will do, boss."

In my peripheral vision, I catch a glimpse of Shadow's smug look. Narrowing my eyes angrily, I ask, "What's the smirk for?"

"No reason at all," he says casually.

"You already know what happened," I state.

"I wouldn't be a very good spy if I didn't already know."

"You would've been a better spy if you saw the sexual harassment lawsuit coming ahead of time," I quip.

"You would have a good point there...if you weren't wrong," Shadow smirks again.

"You knew about it and didn't tell me?" I roar.

"No, there was nothing there *to* know. That's what's odd. The information we've been given isn't adding up. I have suspicions but I won't say until I know for sure," he answers in his typical vague way.

Two hours later, we land in Dallas and I think I'm home free when Fire Chief Greg Floyd calls.

"Mr. Powers, Chief Floyd here. Can you come by your house? I'm here finishing up my investigation and there are a few things I need to talk to you about."

"Sure, Chief Floyd. We will be there as soon as we can," I tell him and then we disconnect. *Shit, this is not what I wanted to do tonight.*

Forty-five minutes later, I'm walking with the Chief into the charred remains of my house. It has taken several weeks for their thorough investigation and all the test results to come back. I suspect that's what Chief Floyd wants to talk about now.

"We've marked the area where it's safe to walk. We had to reinforce some of the flooring, so don't step outside the taped off area," he says as we enter the house.

I follow in his footsteps and ask, "Why am I here?"

"For this," he says as he points to an area of the floor that's noticeably darker than the rest. "The fire started here, in the middle of the floor."

"Arson then," I state flatly. I already knew it but having it confirmed is somewhat eerie.

"Exactly. A fire doesn't naturally start in the middle of the floor. There were also traces of gasoline as an accelerant. Whatever was used to start the fire completely burned up."

"This is just down the hall from my office," I say to Floyd. "He must have heard me in here when he was getting set up. He came prepared to knock me out."

Shadow takes a couple of steps away from us and mumbles a few words into his phone. Seconds later, he rejoins us without saying a word. Chief Floyd and I both look at him expectantly, but he remains stoic and silent.

"Mr. Powers, have you thought of anyone who may have wanted to hurt you or anyone in your house?" Chief Floyd asks.

"No one we are prepared to name at this point," Shadow answers before I can say anything.

"Why is that?" Floyd asks suspiciously.

"They're part of an ongoing Federal investigation that takes precedence. FBI protocol supersedes an arson investigation. When he goes down, the arson charges will be added on," Shadow explains as the Chief and I both openly gape at him.

"Do you have any credentials on you?" Floyd asks.

Shadow pulls out his badge, showing he's an FBI Special Agent. I try to get a look at his name but he flips the leather cover back over just as quickly as he opened it.

"I'll need the official forms in my office first thing tomorrow," Floyd says.

"They're already waiting for you on your desk right now," Shadow replies.

Without further questioning, Floyd takes us around the other safe areas of the charred remains of my house and I pick up the few personal items that are salvageable. A few pictures of my family are redeemable along with a few paintings. As I look around, unusual thoughts and feelings hit me.

*There's nothing in this entire house that I would really miss if I lost it.*

*Every single possession I own can be replaced, as if the original never existed.*

*This house has never been a home – except when Sophia was here with me.*

For the next three weeks solid, my life consists of endless days at work and countless hours in the evening with the contractor to oversee the demolition and the beginning of building a foundation for a new house. Shadow has been, well, my shadow, every step of the way.

"You know you don't have to be there to watch them work," he finally says when he realizes I'm driving in that direction again.

"Yes, I do know," I reply.

"You're avoiding," Shadow replies without emotion.

"I don't avoid," I deny. "I'm making deliberate calculations."

"Keep telling yourself that. Maybe one day you'll believe it."

"Something you want to tell me?" I ask, fishing for information.

"I can tell you that before a sexual harassment *lawsuit* can be filed with the court, a sexual harassment *claim* is required to be filed with the EEOC. There is no claim on file with the EEOC. The paperwork Cheryl has looks real, but I'm ninety-nine percent sure it has been forged. Sophia may be telling the truth about not knowing anything about it," Shadow reveals.

My mind is reeling at this news. I can't form a complete thought, much less a response.

"But her signature was on it," I contest.

"That's part of what I'm still looking into, Dominic."

# Chapter Six

"I had an interesting conversation today," my mom says as she walks into my kitchen.

"Well, hello to you, too, Mom," I reply as I rise to kiss her cheek. "Yes, I have had a good day at work – thanks for asking!"

Mom laughs as she wraps her arms around my neck to hug me. She kisses my cheek and says, "Hello, my son. I'm so glad you had a good day at work. But my news is more important."

"What sort of interesting conversation did you have? While you were out shopping…spending my money…on decorations for my house…that isn't even built yet," I tease her.

She narrows her eyes, playfully threatening me and trying to look as intimidating as possible.

"Fine. I will never tell and you will spend the rest of your life speculating about what I had to say."

I grab my chest in mock pain, "You wound me! I will never know the exact names of the many shades of blue, brown, and pink that you discovered today."

"Have I told you lately that you are a smartass?" she asks while cocking one brow up at me.

Furrowing my brow, grasping my chin between my index finger and thumb, and staring intently at the floor, I respond, "You know, I don't recall hearing that today. Fairly certain you probably told me yesterday, though."

Mom playfully swats at me and I take the bags of decorations she bought and store them in my study. Walking back in the kitchen, I laughingly tell her, "You've been here all of two days and you're already filling up my study with all kinds of stuff! You need to slow down, woman! I don't have enough room here to keep everything you're planning to put in the new house!"

She eyes me speculatively for a moment before saying, "You're right. I think I should hold off on buying anything else for a while."

"Wait–what?" Am I hearing things? My mother just agreed to stop shopping? With my money?

"What? I said you're right. What's wrong with that?"

Now I'm extra suspicious. "Maybe you should tell me about this conversation you had today."

The smile that covers my mom's face is one of pure wickedness. It says she knows something I don't have a clue about. It's the smile a woman uses on a man when she knows he's been caught red-handed and has no way out. It's the scariest fucking smile I've ever seen and my mom is giving me that smile now.

"Maybe it's best that I don't say anything yet, Dominic."

"Oh no, you brought it up. Spill it," I say as I step toward her and that damn grin of hers.

"I will tell you this, Dominic. I ran into Sophia today and it's time for you to talk to her."

I'm literally stunned speechless. This is the last thing I ever expected my mom to say to me.

"I told you what all happened. You were ready to let her have a piece of your mind a few weeks ago. Now you've changed your mind?" I ask disbelievingly.

She gives me a single shoulder shrug and holds my gaze with hers, "You. Need. To. Talk."

"Why does it feel like everyone around me knows something I don't?" I place my hands on my hips, draw in a deep breath that pushes my chest out, and straighten up to my full height. "I've been more than patient and way too calm. My anger has been simmering below the surface for weeks and I'm ready to unleash it. I've gone against my true nature long enough."

"Channel it where it belongs, Dominic. Harrison deserves your wrath, so does Sophia's family, but I believe Sophia deserves to be heard," she wisely counters.

*Sophia's family deserves my wrath?* A memory stirs and I grapple with it in my mind until it becomes clear. "Her mother kept calling her right before the fire," I say. "You think they had something to do with it?"

"I think there's strong reason to think they are somehow involved," she responds. "Are you thinking of going to talk to them?"

I am thinking of doing that very thing *now.*

"Are you going to tell me about your little talk with Sophia?" I answer her question with one of my own.

"No, son. This is between the two of you. Sooner or later, you and Sophia have to sit down and have a long talk. Sooner would be better for you both."

Sunday evening after my mom leaves from her extended weekend visit, I decide it's about time for me to make a surprise visit to talk to Sophia's family in Austin. Shadow has, no doubt, already investigated them, but my mind won't let this rest until I hear it for myself. After a long and heated discussion, I told Shadow he can accompany me or he can watch my ass drive off into the sunset. Either way, he knows I am going so he reluctantly agreed to take a short trip as soon as we can.

"You know if they had anything to do with the attempts on your life, you are walking right into their lair," Shadow admonishes me again on the way to the office Monday morning.

"That's why I have you," I nonchalantly counter.

He gives me a disgusted look and shakes his head.

"Look, I understand what you're saying. Whether they are or not, I want this finished as quickly as possible. If they are, maybe I can find out why or change their mind. If they're not, maybe I can get more information out of them that would help me figure out what the fuck is going on," I explain.

"I suppose it's worth a shot, Dominic. You need to understand that Sophia's father is not one to be fucked with, though. Dude has done some hard time in the past," Shadow reveals.

"Prison?"

"Yes. Got sent up for being an accomplice to an execution-style murder and spent several years in a hardcore, maximum-security prison before he was released. He officially quit the cartel life when he was released, but we both know those ties are never really severed. They may have allowed him to lay low for a while, do a few jobs for them here and there, but if his skills were needed, they wouldn't hesitate to pull him back in."

"I guess that's why Sophia said he disappeared for a while and they went hungry."

"Could be. He was away for a long while, but with her being so young when it happened, she may not have fully realized the time span," Shadow surmises.

I nod but I'm deeply engrossed in my own thoughts and memories. "Sophia told me once that she was really mad at her mother for welcoming her father back in with open arms after he'd been away for so long."

We reach the office and my mind is still trying to put this jigsaw puzzle together with the pieces I have in front of me. Once I'm in my office, the business owner in me takes over and I put those other thoughts away, for the most part. Knowing that Sophia is back at work this week and on the floor below me stays in my thoughts nonstop.

"Good morning, Dominic," Darren calls from my doorway.

"Good morning. Come on in."

"Listen, I won't keep you, but we do need to talk about Sophia," Darren says pointedly.

"What about her?"

"You have to take her back," Darren states emphatically.

"What?" His statement shocks me momentarily and I'm unsure of how to answer him.

"You hired her to be your right-hand person, your go-to person when you're not around. She needs to do her job and not report to me. Whatever happened between the two of you needs to be resolved and she needs to report to you again. She's not doing the job you hired her to do.

And, well, hell Dominic, I'm just too damn old for all this bullshit," Darren bustles.

"For what bullshit, Darren? What has she done?"

"Nothing! She's a great employee and she handles that Rich fellow like he's putty in her hands. Sophia needs to be working with you and learning all the ropes. Not hanging with an old bastard like me who's closer to retirement than he is anything else."

"Let me talk to Cheryl and see what I can do, Darren," I compromise.

"You just need to make it happen, Dominic. I think it looks worse that you moved her away from you if none of that mess is true." Darren leaves my office and my mind is spinning faster than when he walked in.

*Does he have a valid point? Does it make me look guilty?*

Dana walks in with my morning coffee as usual and I decide it's time to have another conversation with Cheryl. "Dana, ask Cheryl to come to my office as soon as possible."

"Yes, sir. Anything else?"

"No. Thank you, Dana."

Half an hour later, Cheryl knocks on my door and I call for to enter.

"You wanted to see me?" Cheryl asks as she walks in and takes a seat.

"Yes. Darren was in here earlier and wants to move Sophia back to me. He says he's too close to retirement to be responsible for her and that it makes me look guilty for moving her away from me," I blurt out.

Cheryl takes a moment to process my words and think through the conversation. She is no doubt playing out every possible scenario in her head. "Do you want to move her back under you, Dominic? That puts you at a greater risk. If anything is said or done that can misconstrued or misinterpreted, you would have no recourse in the matter."

"What if Dana were present during all of our meetings to monitor and be a witness?"

"It's really not fair to put her in that position, Dominic. Besides that, she's been a loyal employee for many years and that would most definitely be used to discredit anything she says in your favor," Cheryl advises.

"Then we'll record our meetings on video. That way, if anything is said, we will all watch it as it actually happened," I offer.

"That could work. If Sophia is wiling to return to working with you and is willing to consent to being recorded while she's in your presence, that could be a useful tactic."

Hitting the button on my phone, I instruct Dana to have Sophia come to my office. Since Cheryl is here, we can get to the bottom of this right now. As we are waiting for Sophia to make her way up, Shadow enters my office and has a seat on the couch on the far wall. His eyes assess the situation and I know he must have heard Dana call Sophia.

Several minutes later, Dana's usual three-tap knock alerts me and my back unconsciously straightens as I wait for Sophia to walk through the door. It's been two months since I've really seen or talked to her. Two months of hell. Two months of uncertainty. Two months of wondering what the fuck happened and how we lost everything I thought we had together.

Two months of being so fucking mad I could spit nails.

Dana opens the door and I see the concern etched in her motherly face. Her eyes find mine and she silently conveys her worry to me, but I have no idea what she's worried about. Until Sophia appears in the doorway, and then I have no doubt of what was on Dana's mind.

Sophia's once radiant skin is now pale and lackluster. Her smile has disappeared, as have the supple curves of her body that I knew intimately. She's lost weight–I can tell that her cheeks are somewhat drawn and her eyes are slightly sunken. It wouldn't be evident to others who didn't know her so well, unlike Dana who saw it immediately. But the subtle changes in her are definitely there. Even with these minor changes in her appearance, she's still the most beautiful woman I've ever seen and I have to keep myself rooted in my seat to not just take her in my arms.

Sophia looks around nervously and I watch with curiosity as she places her hand across her abdomen. "You wanted to see me?" she asks tentatively, her eyes darting from me, to Cheryl, and back to Shadow.

"Yes, Sophia. Please, have a seat," I offer cordially and she sits in the chair opposite Cheryl.

"What can I do for you?" she asks, her voice strong and determined to not show any fear.

"Darren came to me this morning and shared that since he's so close to retirement, he'd prefer to not manage other people. Before we move you, I wanted to ask your thoughts about you coming back to work directly with me," I state without emotion.

Sophia's mouth hangs open from the shock and her eyes search mine. I can only imagine all the thoughts that are racing through her mind. I hold her gaze while giving nothing away. She won't see my anger over her betrayal. She won't sense my confusion over her conflicting actions.

"Yes, I would love that," Sophia finally answers.

Cheryl pipes in, "Your interactions with Mr. Powers would be recorded on video cameras. In the event any further claims are made, the video would be used to either substantiate or negate your claim. Do you understand?"

Sophia's eyes hold mine for a moment longer. She doesn't answer Cheryl's question right away. She acts as if her eyes are physically attached to me and she can't turn her head away. I continue to study her reactions, her body language, and try to ascertain what is going on in her head.

"Yes, I understand and I agree to that. Although, it's not necessary," she finally turns to Cheryl. "I've requested a meeting with you every week for the past eight weeks, except the two weeks I was out after my accident. I've been trying to tell you that-."

"Miss Vasco," Cheryl interrupts. "I think I've made it clear that we are not discussing the case without your lawyer present."

Sophia looks completely exasperated and opens her mouth to blast Cheryl, if the look on her face is any indication. Shadow speaks up from across the room and stops Sophia's impending tirade.

"Can the two of you excuse Miss Vasco and me for a minute?"

Cheryl and I both look at Shadow like he's grown a second head. He wants me to leave my office so he can talk to Sophia without me. *What the fuck?* Shadow rises from the couch and walks over to where we're seated. He stares at me until I finally get up and walk toward he door.

"Cheryl, let's get some coffee," I say and walk toward the door. She rises and follows me out without saying a word.

Cheryl and I stop in front of Dana's desk and wait for Shadow to finish his talk with Sophia. Dana gives us each curious glances but settles her gaze directly on me.

"You should treat her better, Dominic."

Before I can respond to Dana's provocation, Shadow pokes his head out the door and calls for us to come back inside.

"Now, Sophia, tell Dominic what you just told me," Shadow instructs.

"I don't have a lawyer," Sophia speaks clearly and concisely.

I sense a change in her. She started out as a feisty, all-business assistant. When she became my submissive, she also became much more emotional and dependent on me. She now seems to have returned to the confident, mature lady that I first met and I can't help but question how the change came about.

"What do you mean, you don't have a lawyer?" Cheryl narrows her eyes suspiciously at Sophia. "I've been talking to your lawyer and I have the sexual harassment lawsuit your lawyer filed on your behalf."

"No, you haven't been speaking to my lawyer, because I don't have one," Sophia punctuates each word in response to Cheryl's tone. "I didn't file a sexual harassment lawsuit because I wasn't being sexually harassed *and* I don't have a lawyer to file it for me anyway."

Cheryl looks at me and huffs, "Dominic, I don't know what ploy this girl is up to. She's young, inexperienced, naïve, and really needs to take responsibility for her actions. I'm not sure she's the right one for the job."

The anger that flashes in Sophia's eyes is hotter than the surface of the sun. Sophia slowly rises and faces her head-on to rebuke Cheryl's assessment of her.

"You don't know what you're talking about, Cheryl," Sophia starts. "I started college at a very young age, but I worked my ass off in every class. I took the maximum amount of college hours every semester so that I could graduate early. Every summer, I worked as a college intern and I put in as many hours as the executives did, if not more. I learned everything I could from them and used that knowledge to get the project management positions I held before coming here.

"I may be young, but I worked damn hard to get where I am today. You have no right questioning my work history or my ability to take on responsibility. You haven't even asked how well I do my job, so you'd be wise to stop making any assumptions. Any of you're more than welcome to call my former employer, where I interned every summer during college, and ask *them* about my work ethics."

Shadow intervenes and stops this from escalating further. "All of that is true. I checked that out for myself, so I do believe what you're saying. My question is, Sophia, if you didn't file the lawsuit, whose signature is on this paper?"

Shadow removes a single sheet of paper from a manila envelope he placed on my desk. When he hands it to Sophia, her shoulders slump as recognition of the handwriting registers on her face.

"That's my signature. It's my handwriting. Where did you get this?" she asks with sadness filling her voice.

"This is the signature page of the lawsuit, Sophia," Shadow explains.

I watch with amazement as the various emotions play across her beautiful face. First, she's confused as she tries to connect Shadow's words with the paper in her hand. Second, the shock registers as she beings to formulate an idea in her mind of how this could've happened. Third, the pure, unadulterated anger as her eyes blaze with fury and indignation.

"That son of a bitch!" she shrieks, causing Cheryl to jump and Shadow smiles.

"Tell me," Shadow prompts and I listen with rapt attention.

"That is not my signature on a lawsuit, Shadow," Sophia grinds out thought her clenched teeth. "*That* is the signature on my submissive contract with Harrison Dictman."

"How can you tell for sure that's where the signature came from?" Shadow presses.

"There was something wrong with Harrison's printer. Every page had a small dot right in the center of it. Right there," she answered with her finger on the dot. "If you look through the rest of the lawsuit papers, you will probably find that same dot on every page."

# Chapter Seven

***Sophia***

*"I am not your Dom," he enunciates each word clearly and forcefully, leaving no room for doubt. The sobs wrack my body before I can even take the first step out of his home.*

I sit straight up in bed and gasp for air. The tears flow freely down my cheeks and it takes a few minutes for me to calm down. That whole dream of Dominic felt so real–every last part of it, even when I would sit outside of his lake house and wait for him to come home. I felt his hands on me as he brought me such intense pleasure. I felt his breath on my neck and the warmth of his chest against my back. I also felt the crushing pain in my chest when he sent me away.

Swinging my feet off the side of the bed, I decide to get up early and get ready for work. I'm healed enough now to return to the office to work, and there's still that lingering hope that I will see and talk to Dominic today. I know better than to jump up out of bed, but my dream-turned-nightmare about my Dom temporarily disoriented me, and now the morning sickness has me running for the bathroom.

It's going to be a great fucking day.

The aromas of food wafting through the office make my stomach churn as I walk to my office. Even shutting my door doesn't keep them at bay. They float in on the air and surround me. I try to focus on the work I have to do but after so long, I'm making another mad dash for the bathroom. My online searches said the morning sickness usually only lasts for the first trimester and I pray that holds true for me. I take a few minutes in the bathroom to collect myself and brush my teeth.

On my way back to my office, Dana stops me in the hallway.

"Dominic wants to see you in his office, Sophia. I tried to call a couple of times but you didn't answer." Her tone and face holds obvious concern for me. "Sophia, are you all right? You look so pale!"

"Yes, I'm fine, Dana. Thank you. Will you let Mr. Powers know I will be up right away? I just have to finish something on my desk first."

Dana smiles and nods, "Come on up when you're ready, Sophia."

I'm shaking as I sit down at my desk. My hands are trembling and my legs feel like they're made of wet noodles. My already queasy stomach churns again and I grab a saltine cracker out of my bag. The crackers and Sprite are all I can count on to help settle my nausea right now but I can't very well carry them into his office. I nibble and sip for a minute before I attempt to move again.

Walking into Dom's office suddenly feels like I'm walking straight into a trap. Cheryl, the corporate lawyer, and Shadow are both waiting with

Dominic. When he asks if I want to resume reporting to him and working with him, I almost leap out of my chair in excitement. YES! Yes, I want that more than I can express. Even when Cheryl says our interactions will be recorded, I'm fine with that provision. I would agree to anything that gets me close to him again.

Unexpectedly, Shadow asks Cheryl and Dominic to excuse us and I know exactly why. He wants the answers that I've been trying to give to Cheryl for the last two months. True to Shadow's nature, he gets right to the point with me.

"What have you been trying to tell Cheryl?"

"That I didn't file a sexual harassment lawsuit against Dominic. I heard what was said the day the papers were delivered, just before Dominic shut the door in my face," I recall and lower my eyes to the floor. "I was on my way to his office to tell him about my involvement with Harrison and that he was up to something new. But, I was too late."

"So, you are Harrison's sub?"

"I was–but I haven't been for a while now," I answer truthfully.

"But you were when you and Dominic first got together?"

"Yes," I say shamefully. "Harrison said he was sharing me with Dominic but I was supposed to give Harrison information to hurt Dominic. Harrison always said that Dominic killed Carol Ann and he wanted to destroy him for it.

"After I got to know Dominic, and I saw how different he was from Harrison, I knew he couldn't have killed her. So, I told Harrison that it was over between us, I was staying with Dominic, and I wouldn't help him anymore. He threatened me, as usual, kept calling me, and acting more and more desperate. He threatened Dominic's life if I didn't answer the phone every Sunday night. Said he still owned me and I had signed my life away to him.

"I am guilty of helping Harrison in the beginning, when I first started working here. He wanted me to get close to Dominic and find out about Carol Ann's death. But, I soon ended it between us and I was just trying to keep him away from Dominic. It got so out of hand so fast. I was on my way to confess everything that last day, when Harrison called me here, just before the lawsuit papers were delivered."

"That certainly answers a lot of my questions," Shadow says, but his voice doesn't convey any emotion. I can't tell if he's mad, disgusted, or understanding of my predicament. "Do you mind answering a couple of questions in front of Dominic and Cheryl?"

"No, not at all. I've been trying to tell them," I emphatically state.

Shadow nods and says, "One last question– who is your lawyer?"

"I don't have a lawyer," I look him square in the eye and respond.

"Good. I want you to be the one to tell Cheryl that when they come in," Shadow instructs before he goes to the door and calls them back in.

My stomach is rolling as I answer Shadow's questions in front of Dom and Cheryl. Any lingering nausea is completely forgotten when Cheryl insults my abilities to do my job. I've worked hard to obtain the position I'm in now. The sacrifices I made during college and during my summers out of school paid off more than I would've ever imagined as far as my business acumen is concerned. Spending more time with my books than with people may not have been as beneficial to me, however.

When Shadow shows me the signature page of the lawsuit, my first reaction was shame. *Did he just ask me all those questions to embarrass me in front of Cheryl and Dominic?* This was clearly the signature page of my submissive contract. I would recognize it anywhere. When Shadow said it came from the lawsuit paperwork, I have a hard time reconciling the two separate things in my mind.

Then I realized that Harrison used that page to file a fictitious lawsuit against Dominic and I instantly became outraged. If he were right in front of me, I would enjoy inflicting as much bodily pain on him as humanly possible. After I showed them the dot that marred the pages from Harrison's printer, Cheryl snatched the papers up and went through every single sheet.

"Cheryl, take those papers back to your office and call this number," Shadow said as he handed her a business card. "The man who answers is on this case and will work with you on how we're going to prove those fake papers came from Harrison."

"Don't I need his name?" Cheryl asks.

"Nope."

After Cheryl leaves, Shadow pins me with his assessing eyes and says, "I think it's about time the two of you talk and put all your cards on the table. But, I have two more questions for you first, Sophia."

I swallow audibly and nod, dreading what's coming next. Shadow is a former spy. He was a CIA operative for years before joining his friend's security firm. The man knows too much and I'm afraid of what he and Tucker may have recently learned. Will he tell Dominic that I'm pregnant before I can?

He narrows his eyes at me, sensing my moment of weakness and panic. "Carol Ann's death isn't the only reason you helped Harrison, is it?"

He phrased it as a question, but it's obvious he already knows the answer.

"No. It isn't even the main reason I agreed to do it," I answer honestly. My eyes gravitate toward Dominic's and I see the hardness in them. The result of my betrayal, the loss of any trust, and the confirmation that I've done things I shouldn't have echo back at me from his deep blue eyes. It takes my breath and causes my heart to skip a beat.

"What was the main reason, Sophia?" Dominic asks, his voice as hard as his eyes.

"My baby brother, Shawn. He's in trouble, mixed up with wrong crowd. Harrison was threatening him–his life. Harrison has friends on the Austin police department who made the evidence of his crimes *'disappear'* so that his case would be delayed by the state. That gave Harrison something to hold over my head.

"That's why my mom kept calling me. She kept saying that I had to do what Harrison said in order to save Shawn from prison. I finally told my mom and my brother that I was finished covering for him, though. He had to face the charges that were waiting for him and that Harrison wouldn't rule my life any longer."

Dominic's disgusted *'humph'* as a reply is like a knife to my heart. No reason, excuse, or explanation will fix this. The realization that I've lost him forever truly hits me and it feels like a ton of bricks have been dumped on my chest. I fight the tears that threaten to spring to my eyes. My resolution to be strong kicks in and I swallow the hurt down.

Not acknowledging Dominic's spiteful response, I look at Shadow and ask, "What is your second question?"

"Why did you go to Harrison's house that night if you aren't helping him any longer?"

Dominic leans forward after Shadow asks this question, intently listening, and ready to pounce on me after I answer. I can feel it coming–he's going to call me a liar, possibly other things, and drive that knife further into my chest.

"I went because he said he has proof that Dominic killed Carol Ann and he plans to have him arrested with it."

"BULLSHIT!" Dominic yells and I can't help but jump at his outburst.

"She's not lying, Dominic," Shadow replies, his voice low and calm.

"What?" Dominic barks. "So she went to protect me?" he asks sardonically.

"That's exactly why she went, Dominic," Shadow replies to him, but keeps his eyes glued to mine. "She couldn't take the risk that Harrison had something that incriminated you, no matter what the odds were against it being real."

With every cell in my body, I hope that Shadow can feel the appreciation radiating from my eyes and from my heart. He has no reason to stand up for me, to be the least bit supportive, or to believe a word I say, but what he just did means so much to me. Dominic trusts and respects him, so he won't question Shadow's judgment. It's a small victory, but I will take it.

"So what was this mythical proof?" Dominic asks as he turns his eyes to me again.

"I don't know, Dominic. I didn't get a chance to find out," I tell him, keeping my voice soft but neutral. The memories of that night come flooding back to me and I have to mentally shake them away. Shadow sees it in me, though, as his eyes soften and he gives me a single nod of understanding.

"Leave that to me," Shadow replies confidently.

"There is no proof! I didn't kill her!" Dominic yells.

"I believe you, Dominic, but you don't know what this prick has concocted against you," Shadow replies. "Well, kids, I have a few calls to make to get the ball rolling on this. We've wasted two weeks of precious time since then. I will leave you two to finish this talk."

The tension in the room after Shadow exits feels like a living, breathing dragon sitting in the middle of the room. What was once an easy-going connection has become a strained shell of a relationship. Recognizing that I'm wringing my hands in my lap, I straighten my fingers and place my hands on my lap. When I finally dare to look up, Dominic is intently watching me.

"If we're going to work together again, we need to put this behind us somehow," Dominic declares. "So, I'm just supposed to take it on your word that you didn't file a sexual harassment lawsuit against me?"

"What would make you believe me?"

"Nothing. There's nothing that can make me believe *anything* you say," he spits out at me.

I nod while keeping my eyes lowered. My heart breaking all over again at the confirmation of what I knew was to come. "I see," I say quietly. "In that case, I don't see that we can work together anymore, Dominic." Taking a deep breath, I raise my eyes to meet his. "You will have my resignation on your desk within the hour. I just need time to pack up a few personal things from my office."

The shock registers on his face before he has a chance to hide his feelings. He wasn't expecting that reply and, frankly, neither was I. After his declaration, I don't see any other way of handling this. Leaving here is my only option because I can't pretend that I don't love him. Working here with him, living in his company's executive condos, driving his company's car – the reminders of what I had and lost are all too painful.

I can't see him every day and have this pain multiplied every time I hear something new about him moving on without me. The fact that my waistline will soon be expanding to the point I won't be able to hide it is also a huge factor to consider. I still don't know how or when to tell him about that, but right now definitely isn't it.

"You can leave it with Dana," he replies coolly.

Not crying as I rise from the chair in front of him is one of the hardest things I've ever accomplished. I'm walking out of his life, in every way, and he says to leave my final statement with his secretary instead of with him.

Where is the loving, caring Dom I love?

*You killed him and created this version of him.*

Walking to his office door, I can feel his eyes burning into my back. When I reach for the door handle, his smooth, sensual voice calls out, "Sophia." One word from him and my whole body stills, suspends in motion, and waits for his next command.

The heat radiating from his body physically touches mine. The smell of his cologne envelops me and invades my nostrils. That scent has been gone from everything that reminds me of him and makes my heart ache even more to have it so close once again. He is standing behind me, close enough that if I simply leaned back, I could touch him. My hair lightly sways from the closeness of his breath. The only thing I want to do is turn and be taken into his arms.

"You don't have to leave, Sophia," his voice is low and the hateful edge is gone. "You've shown that you can effectively do your job and I'd like for you to stay on with the company. I would appreciate it if you would rescind your resignation."

Letting go of the doorknob, I nod my head in agreement. Turning slowly to face him, his sharp inhale creates a hissing noise as he takes in my face from his up close vantage. His eyes flow over my face, taking in the light green remnants of the bruises around my eyes and on my cheekbones that are hidden by makeup from a distance. His hand involuntarily rises and strokes my face with such tenderness it instantly makes me hope for more. He cups my face with his hand and I lean into the warmth of his touch. My eyes close and I relish in the touch of his skin on mine.

"Did you really go to his house that night to protect me?"

My eyes flutter open, and although my heart wants nothing more than this, my mind knows I'm setting myself up for more pain. Pulling away from his touch, I fix my gaze on his and reply, "Yes, I did, Dominic."

"Why would you do that?" his soft voice asks as his hand goes back to my face again.

He's killing me. One touch at a time, he's killing me.

There's no point in lying about it. My whispered response is from the depths of my heart. "Because I love you, Dominic. I can't tell you how sorry I am for hurting you, but it's not all what you think. I'm not as terrible as you believe I am."

His eyes travel down my body and come to a stop, and he just stares. I look down to see what he's looking at and notice my hand is protectively covering my lower abdomen. When I look back up at him, his intense eyes have locked onto mine and

I can feel him probing my mind for answers. Trying hard to school my expression and not give anything away, I hold his gaze until he speaks again.

"Are you feeling well enough to work? You can take more time off if you need it," he offers with sincerity.

"I'm fine, thank you. I get a little tired easily but that's about it."

He reaches down and takes the hand that's covering my stomach in his hand. My breath catches in my chest when his eyes peer into mine yet again. *He knows. Oh my God, he knows something is up. Do I tell him now?*

"You let me know when you need a break then," he says as he examines my hand. "Do we need cameras installed to be able to work together?"

"If that would make you more comfortable, I'm fine with it. I have nothing to hide…from the cameras."

He noticed the hesitation in my statement. I couldn't say I have *nothing* to hide, because I *am* hiding something for the time being. He knows it, too. There's no doubt about that look on his face. It's not a look of suspicion now–it's a knowing look.

"Is there anything else you need to tell me?"

"I'm sure there's plenty of things I need to tell you, but I'm not sure where to start, Dominic."

# Chapter Eight

My in charge, in control Dom is waging an internal war with himself. He doesn't trust me but he trusts Shadow. My betrayal doesn't make sense to him but my love for him doesn't make sense to him either. He knows there's more to the story but neither of us knows where to start to rectify that. I have really fucked this up.

"What do you want to know, Dominic? I'll answer any and every question you have."

The fire rages in his eyes and I fear what will come next. "Did he have you at any time after I made you mine?"

"No. Not even once," I reply. "He planned to the night I went to his house, but that was against my will and I got away."

He nods, temporarily satisfied with that answer. "When did you tell him you wouldn't help him anymore?"

"After our San Diego trip," I say and his suspicion shines in his eyes so I elaborate. "He had described you as a cold, unfeeling Sir when he sent me to you. He told me horror stories about you and Carol Ann. When I saw firsthand that you were the exact opposite, I knew he either lied or he was completely wrong about you. Either way, I said I wouldn't help hurt you."

"He sent you to me?"

"Yes. When he rescued me from that abandoned building, he asked me a lot of the standard questions you'd ask to learn about someone. I didn't realize it at the time, but he's been grooming me since then. He decided I needed to go to college and major in international business and management. He paid for it all–my dorm, classes, and books.

"After I graduated, I already had a good job with the company I interned with all through college. He said that was a good stepping stone but I needed to aim higher. When this position came open with your company, he pushed me to apply for it. He said he knew I'd get it because I'd remind you so much of Carol Ann, you wouldn't be able to resist me."

Dominic instantly jerked back from me, as if he had been burned. The horrified look on his face melted into anger. "You don't remind me anything about her. That's not a good or bad thing. It's just that the two of you are really nothing alike. For him to even suggest that is more than disturbing."

Shrugging one shoulder, I respond, "I don't put much stock in anything he has ever said now. I've discovered it was all lies and abuse."

"Yet, you thought he had something that proved that I killed her," Dominic narrows his eyes, silently questioning whether or not I believed Harrison.

"I thought he had made up something that would hurt you," I clarify. "Since the day I met you, I haven't believed you were capable of killing her."

"So the day we saw him at the restaurant..." his voice trails off as his memory of that evening takes over.

"He followed us there. I had no idea he planned to start anything with you. But, if you remember, I took my stand beside you. That was my way of letting him know that I wasn't helping him with anything, even though I'd already told him as much."

"So that's why he looked at you and licked his lips," Dominic realizes.

"He only did that to rile you up. It had nothing to do with his feelings toward me."

Dominic turns and walks across his office to the floor-to-ceiling windows. He props his arm up on the window, his elbow bent and his forehead resting on his forearm. I can still see his face in the reflection. He's torn and he's running through everything in his mind.

He shocks me when he speaks, "Do you understand my predicament here? You *admittedly* worked with *Harry Dick-man* against me. There's a potential lawsuit pending, demanding millions of dollars to keep my private life out of the press. Then, you say you're not part of that and that you haven't been helping him this whole time.

"What the fuck am I supposed to believe? You? *Harry Dick-man*? Those are my fucking choices? *You were his fucking sub!"* He yells, the anger returning to him and the feeling of defeat returns to me.

He turns to me in my silence. His eyes are tormented and I don't know how to fix this. I know I have to somehow–there's just too much to lose.

"Is there anything else I need to know right now?"

I shake my head *'no.'* He needs to resolve his feelings for me without the added weight of a baby on the way. When he's decided once and for all, I'll tell him. If I tell him before then, I'll never know if he really chose me or if his sense of duty forced him to be with me for our baby's sake.

"You sure about that, Sophia?" he challenges.

"I'm sure, Dominic," I say with confidence. This is the only thing I *am* sure of.

"Why didn't you tell me any of this sooner?" His voice is both pained and angered.

"I wanted to, Dominic. I started to so many times, but it was never the right time. There's no such thing as a right time. I just kept trying to protect you the way you protected me. I didn't want to lose you.

"But, the day the lawsuit papers were served, that's why I had walked to your office. I'd just hung up from another fight with Harrison. He threatened to tell you and I said I was going to tell you first. I had no idea about those papers, but when I heard the conversation, I knew he'd beaten me to the punch.

"I'm sorry, Dominic. *I'm so sorry*. That doesn't even begin to describe how badly I feel about all of this. I love you and it kills me that I hurt you. There's nothing I wouldn't do to have one more chance, to be able to fix this, to show you how much I love you. I would do anything–*whatever it takes*. Just tell me what I need to do!"

His mirthless laugh doesn't give me hope for us. "I wish I knew what to tell you, Sophia. I just can't see that ever happening between us again. I told you my hard limits and you broke them."

*No deception of any kind. No withholding my body from him.*

"I understand," I reply solemnly. "We'll just be work colleagues then. Is there anything else you need from me?"

Slowly turning to face me, he walks across the room and stops just in front of me. His eyes rake over my face again and I know, deep inside, I can't bear to go through this whole back and forth conversation again.

"Are there any contracts you need to me to take back to my office to work on?" I rephrase my question to convey my intent.

Understanding dawns on his face, and for a second, he looks disappointed. "I'll have maintenance move your office back up to this floor. Since we're working together again, it'll be easier on both of us. Once you're moved, we'll spend some time going over the ones you'll take over."

"Sounds good. If you don't need me right now, I'll go finish my other assignments in the meantime."

Walking as slowly as possible toward the door, I turn the knob and walk out of his office. He doesn't try to stop me this time. It's symbolic to me–I'm walking out of his life. I've explained what happened. I've taken responsibility for my actions. But the damage is irreparable and it's time for us both to move on to whatever our futures may hold.

My problem is–he's the only future I can imagine.

The morning sickness, which has turned into anytime of the day sickness, hits me again like a freight train and I run to the bathroom. The moment I walk out of the stall, Dana is standing at the sink with wet paper towels and hands them to me. Thanking her, I take them from her and walk to the sink to rinse out my mouth. Dabbing the wet towels across my forehead, the cool water brings me some relief.

Dana says nothing but she doesn't have to. The look on her face says it all. She knows. *Shit.*

***Dominic***

I'm pacing back and forth in my office again. It's so fucking hard to concentrate with all this shit bearing down on me. She answered all of my questions but I know she's holding something back from me. That doesn't help me trust her at all. I tried calling her bluff and forcing her hand, but she walked right out the door after agreeing to just be work colleagues.

Running my hand through my hair in frustration, I consider my options once again. Trust her and work with her? Trust her and take her back? Don't trust her and work with her? Don't trust her and take her back?

Just live without her completely?

*Fuck it.* I only live once and I want it to be with her. Deep down, I know I want it to be with her. She didn't save me just to later ruin me. She didn't put herself in danger for nothing. We may have started out under false pretenses, but that's not how we ended.

She was sent to destroy me but she became the other half of my soul. She makes me feel like no one else ever has. My draw to her is stronger than a magnet to steel. I'm tortured without her and

I'm fulfilled with her. She is my love and I am her Dom.

It's well past time I started acting like it. I've been too lenient in my attempt to be patient. It's also time for Harrison to feel the sting of my lash when I teach him the true nature of a Dom. One who is thoroughly pissed off and will have revenge for how his sub was mistreated. There'll be no mistaking the lesson he'll learn when I'm finished with him.

Harrison tried his best, but his best wasn't nearly good enough.

Bursting out of my office, I'm on a mission to talk to Sophia. As I hurry to the elevators, she walks out of the bathroom with Dana close behind her. Sophia's eyes are watery and her color has paled even more. I can't hide my concern as I take in her appearance.

"Sophia, are you okay?"

"I'm fine, Dominic," she lies to avoid the attention I'm drawing to her. Dana, still standing behind Sophia, catches my eye and slightly shakes her head from side to side.

"Dana, would you please get Sophia something to help her feel better?"

"What would you like, dear?" Dana asks.

"Just a Sprite will be fine," Sophia replies, clearly uncomfortable.

"Bring it to my office, Dana," I instruct as I take Sophia by the arm and lead her back to the seat she recently vacated.

"Dominic, I really need to get back to my office," she resists.

"Your boss must be a slave driver to make you work so hard when you clearly don't feel well," I quip.

"It's not that," she protests and tries to stand.

"Sophia, sit down," I say sternly and she obeys. "Tell me what's wrong." My tone leaves no room for argument.

Her eyes dart to the door and I know she's contemplating making a run for it. Sighing heavily, I remind her, "You know I will pick you up and bring you back if you even try it."

Her watery reply cuts me to the core, "Dom, please just let me go." She's trying so hard to maintain her composure.

"You've changed," I muse. "At first, you were a feisty businesswoman who was hell bent on making a name for herself. Then, you became fairly dependent on me and cried frequently. Now, you're more of the feisty lady again, but with sad eyes."

"I've always been the feisty businesswoman, Dominic," she answers, her voice stronger this time. "I cried frequently because every time you did something wonderful for me, I felt guilty over the way we got together. I knew I didn't deserve you, but I couldn't let you go, either."

"You kept saying you didn't deserve me," I recall.

"It was true."

I hear Dana's three-tap knock just before she opens the door and walks to Sophia. She has Sprite and saltine crackers in her hands and I know I must be looking at her like she's crazy. Dana simply says, "Trust me, Dominic."

Dana sets them on my desk directly in front of Sophia. She reaches to grab a cracker and lightly nibbles on it and takes small sips of the Sprite. "Thank you, Dana. This helps a lot," Sophia says.

Dana pats her on the shoulder and gives me a stern look. "She's not feeling well, Dominic. If you can't tell, she has lost weight and she needs to avoid so much stress."

Dana leaves and I take a moment to really take Sophia in. I noticed the hollowed cheeks and sunken eyes, but Dana is right. She has lost too much weight in the last several weeks. She continues to take small bites and small sips as she avoids eye contact with me.

"Sophia, if you're still not recovered, you can take more time off to recuperate. Your job is safe," I promise. "I'd rather you be off to rest and fully heal than push yourself to come back to work too soon."

She stops nibbling and drops her head forward. The pained expression on her face concerns me. "Tell me, Sophia. What's wrong?"

"Don't worry about me, Dominic. *Please* don't. When you talk to me like that, like you care, it just…it just hurts me even more. I'm *trying* to let you go and this doesn't help. I'll be okay." Her voice betrays her words. She doesn't believe them any more than I do.

"Why do I feel like you're still withholding something from me?"

The panic that flies across her face is unmistakable and I know I've hit the target dead center. Now to find out what it is.

"You know I can read you like a book, Sophia. No doubt that I was blindsided by the whole *Harry Dick-man* shit, but that's because he was never a Sir and the whole thing was all too fucked up. Make no fucking mistake about it, though - *you belong to me, Sophia*. I told you there was no going back on us and I fucking meant it. Just because I'm mad doesn't give you the right to withhold anything from me. Not your body, not your heart, and not your mind."

She immediately reverts to a submissive posture–to the one I've instructed her in. Her eyes rise to meet mine, just as she knows I like it.

"That's my girl. You know you can't hide from me, don't you? Your eyes tell me what I need to know about your feelings."

"There's no going back? Even now?"

"Even now," I confirm.

Intently studying her expressive brown eyes, my chest tightens at the emotions I see in them. She loves me and her love shines brightly in them. There is so much sadness in them, too, and she's afraid. She's scared of me?

*What the fuck?*

"Why are you scared of me, Sophia? What have I ever done to make you fear me?"

"It's not that I'm scared of you like that–that you'll hit me or anything," she says tentatively.

"Then what?"

"More than anything, I'm afraid you'll send me away and I'll never be around you again," she whispers, as if she's afraid voicing the fear will make it come true.

"Do you trust me?" I ask, drawing up to my full height and towering over her.

"Yes, of course I do, Dom. But I know you don't trust me."

"That's partly because I *know* you're intentionally keeping something from me. That's deceit–even if it's by omission."

She sits quietly for a few moments, internally debating whether or not to release this vital piece of information that's tormenting her. What she doesn't realize is I'm not giving her a choice. Being apart isn't what either of us really wants. This is a monumental hurdle for us to get over but we have to do it regardless.

"Stop thinking about it and do as I say, Sophia," I demand sternly.

"Can you please sit down, Dom?" she asks, but I hear concern in her tone. Concern for me.

"I will oblige you this one time but my patience with asking is wearing thin."

Nibbling on her bottom lip, she turns in her chair to fully face me. I'm not asking her again and she knows it. I expect an answer from her and I expect it now. I'm finished with being lenient and letting missteps slide.

"First, I want you to understand I didn't do this on purpose. It was never my intent and I was just as shocked as you will be.

"Second, I will respect whatever you decide. If you need time to think about it, I'll give you that, too.

"Third," she pauses to swallow her tears, "just...don't hate me."

"Noted," I respond.

Her eyes dart nervously back and forth between mine. I keep my gaze steady and wait for her explanation.

"Dom...um...damn, this is harder than I thought it would be," she takes a slow, deep breath and then fully exhales it before continuing. "I'm pregnant."

# Chapter Nine

"Dom, say something, please," Sophia prompts me.

*I can't speak. I am literally speechless at her confession.*

"Are you even breathing?" she asks, anxiety rising in her voice.

*No, I don't think I am.*

"How far along are you?" I finally find my voice and my breath. I lean forward toward her and give her my most penetrating stare.

"About ten weeks now," she replies quietly, dropping her eyes to the floor. "I found out in the hospital. The doctor said they did a pregnancy test before doing all my X-rays just to be on the safe side."

*On the safe side*–that phrase kicks me into gear and Shadow's words come back to me. If Sophia is a target now, she needs to be protected around the clock. As much as I'm not ready for what I'm about to say, if she's really pregnant with my baby, I have no other choice. The Dom in me says to take her home and make her beg for release to remind her who she belongs to. The man who just found out he's going to be a father has a deep-rooted need just to make sure his baby is safe.

"Speaking of being '*on the safe side*,' and since you're pregnant with *my* baby–and it is *mine*, correct?"

"Yes, of course it's yours!" she replies with indignation.

"Since you're pregnant with my baby, you're moving in with me so I can make sure you're both safe." My tone and expression leave no room for any argument.

"*What?*" she asks, confusion etched in her beautiful face. It is mixed with a hopefulness that she doesn't try to mask.

To be fair, this has shocked the fuck out of me, but it all makes sense to me now. It's the best–and only–solution for everything that has hit us. "Whoever is behind the attempts on my life is still out there and now could be after you, according to Shadow. The safety of you and my baby is my primary concern. You and I still have things that we need to work through and you need to be reminded that you are *mine*. Moving in with me is the only option that makes sense."

"You aren't mad at me?" she asks timidly.

"I'm not mad about the pregnancy. I'm still in shock since this was the last thing I expected to hear today. But, it actually makes my decision easier," I reason.

The sadness in her eyes multiplies exponentially and she looks completely defeated. "What are you thinking, Sophia?"

"I didn't want to tell you about the baby yet. If you decided you wanted to be with me, I wanted to know it was because of *me* and not that you feel obligated because of the baby."

Standing, I stalk across my office and scrub my hand over my face. Turning back to her, the anger wells back up in me at her deception, but I can't just forget the other things she did for me. "Sophia, I admit that I've been really mad over all of this. *So fucking mad.* But, I knew there was something missing because of the things you did to protect me.

"Hearing the full story from you helped put some of the pieces of this fucked up jigsaw puzzle in place. I can't say I'm *pleased* with all of this, but I know how much you love your brother, so I can definitely see you trying to protect him. You still should've told me, but I should've listened.

"I can't put all of the blame on you. If I'd heard you out before now, so many things would be different. You've admitted to your faults and apologized. It's my turn to do the same."

Her eyes widen and her lips part in shock. She stares at me in disbelief without making a sound for the first several seconds. "Dom, no. *No.* All these months I've been with you, I should've told you. This isn't your fault."

I shake my head from side to side and walk slowly toward her. Stopping directly in front of her, I take her hand and pull her to her feet. "No, Sophia, I acted like a complete ass. You've shouldered the blame and guilt alone long enough. My reaction was rash. I should've had more faith in you and asked you directly. That was stupid…just *stupid*. There's no other word to describe it.

"When those papers were served, I'd just been told about your connection to Harrison. I saw red and I immediately felt like a failure as your Dom. I thought I'd been played for a fool and I automatically believed the worst. You never had a chance to explain or clarify what I thought, and my actions put you in danger. *I'm* sorry, Sophia."

She searches my eyes and my face, looking for any trace of mockery, but she won't find it. Standing this close to her has my senses on full alert as I drink in her natural beauty, inhale her sweet perfume, and long to touch her. I'm still hesitant, even though she's assured me she's not behind the sexual harassment fiasco. I can't give the other employees any ammunition to use against me.

"Does this mean you forgive me?" she whispers to me. Her hands draw into fists at her side while she awaits my answer. "Does this mean you want me again?"

This brave, beautiful lady has endured so much in her short life. The Dom in me wants to take away all the pain and give her only pleasure. He also wants to punish her, lovingly, and drive out any thought, memory, or knowledge of any other man. The man in me just wants to pull her into my arms and tell her that everything will be fine...eventually.

With her question, she's asking me if I want her for more than just my baby she carries. Her heart and mind crave the security and protection only her Dom can provide. But, she needs to hear the words and feel the power of the meaning behind them when I say I want her, I need her, and I love her.

"You are still *My Angel*, Sophia," I pour my feelings into my words, "if you'll still have me as your Dom."

She's been strong and she's kept her emotions under control. She's kept the tears at bay and responded to questions with logic and reason. Until now. The tears she's held back flow like a torrent, running unchecked down her beautiful cheeks. The sobs wrack her body as her shoulders start shaking. I open my arms wide and she rushes into them, wrapping her arms around my waist and clinging tightly to me.

Wrapping my arms around her until she's fully enveloped, I pull her as close to me as two bodies can be and just hold her. My heart broke when I lost her and I feel the same intensity she feels now, we just show it in different ways. My desire to shelter and protect her has increased a million times over now, and not only because of her pregnancy. It's mainly because she's shown her devotion to me during a time when she had no reason to.

I failed her but she only focuses on her actions. Her well-being is my primary concern now, and that is part of my responsibility as her Dom. "Sophia," I murmur against her ear, "my love, calm down for me. It's not good for you to get so upset."

Rubbing her back and gently kissing her head, her body begins to relax against me. Her sobs diminish into occasional hiccups until her breathing finally returns to normal. She sniffles every few seconds, but I can feel the tension rolling off of her in waves. "That's my girl. Feel better now?" I ask, keeping my tone gentle.

She nods but her grip on me tightens, telling me she's not ready to be released yet. I smile and lower my face to rest my cheek on top of her head. Every part of our body is touching, and as my hands roam across her body, I realize just how much weight she has lost. I can feel each notch to count her ribs. Moving my hands further down, I feel her hipbones protruding more and my concern for her health increases significantly.

Quietly soothing her, I raise the question that plagues me now. "Sophia, I asked you earlier, but I want you to thoroughly think about this before you answer. Really consider every remote possibility."

"Okay," comes her muffled reply.

"Do you trust me? Completely, absolutely, and without a single doubt or question? If I told you to do something that's best for you, would you do it even if you didn't want to? Don't answer right away, and give me your completely honest answer."

While she considers my questions, runs through the scenarios in her mind, and weighs her choices, I wait on baited breath. Her answer has to be unequivocally *'yes'* for this relationship to work. No reservations, nothing held back "just in case." This is an all-in or all-out situation and I think she knows that. The part of her mind that is holding onto her fears is what keeps her from giving herself completely to me.

"Dom," comes her watery reply. "Can I tell you something before I answer that?"

"Of course," I reply, knowing that every insight into her thought process gives me an advantage–gives us an advantage.

"When I was seventeen, I left home and lived on my own, on the streets. I graduated high school early since I had enough credits, but you know my home life had become unbearable. I had already lost my mom and my dad before that, but then I later lost my brother–the one person who really loved me and the one I truly loved.

"Then when I met Harrison, I thought he was good. I thought he loved me and would help me, but I was so wrong about him. Then I met you, and you were more than I ever thought a man could be. More than I deserved. But, I fell for you, so fast, so hard. My love for you can't even be described. Then I lost you, too.

"I've lost everyone I've ever loved, Dom. It scares me to know that I would be happiest just giving you all of me, just being completely lost in you. What happens to me if I do and then I lose you? There would be nothing left of me."

Knowing fear was at the root of the problem is one thing. Hearing her describe it in those terms is another. Her question wasn't rhetorical. As her Dom, she needs me to have the answer, to reassure her, and to make the hard decisions so that she doesn't have to do it. The consequences of any decision will be on me, and none of the blame will be on her.

"Sophia, you are mine to love, to cherish, and to protect. I will take the burdens from your shoulders and put them on mine, because I can carry them. I can bear those heavy loads better than you can. All you have to do is let them go, let them fall on me, and I will gladly take them for you.

"You've been strong long enough. The tough decisions aren't up to you anymore. The negative repercussions of those decisions aren't yours to worry about anymore. You're *My Angel*, and I'm your immovable rock. I'm not going anywhere, Sophia. You'll always have me. Lose yourself in me, give me all of you, and let me make you the happiest woman that ever lived."

Those aren't just pretty words and hollow promises I just made her. That is my binding word, my honor, and my love. Everything that means anything to me is in my arms right now–*My Angel* and my child. This is my family and this is what I will protect with swift ferocity. When her body softens, and there's no way to tell where she ends and I begin, I know she's made up her mind. She can't get close enough to me as she prepares to give me her answer.

"I trust you, Dom. Take all of me. I'm nothing but an empty shell without you. I would rather have five minutes of real happiness with you than a lifetime of nothingness without you," she surrenders.

It's such a beautiful thing to watch her submit, to break down her walls, and to lay down her fears. Trusting me to keep my word, keep her safe, and love her through it all fills me with purpose and pride. Sharing the deep love we have for each other is what keeps us going through the darkest hours. Sophia will never doubt my unending love or my unyielding commitment to her again.

### *Sophia*

Can this be true? Am I dreaming? If I am, I don't ever want to wake. The other dream I had about Dom gutted me. It felt so real when he rejected me, but having him hold me and whisper words of love feels more like a dream than reality. I never thought I'd see the day when he'd welcome me back in his arms.

Even knowing there are still issues we have to work through doesn't scare me. His promise to me just gave me all the reassurance I need to know that everything will work out. I finally know what it means to let him in, to let him see the sides of me that I keep hidden from the rest of the world. The old fears no longer matter.

"Dom," I whisper into his chest, "it feels like such a heavy weight has been lifted off my shoulders and from my heart. I've missed you so much."

"I've missed you, too, *My Angel*," he whispers back and sends chills across my entire body. "It's good to have you back in my arms."

"I'm afraid I've made a mess of your white shirt. I'm so sorry about that, Dom. Do you want me to go get you another one?"

"Shhh," he soothes, "that's not for you to worry about, love. It's only a shirt. It means nothing. I have plenty more at home. Speaking of, that's where I'd like to take you now." Placing his hands on my shoulders, he gently pushes me away from his body to look at me as he talks. "Sophia, you've lost so much weight and I am concerned for your health, and our baby's health. I think it's best that you quit working now."

"Am I not doing a good job here?" I ask, the panic threatening to close my throat off.

He smiles warmly at me, "Yes, Sophia, you've been doing an excellent job here. I made the best business decision of my life when I hired you. But, everything that you've been through over the last couple of months is taking a toll on your body. Trust me."

This is the pivotal moment where I have to decide if I'm truly his sub and he's truly my Dom, or if I will hold on to my fear and let it rule my life. No matter what the question is, my answer will always be to choose my Dom. I've learned my lesson in thinking that I can handle everything. I'm strong, but there's more strength in accepting love and help than there is in refusing it.

"I trust you," I reply, conveying that I'll do as he asks. Dom leans down and captures my mouth with his. The feel of his lips on mine again is pure bliss. It's been so long since I've felt him. I want to burn this feeling, his taste, and his kiss into my memory to sustain me for the days when he's away.

Breaking the kiss, but keeping his lips hovering just above mine, he whispers, "Let me take you home now, *My Angel.*"

"My answer to that will always be '*yes*,' Dom. Always."

Using his private bathroom, I clean the streaked makeup from my face and prepare to leave the office. Dom tells me that the few personal items I want to take home with me will be packed up and delivered for me.

As I walk back into his office, he has an amused look on his face. "What are you thinking, Dom?"

"Did you run into my mother out shopping one day?" he asks, catching me off guard.

"Yes, I did and we talked a little. I didn't tell her about Harrison but I did tell her this was all a huge misunderstanding that I needed to fix with you. Why?"

"She wouldn't tell me about your conversation, but she kept saying I needed to talk to you. You didn't tell her you're pregnant?" he asks.

"No," I say, thinking back to our encounter, "but I was standing outside of a maternity store."

Dominic grins and shakes his head, "Yeah, I think she figured it out." He looks up at me, "Ready to go home now."

Home. Home is where the heart is and my heart is with my Dom, so my home is wherever he is. His arm is protectively wrapped around me as Shadow escorts us to the waiting car. Looking around, I realize that I haven't seen Tucker in a while.

"Where is Tucker?" I ask Dom. Shadow tries to hide his grin as he takes his seat behind the wheel and Dom and I climb in the backseat. "What's so funny?"

"Tucker has been following you, Sophia," Dom explains.

"I know he was at one time, but when I was let out of the hospital he said he had other things to do so he wouldn't be around."

"Yeah, that was true for less than an hour but I quickly changed my mind. He's been tailing you and making sure that you were safe the whole time."

"So, does he know about…," I look down at my stomach and back to Dom.

"No, Tucker doesn't know that you're pregnant, but I do," Shadow replies.

Both Dom and I snap our heads in Shadow's direction and my mouth gapes open.

"When did you find out?" Dominic challenges.

"When she was in the hospital," Shadow casually replies. "I told you I wouldn't be much of a spy if I didn't know everything that happens when it happens."

"How do you know and Tucker doesn't?" I retort.

"Tucker is a good guy. Damn good at his job. But he doesn't have the resources I have at my disposal."

I look at Dom, dumbfounded and have no clue what to even ask next. Dom smiles, shrugs a shoulder and says, "He's right. He's damn good at his job. I've learned not to question him because he doesn't tell me shit until he's ready to tell me anyway." Then he quickly adds, "But don't think you can pull that on me, Sophia."

"I wouldn't dare, Dom," I say, teasingly.

"Yes, ma'am, I am going to enjoy reminding you who your Dom is," he replies with a half-threatening, half-sensual tone.

*Oh, Dom, I can't wait for that, either.*

# Chapter Ten

Shadow heads in the direction of the lake house, prompting me to turn to Dominic. "Is your house not finished yet?"

"No, not yet," he says as he moves closer to me. "It will be another couple of months before we can move back in there. We're still at the lake house."

"Where's your normal driver?"

"On his honeymoon. Shadow says he prefers to be in control of the car, anyway," Dominic laughs.

"Don't we need to get my things from the condo?" I question Dom, who opens his mouth to speak but I jump in first. "Let me guess–it's already being taken care of."

He flashes the first full on pull-me-in-and-melt-me smile that I've seen in way too long. "You're learning," he playfully replies and we both laugh. This is the easy-going man I love.

*Oh, shit.* With everything today has already brought, I completely forgot about my plans for an upcoming weekend. I have to tell him but I know he won't like it at all. He may tell me I can't go, but I have to make him understand why it's so important to me to see this through.

"Tell me," he says, interrupting my thoughts.

"What?" His statement catches me off guard since I've been in my own world. Did I miss something he said?

"You just tensed up and you left me here alone for a minute," he explains. "Something's on your mind and you're anxious about it."

"I just remembered my plans for the weekend after next and I don't think you're going to like it," I admit, holding his gaze to convey I'm not withholding information from him.

"Let's hear it," he says reassuringly.

"I'm going to Austin to have dinner with my brother," I state, purposely keeping my tone light and nonchalant.

Dominic doesn't respond right away. He's taking in my statement and weighing all the possible scenarios, risks, and outcomes. He's probably also considering the way I stated it as a given rather than phrasing it as a question that would give him the option to say I can't go.

When his eyes find mine, I second-guess my approach. There's a mixture of hurt and anger swirling in his blue depths. The last thing I want is to cause him more pain.

"I would love it if you came with me," I offer an olive branch.

Dominic inhales deeply and holds it for a few seconds longer than normal. Searching his eyes, I find the same mixture of emotions combined with a hint of suspicion. Regaining his trust will be a long, hard road and I have no misconceptions about it. I understand that I'll have to prove myself many times over. It still hurts to see that suspicion in his eyes, though.

"No, you go ahead. You already had this trip planned and I know seeing your brother is important to you." His voice is devoid of all emotion. Only his eyes give any indication that he's nowhere near pleased with this.

"Dom," my tone is submissive, and my heart is breaking, "please don't be upset with me. This is the first time in years that he's asked to talk to me. I've missed him so much. Even though he's been in trouble, I still love him. Please try to understand. What if it were one of your sisters? Wouldn't you do the same?"

He seems to soften at the thought of one of his sisters needing him. I haven't met them yet, but after meeting his parents and seeing how close his family has been, I know there's nothing he wouldn't do for them. He nods slowly, understanding dawning in his eyes, and he relaxes his rigid body posture.

"I would definitely do the same for them, Sophia," he says as he cups my face with his hand. "What you don't seem to understand, though, is that *your life* is in danger now. You just told your family that you're no longer helping to keep your brother out of trouble, possibly even going to prison. Then, out of the blue, he calls to invite you to dinner, and you're just going to run to him?

"What if that's just a trap? If you go, especially alone, it could all be a setup just to kidnap you, hold you for ransom until they get what they want from me, then they will probably still kill me, you, and our baby."

"It's definitely a trap," Shadow chimes in from the front.

Hanging my head in shame, I feel like an idiot. "Dom, I was so excited to hear from him, I never even considered that. I mean, I know Harrison was holding this over his head, but I just assumed that made Harrison our mutual enemy, making us allies, and giving my brother back to me. I would never, *never*, put our baby in harms way. I feel so stupid."

"Don't," Shadow replies before Dom can say anything. "They were counting on your love and concern for your brother. That's been their M.O. from the beginning. You're going to that dinner, but you won't be going alone. We'll be there and we'll have you covered. Let's get to the bottom of this."

"The fuck you say!" Dominic roars. "She's not your fucking decoy, Shadow, so you can forget that shit."

"Where are you planning to meet him, Sophia?" Shadow asks calmly, as if Dom didn't just bite his head off.

"Quattro Amore, the new Italian restaurant in west Austin."

"Nice part of town, more upscale, nicer homes," Shadow replies. "If they try anything, the people would be more likely to intercede if they see it. If they're up to something, it'll be the quietest, most concealed option."

Shadow seems to be working through the logistics in his mind and not really speaking to anyone in particular. The fury is rolling off of Dominic in waves and rippling through the car. "Shadow," Dom growls through his clenched teeth, "we will talk about this in private."

"Dominic, I'm not questioning your need to protect her and your baby. There will be zero risk to her safety. ZERO. This is our opportunity to either gather more information from Shawn directly or we will figure out what their end game is. Either way, it's worth it to be able to put an end to this once and for all," Shadow reasons.

"You'll be there with me, right?" I ask Dom and squeeze his hand.

"Try to keep me away," he challenges before leaning over to kiss me. This man owns me–heart, body, and mind, and I wouldn't have it any other way. His kiss sets me on fire from the inside out. He deepens the kiss as his tongue slips into my mouth. His hand gently caresses my hair before he twists it in his fist and pulls my head back, giving him the full access he wants.

*Take it. Take all you want. It's yours.*

He pulls his mouth away, but he still holds me by my hair. Leaning his mouth close to my ear, he pulls my hand into his lap to feel his erection straining against the front of his dress pants. Sighing, with deep need coursing through my body, his sexy voice pulls me into him even more as he whispers, "If we don't stop, I can't be responsible for my actions in front of Shadow."

Tilting my head up, so that my lips are touching his ear, I return the favor. "Then hurry up and get me home so we can be alone."

"Shadow, can you not drive any faster?" Dominic growls. Shadow chuckles to himself, but I feel the surge of the increased acceleration as we rush home.

Once inside the house, Dominic leads me directly to his bedroom and locks the door. "Give me a minute to freshen up?" I ask.

"Of course, baby. But don't take too long," he replies as he strokes my cheek with the back of his hand.

Borrowing his toothbrush, I brush my teeth, wash my face, and finish my freshening-up routine as quickly as possible. The anticipation of the plans he has for me makes it almost impossible for me to wait another second. When I open the bathroom door, I find my Dom standing on the other side, his eyes ravenous with need, his bare body proudly displays his readiness, and his hand is held out, palm up, to lead me to heaven on earth.

"Did *'freshening-up'* not include removing your clothes?" Dom cocks a single eyebrow up at me as he leads me into the enormous bedroom.

"How about I strip for you now?" I offer and the slow, sensual smile that crawls across his gorgeous face is the only answer I need.

Gently pushing his shoulders, I guide him to sit on the edge of the bed. Taking a couple of steps backward, my fingers slide down to the hem of my shirt. Crossing my arms at my wrists, I slowly peel the shirt up and over my head, revealing my white, lacy bra. Running my hands down my chest, over my breasts, and straight down my abdomen, I throw my head back in complete ecstasy.

My fingers deftly unzip my skirt and languidly push it down over my hips, swaying them back and forth as my skirt lowers, until it pools at my feet. Standing before him in my matching white, lacy thong, I step out of my skirt and present my body to my Dom for his pleasure.

"Would you like to remove the rest or shall I, Dom?" I submit, giving him the final decision.

He leans back with his elbows on the bed, his sensual smile playing on his lips, and replies, "You've been doing such a wonderful job at it, by all means, please finish."

Thrusting my chest out, I reach behind me to unhook my bra, and hear him groan under his breath. He keeps his need well under control, but knowing that I can elicit this reaction from him empowers me even more. I let the straps fall off my shoulders and slowly uncover my breasts. As it drops off my fingertips to the floor, I turn sideways and reach for my thong to roll it down my legs, bending over as I go.

His arms are suddenly around my waist, lifting me, and placing me on the bed beneath him. "It's been two, long fucking months, Sophia. As much as it pains me to say this, I don't want to wait to have you this time. Any other time, your pleasure comes before mine, but, since you broke way too many rules, you will be punished now."

"Punish me, Dom," I moan.

He pushes my hands up above my head and secures my wrists in the restraints. Crawling down my body, the friction of his skin on mine pushing me to madness, he secures my ankles in the other set of restraints. I'm now lying on my back, my arms and legs spread far apart, and I'm unable to move of my own accord. I'm completely at his mercy, to do with as he will, and surrendering everything I am to him.

My Dom.

He moves to the side of the bed, his hungry eyes rake over my body and gives me chills before he even speaks.

"Did the doctor give you any restrictions? Any precautions?" he asks, his voice kept low as he asks.

"No, everything looks good from the ultrasound."

He nods slowly, taking in my response, and considering his next move. "Good."

He moves methodically, with purpose and intent, and my eyes are fixed on him. My Dom is so handsome and sexy. His stride is confident, his shoulders are broad and proud, and that V on his stomach needs to be licked repeatedly. When my eyes stray back to meet his, the smirk on his face says I have been busted drooling over him.

"Why do I have the feeling that you're enjoying the punishment part a little too much?" His question is rhetorical, I'm sure.

Opening the drawer of the nightstand, he removes the leather flogger with multiple strands, the riding crop, and the leather paddle, and then he places them within reach. His eyes become serious and the tone of his voice matches. Placing his hands on the bed, he leans over so that his face is close to mine.

"Sophia, you're going to receive a punishment fuck now. You are not allowed to come and you will not defy me. This is not for your pleasure – it is so you will never forget who owns your body, who owns you, and the only man you fully trust.

"I will fuck you here," he thrusts two fingers into my already wet center and I can't contain my cry at his welcome intrusion. With quick flicks of his wrist, his fingers move in and out of me and my body responds immediately. "Already so wet," he murmurs against the skin of my breast before he bites my nipple and I involuntarily arch my back, and thrusting my breast even more toward him. "You'd better not come," the tone of his voice conveys a clear warning.

He suddenly withdraws his hand and my body revolts at the loss. I groan loudly in disapproval and his puts his fingers in my mouth. "I will fuck you here, too. Lick yourself off my fingers," he commands and I obey.

A sudden desire to take me flashes in his eyes before it's quickly replaced with the hardness. I'm not used to this Dom, the one who seems to enjoy handing out my punishment and isn't the least bit patient. His method of punishment is so exciting, so raw, and so primal that I can't help but be turned on even more by it. I think this is the point, though–to get me so worked up that I can't help but come and then he can punish me in a different way.

As long as he keeps his fingers in my mouth, I continue to suck and lick them as instructed. Keeping my eyes locked on his, I run my tongue over and around each finger. Moving my head as much as I am able, I lift to take them deeper in my mouth and lower it to draw my lips out to the tips of his fingers. Dom leans across my body and bites the swell of my breast, marking me as his property. The mixture of pleasure and pain swells inside me and makes it hard to focus on my task.

Abruptly pulling his fingers from my mouth, he taps my temple and punctuates his every word forcefully, firmly committing them to my memory. "I will fuck you here. I'm wiping out anything any other man has ever said or done to you *today*. From now on, the only man's words that matter are mine. The only man's touch that you'll remember is mine. I am the only Dom you've ever had or will ever have."

Before I can answer, he flicks the leather flogger across my chest. It doesn't have a sharp sting like a whip does, but after enduring several lashes it makes my skin ultra-sensitive. The quick rotation of his wrists delivers multiple lashes in a short amount of time and soon my breasts are bright red. Dropping the flogger, he reaches over and grabs a silver chain off the nightstand.

When he holds the two ends up in front of his chest, I realize exactly what he has and my audible gasp brings a sexy, sadistic smile to his face. He takes one clamp and places it on my already sensitive nipple, slowly lays the silver chain across my skin, and places the second clamp on my other nipple. The pinching sensation heightens my arousal and I roll my head back in delight.

A sudden tug on the chain brings me back to my senses and creates a new mixture of pleasure and pain. "You will keep your eyes on me, Sophia. Don't make me say it again."

"Yes, Dom," comes my automatic, submissive reply.

He climbs on top of me and, even though I know this is going to be hard on me, I can't help but feel the exhilaration of feeling him between my legs again. He's poised with his face hovering over mine, every inch of our torsos meshed together, and his cock is waiting at my entrance. "You're restrained for a reason," he pierces me with his eyes. "Don't squirm. Don't resist. But, most of all, don't come. You're not allowed to come when you haven't been a good girl."

He thrusts into me to the hilt and his hands hold my face in place, daring me to look away from him as he takes what is his. His girth stretches me to the tipping point between sheer bliss and burning pain. His hips surge into me, over and over, driving harder and harder, until I feel the intensity building low in my belly. The tingling and tickling of an orgasm building tells me I'm about to defy his rule and I try to think of anything else that will delay it.

"I feel your pussy clenching around my dick, Sophia. You better be squeezing me of your own will and not because you're about to come," he says as he drives into me again and again.

After several more minutes, he moves his hand to my breast and removes one nipple clamp. The blood rushes back in, creating a new wave of pain before his fingers skim across my skin to my other breast to remove the second clamp. I cry out from the multiple assaults on my senses. Just as I'm about to have the most intense orgasm ever, he pulls out of me and sits back.

This action causes me to cry out in physical pain. The intense pull is still there, just under the surface, but not quite reached. My nipples are throbbing with the return of blood and my denied orgasm is fading, leaving me unfulfilled and needing more. Now I realize what else is in store for me since my punishment has only begun.

# Chapter Eleven

Dom unhooks my restraints from the bed and tells me to turn over. "I want your ass up in the air and your upper body flat against the mattress," he commands, his voice underlining his unyielding resolve. When I comply, he adjusts my wrists restraints so that my arms are straight out to each side. With my legs spread at his desired width, he reattaches the ankle restraints so that I'm immobile again. This position has always brought more intense orgasms with my Dom and in my mind I'm already dreading the consequences of defying him.

A loud thwack echoes through the room and is immediately followed by an intense stinging on my ass cheek. Opening my eyes, I immediately see that the paddle is missing from its place on the bed and know without a doubt where the stinging pain is from. Four swats later, my ass is on fire and must be fire engine red now. Just when I think I can't stand the pain any longer, he stops and gently rubs it with his hand.

He plunges into me from behind without warning. I'm at the edge of the bed, so he's standing up behind me. His fingers dig into my hips and he uses my body as leverage to push and pull me against him with each wave. The animalistic grunts and feel of determination in his every thrust drives my impending orgasm higher and higher. I feel the bed dip behind me and suddenly there is a change in his angle of penetration.

Fuck! It's killing me as I try to withhold my own pleasure. His hand reaches around and finds my swollen clit. When he takes it between his fingers, I moan appreciatively until he pinches it–*hard*. I scream out, loving every second of it, and he growls from just behind my ear.

"Don't you fucking come, Sophia."

I'm so damn wet now, I don't know how I can stand much more without just letting my orgasm go and accepting the consequences. The only thing is I'm afraid of what it would be. He has much more self-control than I do–he could continue this type of punishment for days, keeping me on the razor's edge but never allowing me to tumble over into the ultimate bliss that only he can bring me.

I bite down on my lip until I taste blood. The boring contract language that I was working on in the office earlier comes to mind. The upcoming dinner with my brother, which is certainly a trick just to get me in Austin, flies through my mind. But with each passing second, the immense pleasure I feel from my Dom brings me back to him, to this bedroom, to this bed, and to him, pumping in and out of me with abandon.

*Oh my god, here it comes…*

"NOOOO!!!!" I scream. He's pulled out at the last second again, leaving me hanging precariously on the precipice of the mother of all fucking orgasms. If I could just move my hands, it would literally only take me a second to send my body into convulsions myself. I can hear him shuffling around behind me, but I can't see what he's doing and I won't even venture a guess.

He makes quick work of removing my ankle and wrist restraints, but he's already considered my plan. "Don't even think about touching yourself," he huffs. "Lay on your side, facing me."

Moving to the edge of the bed, I do as he says, but this time I notice the riding crop is missing. *Shit.* He moves until he standing directly in front of my face and I know instinctively know what's coming next.

"Pull your top knee up until your foot is resting on your thigh," he demands.

Doing so, I note that my legs make the shape of the number four, and this position also gives him full access to my already swollen and throbbing center. Grabbing the back of my head, he holds my hair firmly in his grasp and guides my mouth to his cock. I wrap my lips around him and vigorously work him from base to tip. Wanting to please him because I love him, because he deserves it, and because I desperately want him to please me, I lick, suck, twirl my tongue, use my hand, and try to think of any new move I can try on him.

Just as my unresolved orgasm starts to subside, he moans in pleasure and there's a sensual tap on my clit that sends electricity shooting through my entire body. *Holy shit!* My eyes fly open and I see the riding crop in his hand just as it flies through the air and strikes my clit again, reigniting the fire between my legs. A couple more rounds of this brand of sensual torture, he pulls away from me before he pushes me over on my back and climbs on top of me.

"Take me in your mouth again, Sophia," he insists. Then I feel his mouth on me, between my legs. I can't take much more. The scruff of his beard is an extra stimulant against my clit and the inside of my thighs. When his warm, wet tongue circles my clit, I almost come undone. My legs involuntarily squeeze closed until he pushes them apart.

"Don't do that again. Be still," he says, and I get another swat but this time with his hand.

He continues with his mouth and tongue, adding his fingers for extra torture measures. Reading my body with consummate skill, he stops his ministrations every time I've built up to another mind-blowing orgasm. I'm about to use our safe word, *heartbeat,* because it's too much stimulation with no release in sight, when he suddenly stops completely.

Now, he's lying on top of me, our bodies perfectly aligned and his face is directly above mine. "That's my girl. You took your punishment so well, but I think you're about at your limit. I'm proud of you, my love. You've pleased me so much and now you will get your pleasure."

He pulls my legs up and holds them behind my knees and slowly slides into me. Claiming my mouth with his, he kisses me passionately, lovingly, and thoroughly, as he makes sweet love to me. This is my Dom, the one who focuses on bringing me the most exquisite pleasure I've ever known. This is my Dom, the one who freely gives his love and really doesn't ask for much else in return.

The overwhelming feelings of love I have for him overtake me and my tears flow freely. He knows why, so he doesn't have to ask. His thumbs gently wipe away my tears as he repeatedly thrusts into me. My orgasm builds higher and higher, and I realize now that all the punishment was to bring me to this point–to feel the deepest and strongest feelings I've ever felt. As I reach the ultimate peak of my climax and scream his name, all the worry, stress, and guilt fade from my mind. All that's left is my Dom, our love, and complete serenity.

Over the next hour, my Dom gives attention and love to every inch of my body. There isn't one spot that he didn't lick, kiss, rub, or touch in the sweetest, most loving, and most erotic way. His promise to give my pleasure is kept many times–as I screamed his name over and over again. He made slow, deep love to me, keeping our eyes locked, but letting his love flow freely through them and through his words. The affections he gives me make me feel like a completely loved and fully worshipped woman. All of the punishment he doled out earlier was absolutely worth the rewards afterward.

Dom is sitting up, leaned back against the headboard of the bed, and has me cradled in his arms like a baby. He leans in and gently kisses my face, "You're so beautiful, *My Angel*," he croons. "How do you feel now?"

"Renewed," I say, unable to find a better word to describe it in my state of euphoria. "The cobwebs and clutter in my mind has been wiped clean and I feel at peace now. And this, being in your arms, is exactly what I need right now. I've missed you so much, Dom."

His arms tighten around me in response and he kisses me gently. "I've missed you, too, baby. You have no idea how much."

"I had a dream one night, a nightmare, really. I dreamed I was outside and saw another woman leaving your house. You called me inside and then told me you weren't my Dom anymore. It all felt so real–it was just too much to think I'd lost you forever."

"There hasn't been anyone else, Sophia. Yes, I was hurt, I was mad, and I believed the worst. But deep down, I never stopped loving you," he murmurs in my ear.

This is my home. This is where I belong–wherever this man is will also be where I am. He fills the hole that's always been in my heart. In him, I've found the part of me that has been missing for so long. Maybe it isn't good to be this consumed and attached with another person, but without him, a part of me was dead. I am only fully alive with him.

And I'll stand toe-to-toe and fight *anyone* who attempts to split up my family.

"You must be hungry after all of our bedroom acrobatics, *My Angel*," Dominic says as he opens the refrigerator door. I should've fed you first but I couldn't wait to have you myself."

"I am getting hungry. It's been hard to eat with all the morning sickness I've had. It hasn't been just in the morning–it comes and goes at any time of the day," I admit.

Dominic removes several items and busies himself at the stove. By the time he's finished, I have a steaming bowl of vegetable soup and a grilled cheese sandwich placed in front of me. A very demanding Dom, and father-to-be, takes the seat beside me to ensure I eat it all.

"You've lost too much weight, Sophia," he gently chastises, "and both of my babies needs nourishment." He smiles warmly at me as he inclines his head to urge me to eat.

In between bites, we talk easily to catch up on the last couple of months. When I tell him all about my visit to the obstetrician, he has a sad look when he says he wishes he'd been there with me to see our baby. I jump up from the table and quickly trot to the foyer to retrieve my purse. Dom quickly trails behind me.

"I thought you were going to be sick again," he says when he catches up. "What are you doing?"

I pull out the pictures of our little eight-week old blob and show him the details that the ultrasound technician pointed out to me. He looks at the images in awe at the tiny arms and legs that are distinguishable. "There's a little life growing inside of you. That is so amazing," his voice holds so much amazement. Then he looks up at me, back to serious mode, "Go eat. Now. My baby is hungry."

I laugh and do as he says. That soup and sandwich combination is the best thing I've tasted in the last two months. Dom stares at the images as I eat, going back and forth between the printouts, and I watch him with a smile on my face. Having dreaded this conversation with him at first,

I'm so relieved that he's actually excited about having a baby with me.

"Dom," I cautiously start, "I've been thinking."

He looks up at me and narrows his eyes. "About?" He tilts his head to the side and eyes me carefully as he waits for the next revelation to come out of me.

"Instead of just quitting my job, I could work from home and just go into the office with you a couple of days a week. When I worked from the condo for those two weeks, it really seemed to work out well," I explain and then hold my breath for his answer.

"Why do you want to keep working? I make more than enough to support us," he inquires.

"I enjoy working. Solving puzzles, finding new ways to negotiate contracts with blowhards like Rich Daltry, and making friends in the company. I'm just not ready to give all of that up yet. But, I do agree that my health and the baby's health need to come first."

"I will agree to three days a week while you're pregnant. Two days at home and one day in the office–as long as you're eating and you're both healthy. The first sign of any problem, you will quit working completely and have no stress on you," he offers.

Knowing my Dom as well as I do, I know this is his final offer. He doesn't negotiate like a normal contractor would. He's a *"take-it-or-leave-it"* kind of man. In this case, if I pushed back on the number of days or the terms, I know I can kiss it all goodbye.

"You have yourself a deal, Mr. Powers," I smile and extend my hand for a handshake to seal it.

He takes my hand, gives it a firm pump up and down, and then pulls me into his lap. "It's that important to you?" he asks tenderly.

"It is, Dom. I know you can provide for us, but I love the sense of accomplishment I get from a job well done. It's what drove me to finish school early, to get the best internships in college, and the best jobs after graduation. It's what I know," I explain.

"Fair enough," he says, pushing my hair behind my ear, "as long as you're healthy and happy. I want you to take this week off, though. I can feel your ribs and you've been through way too much. I'm not budging on this one, Sophia."

"You won't hear any argument from me. I'll take this week off to rest and recuperate. Can you work from home this week? You're the only reason I wanted to go back in the office anyway," I confess.

"I do own the company," he reasons. "I can work from home whenever I want."

**Dominic**

"Are these the building plans for Quattro Amore?" I ask Shadow when he unrolls a set of building drawings on the formal dining table. He, Tucker, and I are reviewing our plans for covering the restaurant during Sophia's dinner meeting with her brother this weekend.

"Yes, I want to show you our plan for securing the building. My men and I will be very busy,

Dominic. While Sophia is inside the dining area, her safety will be entirely in *your* hands," Shadow explains, the gravity of the situation is aptly portrayed in his tone.

"Nothing will happen to her on my watch," I vow.

"We'll have communication devices so we'll all be in constant communication, except Sophia. We'll be able to hear her but she won't hear us. If we see someone suspicious, we won't have any way of alerting her. She'll wear a camera so we'll know where she is, we'll see what she sees, and we'll hear what she hears," Tucker explains.

I don't like this one fucking bit. She's been so sick over the past week and has lost so much weight. She really doesn't need this added stress on her of worrying about the true reason behind this meeting. I'm agreeing to this whole fucked up plan for two reasons–the off chance that her brother really does want to see her and make things right between them, or if it is a set up, we'll put an end to it once and for all.

Gripping the table tightly with my arms straightened, I tell them both, "Let's just get this done and over with. I've had enough of fucking around with this. The police have done absolutely *fucking nothing* to find out who is behind the attempts on me. If her family is behind it in any way, I *will* find out, and I will make them pay."

"One step at a time," Shadow absently replies, studying the building layout. "My team will cover every possible exit–four will walk the perimeter, two at the front door, two at the kitchen exit, two at the emergency exit, and one in each bathroom. I'll be in the vehicle outside, monitoring all communications and video feeds. Tucker will have eyes on *you* at all times."

Right, Tucker will have eyes on me. My life has been the one on the line. But right now, it's Sophia's life that I'm concerned about. It must be written across my face because Shadow is carefully watching me, scraping his hand across his chin as he gives me a curious look.

"You do realize this could also be a set up to get *you* in Austin, right? She could just be the red herring that draws our attention away from the real target. That's exactly why Tucker will have eyes on you at all times. This is not up for discussion," Shadow concludes.

"Point taken, Shadow," I agree.

The three of us pour over the plan again, mapping where each person will be, how we'll ensure Sophia's safety, and what we'll do should this turn out to be a simple dinner. None of us believe that is the case, but luck favors the prepared. Shadow and Tucker leave the room and I'm left to stare at the building plans alone.

I've tried to string together the pieces of this mind-fuck puzzle over and over again.

*Harrison Dictman sent Sophia to ruin me with a sexual harassment lawsuit.*

*Harrison claims he has proof that I killed Carol Ann.*

*Harrison has evidence against Sophia's brother, Shawn, which he used to control her.*

*Shawn is facing prison time if that evidence resurfaces. He has ties to the Mexican drug cartel.*

*Sophia's father, Manuel, has a history of being an assassin for the cartel.*

*Sarah, Sophia's mother, kept calling her just before the house fire.*

What the fuck am I missing?

# Chapter Twelve

"Shadow," I call from behind his retreating form.

"Yeah," he says as he turns toward me.

"What did you find out about what Harrison allegedly has on me?"

Shadow and Tucker exchange glances and the corner of Shadow's mouth quirks up. "Tucker will invite himself into Harrison's house and have a look. Harrison hasn't been back home since the night he assaulted Sophia, so it really shouldn't be a problem."

"I don't really want to know," I say, shaking my head. "Just call me if you need bail money." They both laugh as they turn and walk away.

I worked from home today and actually get a lot more accomplished when I'm not constantly interrupted in the office. After work, I took Sophia into the bedroom and we had a rousing repeat of her punishment session, but this time with only her pleasure as the focus. It's a much different experience to withhold an orgasm to further enhance her pleasure than it is to punish. It's much more intimate and much sweeter when she receives her reward. After I lost count of how many times she screamed my name, we both fell on the bed in exhaustion.

"You really need to quit taking advantage of me before I've had a chance to eat dinner," I playfully chide her. "You just zap all of my energy."

She laughs and playfully swats my arm. "It's about time for you to feed me, isn't it?"

"Yes, love, I'll gladly feed you," I reply suggestively.

"You are insatiable! And I love it–but right now, we need real food," she says lovingly.

"Your wish is my command, my love." I help her dress and wrap my arm around her as we walk to the kitchen.

Hours later, we've had dinner and Sophia says she's going to soak in a hot bath. I'm tempted to join her, but I head back downstairs instead. I'm caught up in my own thoughts of how my life has simultaneously become so fucked up but also became so right. After Carol Ann's death rattled me, I questioned my ability to be a Dom. Sophia's association with Harrison shook me at first, but my resolve to show them what kind of man I am is strong. Now, after learning the truth, Sophia is back in my arms and we have a baby on the way.

These thoughts swirl in my mind mixed with memories of everything else that's happened, but no matter how hard I try, I can't see the complete picture. Recounting each incident, turning them over and over in my mind, it takes me a moment for the beeping noise to register.

*The alarm at my office has been tripped.*

Tucker is already on the phone with the building security, giving them directions as he rushes toward the door to the garage. "Lock down the building *now*. Stop the elevators and lock the stairwell doors. Post guards at every exit and coordinate with the police when they arrive. No one gets in or out until we get there."

Shadow and Tucker stop their urgent movements to glance at each other and then at me. I know what they're thinking. *Who gets to stay behind and babysit Sophia and me?*

"Go ahead, Tucker. I'll stay here," Shadow says. "You'll be able to recognize if the intruder is an employee or not."

Turning to me, Shadow says, "I know you're capable to taking care of yourself. But, this may be a diversion to get us away from you so someone else can sweep in. I'd rather err on the side of caution until all of my questions are answered."

I nod in response and pace the expansive den back and forth. "I'm going to visit Sophia's family while we're in Austin for her dinner meeting this weekend. Even if it really is with her brother, even if he really does just want to be a part of her life again, I'm still going to talk to them," I decide, more to myself than to Shadow but I see him nod his head in agreement.

"I told you I've done some digging around on them. Seems Shawn has some pretty serious charges against him and he's only free because the evidence has been 'misplaced' somehow. The only way that can happen is if Harrison has some low friends in high places within the Austin Sheriff's Department," Shadow relays.

"What kind of charges?"

"Driving under the influence, negligent homicide, and drinking underage," Shadow replies solemnly. "He was driving drunk and high, with friends in the car. He lost control at high speed, hit an embankment, and flipped the car. He walked away with minor bruises, scrapes, and cuts. But his girlfriend, who was in the seat beside him, died at the scene."

"What evidence is missing?"

"The blood sample that proved his alcohol level and the drugs that were in his system at the time of the wreck. If it doesn't turn up soon, his lawyer will file a motion to have the evidence suppressed since they didn't preserve it properly and the chain of custody is in question," Shadow explains. "If it does turn up, the judge can deny the motion and allow it to be admissible in court."

"So, he's either looking at a long time in prison or getting off scot-free?" I ask incredulously. "How is he out of jail if he's awaiting trial for negligent homicide?

"The judge set his bail at half a million dollars and his family posted the money for the bond," Shadow replies as he cocks one eyebrow up in suspicion. "That's fifty-thousand dollars cash someone had to put up to get him out. That's a lot of money for them."

"They had to get help from *someone*," I agree.

"Follow the money. That's where the bad guys are," Shadow muses. But we both know it's the truth. Follow the money trail and it'll lead us right back to the person behind it all.

"The way Tucker drives when he's alone, and the light traffic at this time of night, he should be there in thirty minutes."

Shadow shakes his head and quirks one side of his mouth up, "They won't find anyone in there. It's just all way too convenient. A few days after you and Sophia get back together and she's here with you? No, this is definitely a diversion tactic. But, from what is the question."

"Are you saying you think Sophia is in on this?" The surface temperature of the sun would be considered the North Pole compared to me right now.

Shadow instantly snaps his head around to look at me when he recognizes the inflection in my voice. He calmly replies, "No, Dominic. That's not what I'm saying at all. I'm saying *someone* is using the circumstances to their advantage, but it's not Sophia."

The seed of doubt has been planted and I won't rest until I see for myself. Sophia claimed she wanted to take her bath right before all of this happened. What if she called someone–like *Harry Dick-man*–to give him the green light to break in? What if she is just playing me again? Calming my mind, I take a deep breath and make my move. Taking the stairs two at a time, I quietly creep toward the master bedroom. The door is already slightly ajar, allowing me a stealthy entrance.

The lights are off except for a small reading lamp in the far corner of the bedroom. Sophia is curled up with my pillow, her face nearly buried in it, and a folded washcloth across her eyes and forehead. My heart thaws again at the sight of her asleep in my bed. Her hair was obviously wet but has begun to air dry, the smell of her body wash still lingers in the air, and her damp towel is on the floor beside the bed. She did take her bath, climbed in the bed exhausted, and is using her Dom pillow to help her rest.

When I take a step toward her, she suddenly flies out of bed and sprints to the bathroom. Concern fills me and I rush to the doorway, finding her on her knees, hunched over the commode. She looks so thin and frail in her nightgown–so much more so than just over two months ago when I shut her out of my life. Regret and guilt eat away at me for all the time we've been apart and thoughts of how hard it must have been on her saturate my mind.

Running cool water over a clean washcloth, I wring it out and hold it against her forehead when she stills. "Are you finished, baby?" I ask gently. She simply nods her head and begins to stand. I help her up and she moves to the sink to brush her teeth. I can't stand it any longer. She looks like she's about to fall over right in front of me.

"Let me carry you," I state, but wait for her to agree since any sudden movement is likely to make her feel sick again. She doesn't answer verbally, but she wraps one arm around my neck and I bend to hook my arm behind her knees. She lays her head on my shoulder and I pull her close to me.

"You feel so cold, baby. Do you want me to lie down with you and warm you?" Again, she only nods and I carefully place her in our bed. Quickly shedding my clothes, I crawl in the bed behind her and cocoon her with my body. My arms wrap around her, my entire upper body is flush with hers, and our legs are entwined. A shiver runs through her before I feel her becoming warmer.

"Have you been sick the whole time you've been up here, Sophia?" I whisper.

"Yes," she answers weakly.

"Was today too much for you? Did I cause this?" I have to know if this is my fault. If my decision to playfully punish her, then thoroughly love her, drained her of all her energy and brought on this sickness…

"No, Dom, you didn't cause it," she whispers back. "Well, you kind of caused it," she amends and my heart jumps up in my throat. "You impregnated me, so that makes it your fault," she jokes.

Blowing out a long held breath, I really want to chastise her for that little prank. But, I know there's no way she could've known how responsible I feel for wearing her out. "Are you sure it isn't because I was too rough on you today? Or because you were too weak to endure everything?"

She rubs my arm lovingly, "I'm sure, Dom. It's been a regular occurrence for a while now. Morning sickness my ass–it's morning, noon, and night. There's no rhyme or reason to it."

"You're going to the doctor tomorrow, Sophia. You've lost too much weight and I want to know that you're healthy." I can't keep the concern from my voice on this. She needs to know how important her health is to me. She needs to know how important *she* is to me.

"Okay," she agrees. The fact that my feisty little sub doesn't argue that she needs to see a doctor alarms me.

"Do we need to go now?" The alarm at the company can wait. Tucker is more than capable of handling it without me. My first concern and responsibility is right here in my arms.

"No, I just want to sleep," she says, the fatigue overtaking her. Within a few minutes, her breathing slows and becomes steady. Her body is warm and she seems to be resting comfortably.

Easing out of bed, I quietly grab a pair of lounging pants and walk back downstairs to find Shadow.

"Have you heard from Tucker?" I ask, running my hand through my hair and glancing back up the stairs.

"He's there, but he's busy securing the building. Is everything okay?" he abruptly changes the subject.

"Sophia is sick. It may just be normal morning sickness, but she's lost too much weight. I'm taking her to the doctor tomorrow and I'm not leaving her tonight."

"Understood. We got it," Shadow replies just before his phone rings. "Yeah," he answers.

After a few clipped responses, I gather that Tucker is talking to him and he's just taking all the information in. It's hard being on this side of the conversation with Shadow because the mountain gives nothing away. Several minutes later, he disconnects with Tucker and I wait for an update.

"No one was found and he said they combed all the floors that are assigned to your company. There was nothing taken, but your office was broken into and some papers were disheveled on your desk. After they secured the office, Dana went in and checked the papers. She said they were a contract she had printed earlier in the day and left for you to review. The pages were numbered and they're all there. The security camera feed shows someone wearing all black, including the ski mask that covered his face and the black gloves that covered his hands.

"The strange thing, though, is when he jimmied the door to your office, he had papers in his hand. When he ran out, there were no papers. Something was *planted* in your office and only you would know what wasn't there before. When you and Sophia finish at the doctor, we need to go through everything carefully. Whatever he left behind was worth breaking into the building and risk getting caught," Shadow explains.

The cameras don't capture what happens inside my office, for obvious reasons, but it's really unfortunate in this instance.

"I need to go work off some of this pent up energy. Do me a favor and listen for Sophia. If she gets sick again, come get me. I'm concerned about her getting dehydrated."

"Sure thing."

The gym in the lake house is nowhere near the size of the one that was in my main home, but it'll do for tonight. I change into some gym shorts and running shoes that I always keep in here and prepare to work out my frustration. Hitting the treadmill, I continually increase the speed and incline and run until I don't think I can take another step. Checking the time, I realize I've been at this for about an hour on full throttle. After a quick shower, I rush up the stairs to check on Sophia again.

Approaching the door, I soften my steps and ease into the room. She hasn't moved from the position I left her in. Slipping back into my spot behind her, I envelop her with my body and place a soft kiss on her head. "I love you, *My Angel*," I whisper softly before sleep overtakes me. As I begin to drift off, I realize that holding Sophia in my arms relaxes me more than anything else. Even with the shit storm going on at my office now, the most important part of my life is here with me and everything else can wait.

***Sophia***

I'm being pulled out from the deepest slumber I've had since I lost Dominic. The bed is more comfortable than I remember and I'm warmer than

I've been in weeks. Moving slowly, I try to turn over but there is a hard wall behind me, and I feel a thick, muscular arm snaked around me. Forcing my eyes open, my heart flutters and I almost cry from happiness.

I would recognize the intricate design of those tattoos anywhere. *My Dom.* I love waking up in his arms and every morning is like the first time all over again. The memories of last night flash before me and I recall him helping me when I was sick. He carried me to bed and I could feel the concern radiating off of him. For a few minutes there, I thought he would take me to the emergency room and demand that they "fix" me. Just the fact that he helped me in the only way he could makes me fall deeper in love with him.

Twirling the ring he gave me on my finger, the inscription still holds so much meaning to me. "*My Dom's Angel.*" It's my collar from him, the symbol that I belong to him, and he said it was to never come off. "*There is no going back,*" he said when he gave it to me. I thought I understood what he meant at the time, but it is all so much clearer to me now.

Even when we were apart, I was still his and this ring stayed on my finger. My heart, my mind, and my body knew I still belonged to him. I knew without a doubt there could be no other man for me after loving my Dom. Now that I have him back, there's nothing I wouldn't do to keep him. He wants to take me to the doctor today because he's worried about me. If such a small thing would give him peace of mind, I'd never deny him that. I'm sure the doctor will just explain that this is a normal part of pregnancy but he'll feel better hearing it from Dr. Perry.

"Good morning, my love," I hear his husky morning voice from behind me.

"Good morning to you," I turn my face over my shoulder and respond. He leans in and plants sweet kisses on my eyes, nose, and chin.

"Did you sleep well?"

"Better than ever," I say honestly. "Did you?"

"More relaxed than ever, baby," he snuggles in closer to me, burying his face in my hair. "How do you feel this morning?"

"I just have to lie still in bed for a few minutes after waking. If I try to jump up right away, it usually makes the nausea worse," I explain.

"Lazing in bed it is, then," he chuckles. "We're still going to the doctor today."

"Okay, Dom," I agree and he raises his head, concern filling his eyes.

"Are you worse than you're telling me?"

"No," I smile at him, "I just know you won't rest until the doctor tells you it's all normal and I'm fine."

The concern hasn't faded from his eyes but I see gratitude swirling in them, too. He knows I'm agreeing to go for him, not for me. It's a small sacrifice–spend a little time in the car and in the waiting room with my Dom, just to see the doctor and hear that my symptoms are normal. That's why his next words shock me so much.

"I'm not so sure this is normal, Sophia. I didn't realize how much weight you've lost until I really looked at you in your nightgown last night. If the doctor says you need to go on bed rest until the baby is born, there'll be no argument. That means no work, no trip to Austin, *nothing*. If I made it worse by tiring you out too much yesterday, I'm so sorry and I'll do everything I can to help you feel better."

Slowly turning in his arms to face him, I lovingly stroke his face. "Dominic, you didn't do anything wrong. I felt fine the whole time we made love yesterday. You took good care of me. It wasn't until after dinner that I felt sick and I've done that so many times, I should've known to only eat a light meal in the evening. It's not your fault."

He nods, but I still see the question in his eyes. When the doctor says so, he'll believe it. I love that he cares for me so much. I love that he takes such good care of me.

I love how he loves me.

# Chapter Thirteen

"Sophia Vasco," the nurse calls from the open doorway.

Dominic and I rise from our seats and follow her to the weight scales. As she adjusts the counter-weights, she states my weight and then begins to write it in my chart. The alarm in her voice catches me off guard when she realizes the difference.

"Sophia! Why have you lost six pounds since the last time you were here?"

"I've been sick all the time. I've had a hard time keeping anything down," I explain and feel the tension rolling off Dominic in massive, crashing waves. I'll be on complete bed rest with an electric wheelchair to cart me back and forth to the bathroom by the time he's finished with me.

"You should've called us, sweetie," the nurse says. "It's not good for you to lose that much weight when you're pregnant."

She escorts us to an exam room, tells me to undress and put the hospital gown on, and then leaves Dominic and me alone. He helps me undress then he helps me into the hospital gown before circling his arms around me and pulling me close to him. His warm hands are splayed across the bare skin on my back and he smells so good. I love his scent–his woodsy cologne mixed with the purely dominant, alpha male scent that only belongs to my Dom.

He tenderly strokes my back, along my spine, before he says, "Hop up on the table and get off your feet, baby."

I smile at him but I do as he says. "Are you going to be this overprotective for the next seven months?" I laugh.

He gives me a real smile, the one that can break hearts and melt glaciers, before his answer makes my heart swell with more love than I knew I could even feel. "No, baby, not for the next seven months. For the rest of your life."

He stays at my side, his arms wrapped protectively around me, his head nuzzled against mine, until the doctor walks in the room. "Hi, I'm Dr. Tabitha Perry," she says as she shakes hands with Dominic.

"Sophia, I hear you've been very sick and have lost six pounds." Her voice conveys concern and I feel Dominic tense beside me.

"Yes, the morning sickness isn't following the rules. I've been sick all day and night," I explain. "Dominic was worried about me last night when I got sick again and wanted me to come see you as soon as possible."

"Morning sickness is a bit misleading," she smiles, "because it's not always morning when it hits. The problem comes when you're not able to keep nutrients in your body to feed the baby. The baby will first steal what it needs from you, but when that's depleted, then you both suffer."

I notice, with deep foreboding, that she hasn't said it's normal to be this sick. Casting a weary look at Dominic, I see the worry in his eyes, too. "What do I need to do?" I ask Dr. Perry, terror and panic rising in my throat.

"Let's do your exam, get your blood work back, and we'll go from there. In the meantime, I will give you a prescription for anti-nausea medication that will help you keep your food down."

"Is that medication safe the baby?" Dominic asks.

"Yes, pregnant women have safely used it for many decades now. Your mother probably even used it with you," Dr. Perry explains before having me lie back on the examination table.

"Have you seen any spotting or bleeding?" she asks as she checks my stomach.

"No." I'm so scared now. It's *not* normal to be this sick and I shouldn't have let it go on so long.

"Any cramping? Either in your lower abdomen or in your lower back?"

"No." *Oh my god, why is she asking all these questions? What's wrong?*

She nods, "I'm going to check you now. Put your feet in the stirrups and scoot all the way down to the edge of table."

Dominic helps me move down and I know it's just so he'll have something to do, something to contribute, and something to help distract him from his thoughts.

"Dr. Perry," I start apprehensively, "I have to ask you an embarrassing question."

"Sure," she laughs. "I assure you, I've heard them all and nothing will shock me."

"Will…vigorous…sex hurt the baby? Or make the morning sickness worse?" I'm so glad I'm lying down, staring at the ceiling, and can't see her over the sheet draped across my legs.

"No, not at all. Your baby is well protected in your uterus, surrounded by amniotic fluid, and padded with your internal organs. At most, the baby would be rocked to sleep," she assures us.

"What if it overexerted Sophia?" Dominic chimes in. "What if it took too much of her energy?"

"Still wouldn't hurt the baby. Sophia may want a nap afterward, but a healthy, even *vigorous*, sex life won't hurt the baby in a normal pregnancy. There are very few circumstances where we have to worry about that–previous preterm labor, if she had a cervical mesh inserted, or other similar known medical issues."

Dominic releases an audible sigh of relief and reaches to take my hand in his. Love shines in his eyes and I give just as much love back to him.

"It's still too early to hear the baby's heartbeat with the fetal Doppler," Dr. Perry says as she stands. "As of now, everything looks normal except your weight loss. We have to turn that around immediately. Major organs are forming now and the baby needs all the nutrients he or she can get.

"Take your medication, eat smaller but more frequent meals, and keep something on your stomach at all times. Many women have found that if they let their stomach get completely empty, the sickness is much worse. Keep crackers beside your bed and nibble on them before you even lift your head from the pillow. You should see major improvements soon."

"Thank you, Dr. Perry," Dominic says sincerely as he shakes her hand, clasping her one hand with both of his.

I have a feeling that my loving, possessive, protective Dom is about to amp it up to the one-thousandth degree.

After making several phone calls when we left the doctor's office, he has managed to have *all* of his work and my work delivered to the lake house. Christine has stocked the kitchen with every type of food the grocery store carries. Dana has bought multiple pairs of comfortable, but stylish, pajamas so the baby and I will always be well taken care of.

"When does it say to take your medication?" he asks.

"Every twelve hours as needed for nausea and vomiting."

"Are you nauseous?" he asks, eyeing me speculatively.

"Not at the moment. I actually feel pretty good for a change. You did hear that she said a healthy, vigorous sex life is still okay, right?"

He smirks, such a sexy grin, "Oh, I heard her, Miss Vasco. Just wait until I get you home."

"Thank you, Dominic," I say. My tone reflects my seriousness as my overwhelming gratitude overcomes me. Pregnancy hormones or not, his nurturing side astounds me.

"For what?" he asks, clearly puzzled.

"Everything," I say simply. "You've given me so much without asking for much at all in return. I was broken when I came to you. I'd lost my true self and you helped me find it again. It may be hard to believe, but I wasn't always so dependent on others. Somehow, I made it through college, internships, and even thriving in a very demanding position at work, but I let Harrison push every self-destruct button I have.

"The only thing I don't regret about meeting him is that he sent me to you. I've told you many times that I don't deserve you, but I can never let you go now. I mean that with all my heart, Dominic.

Even when we were apart, I picked myself up and carried on because I had to. It wasn't easy, but I found some of the strength I lost somewhere along the way. That's because of you."

He smiles warmly at me and shakes his head. "That's where you're wrong, Sophia. Submitting to someone else, allowing them to decide what they do to you, and surrendering your complete trust in such a beautiful act of faith–*that* is strength. You've always had it. You may have misplaced it for a short time, but it's always been there."

Leaning over the center console, I gently stroke his face before placing soft kisses along his jawline. Continuing up to his ear, I gently take his earlobe in my mouth, lick around the edge, and pull it between my teeth and lips. Dominic groans and moves his hand to my leg. Darting my tongue out, I lick down the path from his ear to his collarbone. "You taste so good, Dom," I murmur against his skin.

The growl that rumbles through his chest sets me on fire. Sliding my hands down his chest, I skim my fingertips over the ripples in his abdominal muscles and rub my palm across the bulge in his pants. Deftly unbuckling his belt, unbuttoning and unzipping his pants, my hand wraps around him and I begin stroking him up and down.

Dropping my head into his lap, I take the mushroom shaped tip into my mouth and he moves his hand to the back of my head. As I circle my tongue around the tip of his cock, I'm feeling playful, so I tease him with my mouth. Fully opening my mouth, I lower my head slightly but refuse to take him in fully just yet. Raising my head again, I pay more attention to the underside, flattening my tongue against him from tip to base.

His fingers grip my hair and he pants, "Baby." His pleasure-filled tone spurs me on further. Licking my way back to the top, I wrap my lips around him and spiritedly pleasure him. My hand and mouth work in tandem, his hips jerk upward and his grip on my hair tightens in response. Taking him as far in my mouth as I can, I relax my throat muscles and allow him to hit the back of my throat. Moaning, I feel the ripples crash through him as his body stiffens.

"Fuck, Sophia," he says between clinched teeth.

Swallowing, so that the muscles constrict around him, I lightly shake my head from side to side. This earns me another growl of praise. "*Holy shit, Sophia!*" He sucks in a sharp breath and holds it in. I keep working him, my warm, wet mouth taking his length and girth as much as possible. His one hand that's still on the steering wheel is fully extended, his knuckles are white from his tight grip, and his hand in my hair is slightly tugging on it.

"Fuck, it's hard to focus on the road with your mouth on me," he praises.

Increasing the speed and pressure, my head bobs up and down in his lap until he says, through gasps, "I'm…about…to," before he's unable to hold back any longer. His release shoots into my mouth and bathing it in his warm, salty taste. I keep going until I'm positive I've taken all he has to offer and lick up every last drop. His entire body instantly relaxes as he melts back into his seat.

When I raise my head up, he looks at me with both surprise and adoration. "What was that for?"

I smile at him and respond, "You just tasted too good for me to stop."

He quirks one eyebrow at me and gives me his sexy smirk. "I know exactly what you mean and I'll show you as soon as we get home," he promises

Tingles run through my body at the thought of what's in store for me. "You need to hurry and get us back home then."

When we walk through the door, I immediately know that our afternoon delight will have to wait a little longer. Tucker and Shadow are at the kitchen table, deep in conversation. Their brows are drawn down and the air in the room is crackling with testosterone. Dominic senses it, too, because his stance immediately changes as he shields me with his body.

"What is it?" Dominic asks.

Tucker responds without looking up, "Something you need to see for yourself, Dominic."

When Tucker uses his name, it's always bad. It's always something that will be more than upsetting. This is his way of establishing they're on the same team and that Dominic doesn't have to face the problem alone. Dread and alarm fill me until I feel the anxiety swelling in my throat. Even

Shadow has a concerned look on his face and that is definitely not normal.

"Show me," Dominic replies stoically.

"Maybe you should have a seat first, Dominic," Shadow suggests, but holds out a piece of paper anyway.

I suddenly can't breathe. My brain and muscles seem to have forgotten how to draw in oxygen. My feet are rooted to my spot on the floor, my heart is pounding in my chest, and the blood is roaring in ears. Opening my mouth to speak, I can't form the words. I recognize that paper. *How can this be?*

Dominic snatches the paper from Shadow's hand but doesn't take a seat. I think he may be somewhat insulted at the suggestion that he would need to take this siting down. For several long minutes, Dominic is eerily silent. I'm not sure he's breathing either. Shadow and Tucker keep their eyes trained on Dominic, both unable to hide their concern in their normally indifferent expression.

Dominic's voice is low, controlled, and downright scary when he asks, "Where did this come from?"

Tucker meets Dominic's stare and, with a calmness that betrays his facial expression, he drops a nuclear bomb. "I paid a visit to Harrison's house today. This was in a file with your name on it."

Without another word, Dominic's confident, determined stride carries him up the stairs and into one of the spare bedrooms. After several minutes, he returns to the kitchen and is holding a second paper, his gun shoulder holster, and his Glock .45. He lays them on the table as he adjusts the holster and pulls it over his head before securing it in place.

"Boss, let us handle this," Tucker says soothingly, trying to reason with a very determined dominant man. "It's best that you stay out of it for now."

No one seems to remember that I'm here. My hand found the countertop and I'm gripping it so tightly I'm sure there will be finger indentions in it. Curiosity is killing me. I want to ask what's on the paper, but I don't want to at the same time. Looking at it, I instinctively know what it is but not what it says. The only thing I know for sure is that one paper is about to change my life.

"Tucker, if you think I'm not going to kill that son of a bitch, you're fucking crazy," Dom growls.

"What is it?" I finally manage to speak, my voice meek and unsure, conveying exactly how I feel right now. Three heads whirl in my direction but my eyes are only trained on one of them. Dominic looks slightly confused for a second, as if he's questioning why I'm here, then his eyes change with realization.

"Sophia," he says softly, his voice a stark contrast from the tone he just used with Tucker. He's searching for the words to say. He doesn't know how to tell me without hurting me. His eyes stray to my stomach and my hand quickly draws up to protect our baby. He drops his eyes to the floor just in front of me and I feel my heart break because he won't look at me–he can't look at me.

"What is it?" I ask more forcefully, drawing my shoulders up to stand tall. I'm no one's doormat. I willingly submit to Dominic because he's earned my trust, he takes care of me, and he shows me he loves me. After the events of the last several minutes, I'm not feeling real submissive and it doesn't appear that I'm his first priority.

Dominic takes a step toward me and I take a step backward while slowly shaking my head back and forth. I will not be placated with *"trust me"* or *"everything's okay"* this time. Dominic's head drops to the paper still held in his hand. He takes a deep breath and fully exhales it, clearly still torn on what to say. In my peripheral, I can see Shadow and Tucker looking at me with a mixture of compassion and pity.

"It's the second page of Carol Ann's letter to me. The page that has been missing," Dominic replies solemnly.

My heart ceases to pump in my chest.

***Dominic***

*Sir,*

*I can't believe we have been together for a whole year. So much has happened in our short time together. I often feel that I've brought more sadness than happiness to your life. You have brought me nothing but happiness and I want you to always remember that. No matter what storms have hit, you have been my steadfast rock in the turbulent seas.*

*Never doubt the good you've done for me. Never doubt my appreciation for you. And never doubt my love for you. I'm paralyzed at the thought of losing you and I know I could never live without you. Through all of my problems, it's been your love that has pulled me through. I love you, My Sir, and there's nothing about our life together that I regret. I'm sorry for the trouble I've caused for you.*

I memorized those words and can recite them backwards in my sleep. The rest of the letter, the page that Tucker just handed me, is now seared into my memory. The conclusion of Carol Ann's thoughts on the worst fucking day of my life will haunt my dreams, interrupt my sleep, and forever be cursed by the '*what-if's*'.

*What if I had just stayed home that day?*

*What if I had made it home earlier?*

*What if….*

I'm frozen in time as I read her words. Picturing her in my mind, I can see her face as she writes each line. She's sitting at the desk, her left arm at a ninety-degree angle as her hand supports her head. The right side of her lip is between her teeth as she concentrates on her wording. She lives in these words and I can feel her emotions bubbling up and spilling over onto the page.

*Through all of our troubles and trials, one thing has remained constant: our love. It has never waxed or waned. Not when my parents objected to us not being married before living together. Not when my brother tried to shame us for our choices. Not even when my fear of leaving the house put a damper on socializing or traveling.*

*I made a new resolution today and, with you, I will keep it tomorrow. Enough of my life has been lived in fear and shame. No more. You've asked me to go with you on business trips before but I wasn't able to go. I want to go with you on your next trip. I want to spend every minute with you that I possibly can. Tomorrow, I want you to take me shopping for new clothes.*

*Oh, and some of them will have to be maternity clothes. ☺*

*With all the love in my heart –*

*Carol Ann*

*(P.S. I didn't really drink the champagne.)*

# Chapter Fourteen

Carol Ann was ripped from my arms, my life, and my heart way too early. Now, reading these words, I can't help but think about all the ways my life has been forever changed in the blink of an eye. I mourned her death, I blamed myself, I questioned my Dom abilities–but I was robbed of the time to mourn my unborn child.

My paternal rights were denied in every imaginable way. I would never see that baby born, teach it the things only a father can, and watch it grow every single day. My baby that Carol Ann carried has never been recognized, named, or even memorialized in death. *Robbed*–of all the things that can never be and all the things that should have been.

The rage hits me like a freight train and my sole purpose has become killing *Harry Dick-man*. A terrible and violent death is too good for him, but that's what he'll receive nonetheless. Without a clue as to where he is hiding, I bolt up the stairs to retrieve my gun.

When I reach the top of the landing, I have a sudden need to retrieve the first page of the letter from Carol Ann. It was one of the things I saved from the house fire–one of the few personal items that survived. After I double-check that the handwriting and the paper match, I unlock the secret safe and grab my Glock .45 and my shoulder holster.

He is dead. He just doesn't know it yet and he won't know I'm there until I want him to know.

Bounding back down the stairs with my possessions in hand, I lay them down on the table, ready to double check the clip before I head out to find him. I've zoned everything else out in my red haze of fury. I'm barely cognizant of Tucker trying to talk me out of what he knows I'm planning. After leveling him with my *don't-fuck-with-me* stare and response, I continue with my plan.

Until I hear a small voice calling from behind me.

*Sophia.*

The shock of that page completely floored me and I had thought of nothing else until she spoke. Her voice pulled me back from the deep pits of the revenge that I was plotting. Looking at her now, the shame fills me at how quickly I changed from the man who just brought her home from the doctor's office to the man who forgot everyone and everything else in his life.

*Doctor's office.*

My eyes drop to her midsection and I think about the baby that Sophia now carries. *My baby, my blood, my life.* My need for vengeance is completed deflated now and all I want to do is hold Sophia in my arms. An unconscious signal sent from my brain makes my feet move toward Sophia, the exact direction my heart naturally gravitates to anyway. But she moves backward, away from me, and shakes her head *'no.'*

She knows and I've hurt her terribly, but she stands proud and demands to know what I'm still gripping in my hand. The doctor has just said she's lost too much weight. We had to pick up prescription medication to help her even eat to keep herself and the baby nourished. The last thing I want to do is add to her stress by telling her anything about this.

But I can't lie to her.

"It's the second page of Carol Ann's letter to me. The page that has been missing," I painfully admit.

The color drains from her face and she stands transfixed. Raking my hand through my hair, I blow out a frustrated huff of breath. Seeing my reaction to this letter cut her deeply, I know this without a doubt. It will appear to her that my feelings for Carol Ann are ruling me and that my feelings for her are inferior. Nothing could be farther from the truth.

"Sophia, are you feeling sick? Do you need your medicine?" I purposely keep my voice gentle.

Her chin begins to quiver but she's fighting the tears with every ounce of pride she has in her. Taking a deep, calming breath, her countenance changes and her features become hard. I can see her shields going up to protect herself from further pain. What she doesn't understand is I'll do whatever she needs me to just to keep that pain from her.

Her next question hits me in the chest like a twenty-pound sledgehammer.

"Why would Harrison have that page of her letter if it was in your condo when she died?"

The breath has been knocked out of my lungs and my mind spins with various scenarios, but none of them are plausible. In my shock of just now learning that Carol Ann was pregnant, and in my haste to exact revenge, my only consideration was that Harrison kept this from me for the past two years. The interrogatives of the details didn't even occur to me–that's how far gone I was in my own world.

The distant sound of a chair scraping against the floor comes from behind me, but there's no connection between it and my brain. All the questions swirling in my head are so loud, it's as if there are fifty people talking at once all around me. Strong hands grip my shoulders, push me downward, and my legs obey. My eyes are grounded to Sophia's but I can't even respond intelligently.

"Dominic, let me have that," Tucker says as he pulls the letter from my hand.

Snapping out of my stupor, I realize Sophia has asked the million-dollar question. *Exactly how did Harrison get that page?* Carol Ann hid it in our apartment. Granted, it was in a spot she knew I would find it, but that was all part of our game.

"I don't know how he got it, Sophia. But I need to find out."

"What does it say?" She narrows her eyes and dares me to lie to her.

"You can read it, I won't keep it from you. But I'd rather you didn't for a few more weeks, until we're well past the first trimester." I could be more forceful by outright saying she can't read it, but that would cause her just as much doubt and anxiety. "I'm asking you to please wait, Sophia."

Her eyes fill with tears but she blinks them back, swallows the heart I know that is in her throat, and extends her hand toward me, palm up. Her hand is shaking, without a doubt scared to read it, but equally scared to not read it.

"Guys, can you give us a minute?" I ask Shadow and Tucker as I stand and pick up the letter. Their reply is to leave the house completely. Knowing Tucker, they are just waiting on the front porch to give us a little privacy.

"Sophia, I need to explain my reaction to this letter before you get upset over it," I begin. "All I could think of was that this part of the letter has been in Harrison's hands for the past two years. All this time that I've questioned my worth as a Dom, questioned what I could've done for Carol Ann, and even that Harrison blamed me for her death. He could've spared me all of that."

"Let. Me. Read. It," she challenges.

Staring down at the letter for a minute, I know this will not go over well. I'm torn between what's right and what's best–they're not always the same thing. What's right is not keeping Sophia in the dark. What's best is that she regains her health to protect herself and the baby. Before I change my mind, she pulls the letter through my fingers and begins to read it.

I know the very second she reaches the last line of the letter. Her mouth drops open, her hand quickly covers it, and her eyes squint to mere slits as the pain stabs through her heart. Her shoulders slump and the wounded look on her face kills me. The paper floats to the floor as she uses both hands to cover her face and her body shakes from her sobs.

Placing my hands on her arms, I begin to pull her into my embrace but she extends her arm, pushing against my chest to keep me at bay. "Sophia, baby, I know what you're thinking. This letter was a complete shock to me, though. I had almost two years of pure *hell* before I found you. He tried to fuck that up, too. He *deserves* to pay."

"It's selfish of me, but I can't say I'm not jealous of what you had with her. I can't even explain what I feel right now. I'm ashamed that I'm jealous over someone you loved in the past, knowing she's gone. It comes down to this, really," she takes a deep breath, "It just seems like she was better for you than I am."

"I love *you*, Sophia, more than I've ever loved anyone. It was a shock to find out she was pregnant when she died after all this time and it's wrong that he knew all along. A baby I never knew about was buried with her, but never mourned or even recognized. These are the things I'm battling. But, no matter what, I never want to make you feel like you aren't the most important person in my life. *You* are the only one who has ever called me Dom."

She sniffles, wipes her face off with her hands, and gives me a rueful smile. "These pregnancy hormones are really doing a number on me, Dom. You may have to be more patient with me than ever," she says on shaky breath. "That was definitely a shock to me, too. It hurts, I won't lie, but I have to consider how *you* must feel. Finding out this way and after all this time must be just terrible.

I open my arms and she willingly walks into them. Those walls she put up are coming down and we are growing stronger together. The realist in me can't help but think, *what's next?*

Even though I know there are a million files I need to comb through to figure out what was left in my office, I put it off for another day. Even though every ounce of me wants to leave, hunt Harrison to the far corners of the earth, and beat the ever-loving shit out of him, I wait it out. Even though I want to comb through every detail of this letter until I figure out what the hell is going on, I push it aside. For the rest of the night, my only priority is to ensure Sophia knows *she* is my priority in every way.

"I have an idea. Let's just spend some time together doing nothing. We can watch TV or we can put a movie in to watch, make some popcorn, and lay around on the couch," I offer. She doesn't look pleased.

"Dom," she narrows her eyes at me, "a huge weight has just been dropped on your shoulders. Another maddening piece of the puzzle has just been revealed and it makes even less sense than everything else we know. Someone just broke into your office and left something–there's no telling what that was! But you just want to veg out on the couch and watch movies?"

"Your needs come first with me, Sophia. I want nothing more than to hold you in my arms, shower you with love, and give you all my affection.

You're the one I want to spend my life with, *My Angel*, and you're the one who matters the most to me."

"Everything won't just go away, you know?"

"You're right, it won't. It'll still be there for us to deal with tomorrow. Even if we stress over it all night, it'll still be waiting for us tomorrow. I think we've both had enough for today and we just need time to decompress."

"A few minutes ago you were ready to go hunt him down and kill him. What's changed?"

"My priority."

**Sophia**

Dominic and I are stretched out on the couch with a movie playing in the Blu-ray player. The extra wide couch gives us both room to lie down–Dominic is on his side and I'm on my back next to him. His hand is under my shirt and he has been gently stroking my stomach the last couple of hours. He suddenly pushes himself up and hovers above me, with his arms framing my face and caging me beneath him.

"You are so beautiful, Sophia," he says tenderly before lowering his head to kiss me. His full lips brush against mine before I feel his tongue against the crease in my lips. Opening my mouth, I give him full access to plunder my mouth with his soft caress. My Dom is the best kisser, melting me where I lie and making me instantly wet for him.

Pulling away from me, his sexy smirk tells me he knows that he's already primed me for whatever he has in mind. Sliding down my body, he skims his mouth across my shirt and I can feel his hot breath through the thin fabric. My hands instinctively rise to run my fingers through his hair. Using one hand to hold his weight, the other lifts my shirt and pushes it up to expose my stomach.

Settling between my legs, Dom splays his hands out across my belly and places loving kisses across my skin. Just the feel of his lips on my skin causes chills to rush across my skin and the need to feel him inside me becomes overwhelming. His warm tongue bathes my quickly heating skin and I moan in pleasure. He unzips my pants and pulls them down off my hips.

Then he completely stills.

Opening my eyes, I see him staring at the area around my navel. His hands frame it and he kisses it softly. He whispers something against my skin but I can't make out the words. As I raise my head to ask him, I realize that he's whispering to the baby, carrying on a full conversation without me. I can't help but smile at him and wonder what they're talking about.

The words of Carol Ann's letter return with a vengeance. Dom must be so distraught about what he just found out, but he's focused on me now. *Does this help him work through it? Or does it remind him even more of what he lost?* It's not that I'm exactly jealous of her or the baby she carried. Looking at all the ways that Harrison has hurt him is bad enough. Knowing that I helped bring that pain to Dom kills me.

"What are you two talking about down there?" I ask playfully.

Dom lifts his eyes up at me, mischief shining brightly in them, "That's for us to know and you to find out."

"That's not playing well with others, Daddy," I jokingly reply. The look of complete shock on his face surprises me. "What?"

"I'm going to be a *Daddy*," he says slowly, as if he has only just realized this in spite of already knowing I'm pregnant. "We're going to have a miniature version of you running around, calling me Daddy, and I'll be wrapped around her little finger."

"It could be a miniature version of *you* running around, calling you Daddy, and I'll be wrapped around *his* little finger," I point out.

"We have to tell my parents," he says out of the blue.

I'm having a hard time keeping up with his moods tonight.

"Yes, we do. What's with the urgency and abrupt subject changes?" I laugh.

"It just hit me that there's a small human growing inside you," he says in awe. "My mom will want to help. My sisters need to meet you. I need to push the contractor to finish the house so we can fix up a nursery. We have a lot to do."

His voice is so animated and this is the most excited I've ever seen him. Being included in his plans for the future makes me feel more confident in our relationship. The way he shows love and attention makes me feel like the two months apart were just a horrible nightmare. I feel hope for the first time in a long time.

"What are you smiling about?" he asks, drawing my attention back to the here and now.

"I didn't realize I was smiling. But, I was just thinking about how excited you sound. It feels good," I admit.

He leans down to my stomach again, cups his hand around his mouth, and whispers something else to the baby. Then he grins at me, his sexy, mischievous smirk makes me smile in return. "What are you saying to our baby?"

"I just told her that I am excited to be her Daddy, but she better be good to her Mommy," he smiles as he pulls my pants off the rest of the way.

"And, I told her that I'm about to be *very* good to Mommy."

Fireworks in every color imaginable ignite behind my eyelids when his tongue presses against my core. His big hands snake under my behind, lifting my behind in the air and leaving my back flat on the couch. His tongue is like a finely tuned instrument, bringing the most exquisite pleasure in powerful, uncontrollable waves that crash over me again and again. His fingers work magic inside me, stroking the single spot that intensifies the feeling, while his warm tongue circles my clit.

The speed of his hand increases as he brings me to climax, my orgasm soaks me and he licks all the evidence of it away. I scream out in ecstasy before my body completely relaxes from sheer exhaustion. "You taste so fucking sweet, baby," he murmurs against my clit, the timbre of his voice vibrates through me. "Delicious," he says as he licks my sex from bottom to top.

He quickly sheds his pants and crawls up my body until he's fully seated between my legs. Pushing into me slowly, he fills me up, stretches me with his girth, and I gasp in delight from the feel of him inside me. He moves slowly at first, keeping my face held in his palms, and keeping his eyes on mine. "Don't take your eyes off mine, Sophia. I want to see what you're feeling. I want you to know you're *mine*."

*I've always been yours, Dom.*

# Chapter Fifteen

For the last few days, the four of us combed through every file from Dominic's office. Dominic's study was full of boxes, stacked chest high and neatly lined along the walls. We each took a wall and started working through the files with a fine-tooth comb.

None of us really knew what we're even looking for, so it was actually *worse* than looking for a needle in a haystack. When I asked Shadow what I should keep my eyes peeled for, his reply was simply, "My gut says you will know it when you see it."

At the time, my sarcastic reply was, "Well, that's helpful."

Actually, it turns out that it was indeed helpful. "Oh my god, I think I found it," I call out to the others. My tone is steeped in worry, even to my own ears.

Shadow and Tucker make a quick move toward me but Dominic stands still, holding the file that he's been looking through, and waits. His eyes search mine, asking questions that I can't find the words to answer. He sees it in my eyes, though. Knowing me as well he as he does, he sees the concern, he feels my worry, and he senses my anxiety.

When Shadow and Tucker both read it while looking over my shoulder, Dominic puts his file down and swiftly moves across the room. No doubt that he also sees the shocked look they both wear. The last few days have really been hard on me, alternating between admitting that I'm jealous and angry that Carol Ann was pregnant with Dom's baby and being upset that she died while pregnant with his baby. The emotional roller coaster has become the very basis of our lives and I'm so ready for the drama to stop.

That's not happening today, though.

Dominic snatches the paper from my hand and paces in the study as he reads it, and rereads it. "That son of a bitch!" he roars, causing me to jump from being startled.

With his voice thick with sarcasm and anger, he reads the note aloud.

*"If you're reading this note, it's because I'm dead. I've become frightened of Dominic Powers. His abusive and controlling ways have escalated and I fear for my life. If I die under suspicious circumstances, he should be the first person you investigate.*

*"I've tried to leave, but he keeps me prisoner in our condo. I'm afraid of what he'll do to me if I try to leave again. If I die, just keep him from doing the same to another woman. –Carol Ann Dictman"*

Dominic's face turns multiple shades of red as the anger in him rises. Tucker calmly walks over to him and takes the note from his hand. He studies the handwriting between this note and the other one Dominic has from Carol Ann. "The handwriting is strikingly similar but there are some discrepancies," Tucker says calmly.

Shadow and Tucker sit at Dominic's desk and carefully examine every letter of every sentence. Shadow makes a phone call and we only hear the clipped end of the conversation. When he's finished, he says he has a contact in the Dallas FBI office that is a handwriting analysis expert and will look at the letters. Shadow leaves, taking the letters with him, and Tucker stays behind with us.

The only thing I know to do that may remotely help calm Dominic is to wrap my arms around him. "We'll get through this together, Dominic," I whisper to him and his arms tighten around me.

"You know, it's my job to reassure you," he murmurs back to me.

"I'm a tough girl. I can support and help my man sometimes, too."

"You do, love. You do," he sweetly kisses my hair.

Friday is here and I wonder how the week has flown by so quickly. Today is the day that I've both looked forward to and dreaded. We fly to Austin today and meet my brother at Quattro Amore for dinner tonight. At least, I hope it's my brother. Just in case, we have a whole team of security personnel flying with us that will be positioned all around the restaurant.

"Stop wringing your hands, my love. It'll be fine. You won't leave my sight and we have enough manpower to shut the whole place down," Dominic smiles, reassuring me. I look around the plane and I know he's right. I have nothing to worry about with all these people helping us.

"I'm nervous either way, Dominic. I love my brother, and I want to see him, but I just don't see it going well if he starts on me about helping get him out of trouble," I confess my fear.

"Babe, if he puts his needs before yours, you don't need him in your life."

"I know. But he's my little brother. It's not so easy to just let him go," I reply and look into my Dom's eyes. "He doesn't come before you, though. If I have to choose, it will always be you." Pulling my hand to his mouth, I watch his full lips kiss the back of my hand and I want to lean in and capture the kiss with my lips.

It's a short flight to Austin on his private jet and the landing gear is suddenly touching down on the tarmac. Taking a deep breath, I steel my nerves and face whatever is ahead of me. My pregnancy hormones coupled with my overactive nerves have wreaked havoc on my morning sickness today. I only took half of an anti-nausea pill before we left in hopes that it doesn't make me too groggy to fully function. So far, so good.

Two black, full-size SUVs with black tinted windows are waiting for our entire entourage. Dominic sits by me and moves in as close as he can get. His hand slides across my waist and covers my stomach, shielding our baby and warming me from the inside out. I glance up at him as he's talking to the security team and realize that he's not even aware of the gesture.

"Why are you looking at me like that?" he whispers to me.

I look down at his hand and back up at him. "Oh, no reason."

The smile he returns is the one that melts me every time. "It just comes naturally, I guess," he shrugs.

Two blocks from the restaurant, we stop and I take a taxi the rest of the way to the restaurant. This huge security team would definitely draw attention if we all pulled up to the front door at once, so our arrival is staggered. The other SUV went on ahead so the men can get into position at all the exits. The taxi will deliver me next and I will stall before going to the hostess. The second SUV will be immediately behind me. I know I'm well covered, but I still wonder what I'm walking into.

When my driver arrives at the restaurant, I fumble with my purse before giving him my credit card. After waiting a few minutes for him to figure out how to use the credit card reader and print my receipt, I know the second team is already in place and ready for me. I just have to remember, in my nervousness, to keep my hands off my necklace that's really a camera. Shadow also put a tracker inside the hem of my shirt for double safety measure.

Quattro Amore is more than opulent-it is the very definition of debonair. The wait list for reservations is long and exclusive, making me question how Shawn even got on the list. The live performer croons a romantic ballad in her sultry voice on a floor-level stage. There's a small dance floor immediately in front of the stage and a few couples are swaying to the music. On shaky legs, I approach the hostess and give my brother's name. "Hi, I'm meeting Shawn Vasco here. Has he arrived yet?"

The hostess checks the list and smiles, "Yes, he has. Follow me."

The butterflies in my stomach are more like bats flying around. As we turn the corner in the five-star intimate restaurant, I catch a glimpse of Dominic intently watching me. He's only letting me know where he is for my peace of mind. Once he steps back into the shadows of the dimly lit dining area, he completely disappears from sight.

As we approach the table, I can only see the back of the man that is waiting for me. Walking around to the other side of the table, I crane my neck to get a good look at him. My breath hitches in my chest and I grip the padded, high back of the chair in front of me. His eyes rise to meet mine and he quickly stands.

"Hi, sis," he says hesitantly.

"Hi, Shawn," I reply on an exhaled breath. I wasn't sure what to expect on the way here and now I'm even less sure of why he wants to see me. Drawing on all my strength, I decide to just dive in as I take my seat. "I was surprised to hear from you. Especially now. You made it clear you didn't want anything to do with me. So, why have I traveled all the way to Austin for dinner?"

His shock turns to shame as my words sink in. He nervously clears his throat and fidgets in his chair as he searches for the words. But I refuse to help him by filling in any of the silence. I'll sit here and stare at him until he answers me. All this time, I've romanticized how close my brother and I were, but the truth is that he betrayed me. He left me and blatantly said I embarrassed him.

"I know I did, Sophia, and I'm sorry for that. I was younger and even more of a fool than I am now. Can you forgive me?"

Leaning back against my chair, I tilt my head, narrow my eyes, and intentionally rake my eyes over him. Something is off in this whole scenario. Something is terribly wrong and I feel like I'm being completely set up. The only thing I know to do is to try to keep him talking so we can figure out what he's planning.

"Why now, Shawn?" I ask accusingly. "Why is it suddenly so important for you to see me to talk to me? We have these nifty new gadgets called phones."

His nervousness increases as he answers, "I needed you here, Sophia."

The waitress suddenly appears with bread and fills our water glasses. I didn't hear a word she said about the specials for today. I have a strong feeling we won't be here long enough to actually eat anything. When she finishes her spiel and leaves our table, I glare at Shawn.

"Why do you need me here, Shawn? Stop being so vague and answer the question."

"Because I don't want to go to prison," he replies, his voice barely audible but I know exactly what he said from the look of shame on his face.

"So, you'd give up your pregnant sister to a demented madman to save your own ass from a crime you committed," I state with disgust. My brother is long gone. The young man that sits across from me is barely a shell of the boy I remember. "You really are a piece of work."

"Pregnant?" he replies, his voice and face conveying his complete shock.

"Yes, just over three months now. But why should that matter to you? Does it make you think twice about what you're doing?" I spit out at him.

Shawn drops his head and stares into his lap. He's so ashamed he can't even lift his head to speak to me. I'm so hurt that I'm only barely holding back the tears. The anger outweighs the hurt, though, and prevents me from being a blubbering mess. A tall figure steps up beside Shawn and lightly clears his throat. My eyes are already fixed on him when Shawn's head quickly jerks up to look at him.

Harrison.

Without another word, Shawn vacates his chair and I watch his back as he walks away, toward the door. He used my love for him against me and helped Harrison with his vendetta against Dominic. Cutting my eyes back to Harrison, the scowl on my face no doubt tells him exactly how I feel about him being here. But that doesn't stop me from telling him.

"*What the fuck* are you doing here, Harrison? What do you want from us?"

"What I want is for Dominic Powers to lose everything. I want his company gone. I want him to lose you. I want to completely destroy him," he states plainly as he butters a slice of bread.

"Why? What did he do to you?"

"You mean besides kill my sister? Oh, well, if that's not enough then I'll tell you the rest. He thinks he is so good–sitting on high and looking down his nose at the rest of us. Carol Ann, she tried to get him to give me a job but he wouldn't do it. He said I wasn't good enough to work for his precious company," he sneers.

"So, you're doing all this because he wouldn't give you a job?" I try to clarify, dumbfounded at his lack of reasoning.

"Don't you see? He's no better than me. What's he got that I ain't got? Nothing, that's what! With his big houses, all his money, his cars, and the women falling at his feet, willing to do whatever he wants them to. He just thinks he's all that. But he's not, he'll see. I'll show him what Harrison Dictman is made of."

"This whole thing has been about your jealousy? You just want to be Dominic, have what he has, and make him look bad?" I ask incredulously.

"He wouldn't give me a job! Said I wasn't good enough!"

"Did he say you weren't good enough or that you weren't qualified?"

"Same difference," Harrison dismisses my question.

"So, you wanted a high-paying job at his company and he told you that you weren't qualified for it," I rephrase. "That made you mad and jealous, so you set out to hurt him because of that."

Harrison just stares at me but I know my words are taking root. Surely he has to see how insane this whole scenario is.

A slow, evil grin creeps across his face and his eyes glow with anger. "I heard he took you back after everything you've done to him. He ain't too bright then, is he? I guess you're his weakness but he needs to learn that you're mine. You signed the contract–that makes you mine. I am your Dom and you will call me that from now on. I will show that pussy-boy how a real Dom treats his women."

Harrison's face suddenly drops and he completely loses all his bravado. His mouth gapes open as he stares at something just over my shoulder. When I turn to look, I see my Dom walking toward us. His stride is confident, his face displays his determination, and his entire aura screams *'try me, I dare you.'* Even with the low lighting, I can see his blue eyes alight with fire. People eagerly move out of his way and turn to watch his purposeful gait.

Dominic walks right up to our table and stops mere inches from Harrison. His hands are balled into tight fists and, just as I'm sure he's about to knock Harrison out cold, he turns his gaze to me.

"Sophia, my love, they're playing our song. Dance with me," he commands. It's not a question or a request. It's my Dom, being dominant, and showing Harrison that it takes more than a heavy hand to be a real Dom.

Quickly rising to my feet, Dominic takes my hand and leads me to the dance floor. The soulful singer has just started a beautiful rendition of *I Can't Help Falling In Love With You*. Dominic wraps his arms around my waist as I wrap mine around his neck. We sway back and forth, but he keeps my back to the tables so he can watch our surroundings.

"So this is our song?" I coo up to him.

"It is definitely our song, baby," he says and gently kisses me. "I had to get you away from him. He has something in his pocket and I wasn't about to risk your safety for even one more minute."

I shudder at the thought of what he may have to force me out of here with him. Dominic feels it and pulls me into his arms even tighter.

"There's no way I'd ever let anything happen to you, Sophia. You're my heart and my love. I'll protect you with my life. I need you with me, every day, and in every possible way."

"You've got me, Dominic. I'm yours forever. When you said there's no going back, you were right. There's no way I can go back to a life without you."

We dance until the song ends and, by then, I've almost forgotten about Harrison. The words of the love song washed over me and made me realize exactly how precious our love is. I really can't help falling in love with him and it happens over and over every day. My love grows deeper, stronger, and becomes a living part of me.

When we turn to exit the dance floor, I see an empty seat where Harrison had been. Looking around nervously, I grip Dom's arm in fear. He leans down to my ear and whispers, "Relax, love. He's long gone. A couple of the security guys are following him to see where he goes. We were counting on him showing up."

"What did he have on him, Dominic?" I have to know.

He exhales in a huff, considering whether or not to tell me. "A stun gun."

*Oh my god. I think I'm going to be sick.*

# Chapter Sixteen

***Dominic***

Sophia and I are sitting in the backseat of the SUV with Shadow and Tucker in the front. Sophia has been quiet on the way to our hotel. She's lost in her thoughts and she's dwelling on her brother's betrayal. Taking her hand in mine, I lace our fingers together and lightly squeeze. Her rich brown eyes find mine and I can feel her reaching out to me, asking me to throw her a lifeline. I have just very thing she needs.

When we reach the hotel, she finally smiles when she sees we're turning into the Four Seasons. "Your favorite," she says with a nudge to my side.

Shadow and Tucker get out of the car. Shadow goes inside to check-in and get our room keys while Tucker stands guard outside.

"*You're* my favorite," I say warmly. The words are true but I'd like to see a brighter smile on her face.

Her smile fades, but the look she gives me in return is one of pure adoration. She leans in and kisses me softly on the lips. Her hand strokes my jawline, scrubbing my faded beard. "Love doesn't even come close to describing my feelings for you. If I had to choose the best moment of my life, it would be the moment you made me yours. And I've been yours since that day, probably even before. *You* are my forever."

"Not that I don't love hearing you say that, but where is this coming from?"

"You have a close relationship with your family, so if you had to choose between them and me, there's no contest. You'd always choose them. It's not the same with my family, Dom. I'll never choose anyone over you," she says solemnly. "You're all I have. I have no one else."

I knew if her brother actually showed up, it would be hard on Sophia. From what Shadow has told me about Shawn, he's in way too deep to think of anyone but himself. He more than proved how weak he is when he offered up his sister as payment for his crimes. I wanted to pummel the bastard when, like a fucking coward, he couldn't even look her in the eye.

Her words are meant to reassure me that she won't betray me to help her family when this situation escalates. Her eyes ask me to believe that she's on my side and to trust her love for me. What she hasn't realized is I already do believe her on both counts.

"It's time to get you alone in our hotel room, Sophia," I murmur against her lips as my hand wraps around the back of her neck. Pulling her to me, I claim her mouth with mine, stake my territory with my tongue, and exert my dominance with my hold on her. She willingly submits, instantly succumbs, and becomes like putty in my hand. "Upstairs."

We exit the vehicle as Shadow approaches with our room key. "Presidential Suite," he says with a smile. Shadow, Tucker, and I grab our suitcases from the back and move swiftly to the elevators as the valet parks the car.

Shadow performs his standard check of the room before leaving us alone. After I lock the door behind him, I turn to Sophia and the need to devour her nearly overtakes me. Her return smile says she's ready to be devoured.

"You have to eat first, Sophia," I say calmly. "My baby girl and my baby both need food."

Sophia takes a haggard breath and nods, "You're right. I lost my appetite at the restaurant, but I do need to eat."

"Especially for what I have planned for you tonight," I hint. "You'll need all the energy you can get."

"By all means, let's order room service this very minute," she purrs. "You don't want to keep your girl from her dessert, do you?"

"*My Angel*," I say with a shake of my head, "my girl *is* dessert tonight."

Picking up the phone, I dial room service and order our meals after Sophia chooses what she thinks she can safely eat. She gives me a curious but excited look when I order strawberries, chocolate, whipped cream, and honey. "Oh, and can you include a couple of paraffin candles from the spa, too?" I ask the concierge before hanging up.

"Candlelight dinner for two?" she asks with a shy smile.

"Something like that."

When everything arrives, she gives me a suspicious look when I put one candle to the side and light the other one. The spread of food is laid out on the table in front of us, but I put the strawberries, chocolate, whipped cream, and honey aside with the candle. Wiggling my eyebrows at her, I wordlessly tell her exactly what my plans for dessert are.

"Are you ready, my love?" I ask when the last of our dinner is consumed. Taking her hand, I help her stand and pull her into my arms. My mouth finds hers and I thrust my tongue in, enraptured with her taste and burning to take her right here on the table.

She has other plans, though. She pulls away and says, "I have a surprise for you. Give me five minutes?"

"Four. I can't wait a second longer than that," I concede and she rushes off to the bedroom. I hear the zipper of the suitcase and then the bathroom door clicks shut. While she's busy, I gather my surprise for her and take the ingredients into the bedroom. "You have three minutes and I'm coming in after you," I call out in warning and chuckle when I hear her squeal in response.

Gathering my supplies from my suitcase, I fashion a makeshift rigging system by typing my red, nylon rope to the chandelier hanging above the bed. The other surprise is lying on the bed directly in front of the rope. I quickly shed my clothes and wait in position for my girl to come out. She will never know it, but I just about swallow my tongue when she opens the bathroom door and I see my surprise.

I've never seen anyone who looks as fucking hot as she does. She's wearing a tiny, black leather thong that ties on each side. Her matching black leather bra is cupless, so the leather straps only form a frame around her breasts rather than cover them. Her thigh-high, black leather stiletto boots complete her ensemble. I'm instantly hard as a fucking rock and my cock twitches when she licks her lips in response.

She saunters over to me, her hips swaying seductively as she approaches. She stops in front of me, extends her arms to the side, and positions her feet hip-width apart. Not even trying to hide the lascivious perusal of her body, I slowly rake my eyes up and down her body to drink in every inch of her. I reach out to feel the leather thong first. Then I drag my hand up her body–over her sexy stomach, across her navel, up her breastbone, across her throat, and stop at her luscious lips.

Taking my finger into her mouth, she draws it in, wraps her lips around it, and strokes it with her tongue and holds my hand with both of hers as she pulls her head back. Wrapping my other hand around her neck, I pull her to me and crush her mouth with mine. Our tongues twist and caress with an urgent, fiery need. She moans softly into my mouth and leans her supple body into mine.

Pulling away from her with the strength of a thousand men, I walk slowly around her while she stands still. Her long, reddish-brown hair cascades down her back in gorgeous wavy curls. Pulling the strings on both hips, her thong drops to the floor. I wrap one hand around her hair and tug on it, bending her neck backward as I run my finger down the center groove of her back, to her perfectly round ass, until I reach my favorite spot between her legs.

She's breathing faster now, waiting for me to bring her to the highest highs. I smile to myself, knowing that she thinks she knows what's coming next. Brushing my fingertips over her clit with just enough pressure to make her wetter, I growl into her ear, "Whose is this?"

I thrust my finger inside her and she moans, "*Yours, Dom.*" I quickly withdraw my hand and walk away from her. When she groans in frustration, I shoot her a disapproving look and she instantly submits.

I *tsk* at her, "You'll be punished for that." Inclining my head towards the bed, I curtly command her, "Get on the bed, in the center, up on your knees."

She moves briskly to assume her position on the bed, beside the red rope. I watch her carefully as her eyes dart to the rope and then to the other surprise lying on the bed. She then turns her gaze to me and waits. There is no fear in her eyes. No worry, no question, and no doubt–there is only complete trust. She has fully submitted to me and that fills me with so much pride I can barely contain it.

"I hadn't planned to do this with shoes on, but you look too fucking sexy in them to take them off. I have to see you–your hands tied and the spreader bar between your legs while wearing them."

Her response is to raise her hands above her head. Moving quickly out of sheer desire, I wrap the red rope around each wrist several times before wrapping them together and tying it with a slipping reef knot for a quick release. The dark red rope is a stark contrast against her creamy skin and black leather lingerie.

"Don't pull on it," I command. "It's not intended to be a suspension. Your level of submission to me will dictate how still you remain. If I have to hog tie you to make you be still...," I purposely leave my threat hanging in the air. I take the rest of the red rope from the suitcase and put it beside the spreader bar before I move behind her on the bed.

My chest is flush with her back and my cock gently nudges her ass. Slowly surging my hips forward, I rub it in the crease between her perfect heart-shaped cheeks. Grabbing her hips, I wrap my fingers around her hipbones and continue teasing her. Snaking one arm around her, my fingers find her clit as I apply pressure in small circles. She wants to move, to squirm, and to ride my hand until she comes all over me. But she knows better.

Jerking my hand away before she gets too close, she makes no sound in retaliation this time. I stroke her ass with my hand, quickly slap it and watch it turn red in the shape of my hand. Sophia softly moans in pleasure but remains in place. *That's my girl.* Her reward is immediate as I reach between her legs from behind, stroking her already wet center and thrusting my fingers deep into her.

Crooking my fingers, I find that spot and pull her tight against me as she soaks my hand.

Grabbing the end of the rope, I tug on it and release her hands. She lets them fall limp in front of her. I unwrap the rope and cast it aside. One at a time, I pick up her wrists and massage them as I also pull her up to a standing position. "You didn't tell me they were going to sleep on you, so I'm assuming they feel okay?"

"Yes, Dom, I'm fine," she replies in her lust-laden tone.

"Good. I'm not finished with you yet," I promise and she smiles her *come-hither* smile. I pick up the spreader bar and she moves her feet wider apart until the bar just fits between her ankles. I quickly tie the bar in place then pull her arms behind her back to tie her elbows together. This tie pushes her breasts forward, and I move around to her front to enjoy the view. In her current leather straps, she looks *absofuckinglutely* edible.

Taking one breast in my mouth, I suck and bite her nipple while massaging her other breast. Changing positions, I give the other equal attention. Dropping to my knees in front of her, I suck her clit into my mouth and scrape the sensitive nub with my teeth. She can't grab my hair like she usually does so she's forced to accept all of the pleasure without moving. My tongue darts in and out of her and she screams my name when I add my fingers to the assault.

"Dominic! OH MY GOD!" She shrieks and the evidence of her pleasure flows onto my tongue. She tastes so fucking good. I dip a strawberry in the whipped cream and take a bite of it before thrusting my tongue in her mouth. The mixture of her essence and the fruit is exquisite. I then feed her the rest of the strawberry before giving her a bite of the chocolate. Tasting her clit again with this new flavor combination will make me crave chocolate and strawberries every day.

Standing, I lick the remnants of her off my lips and she watches with hooded eyes. I light the candle and remove it from the candleholder. As the wax heats and melts, it drops onto her breasts and covers them. Her exposed posture mixed with the heated drops on her bare skin is like an aphrodisiac to her. With each trail of wax that covers her beautiful body, she coos and writhes in pleasure.

"Bend over," I demand.

Bending at the waist, her face is directly in front of my dick that's hard enough to cut fucking diamonds. Her mouth opens and my hips surge forward of their own accord. Her warm, wet mouth feels fucking incredible and my tempo unconsciously increases and her head bobs back and forth eagerly.

"Mmmm, baby," I groan, "you're so good with your mouth." But I stop her because this is not the way I want to come tonight. Moving around behind her, I grasp her bound hands in one of mine and warn her, "Get ready."

Before she can respond, I slam into her from behind and she cries out in pleasure. "AHH! DOM!" Over and over, my hips pump into her wetness until I feel the familiar quiver and tightening of her inner walls. Moving my hands to her hips, I pull her back as I thrust forward, driving into her relentlessly until she's screaming and I'm growling her name in rapture.

Staying inside her, I quickly untie her arms and help her up to an almost standing position. My front is again flush with her back and my arms are wrapped around her from behind and hooked up across her breasts. "I don't want to let you go," I whisper in her ear.

But I can't leave her legs tied any longer, so I reluctantly pull out of her and finish untying her. Pulling her with me, I sit on the edge of the bed and she sits on my lap. I hold her close to me, lovingly stroke her, and whisper to her to reassure her. "You're so beautiful, baby. I love this outfit and you completely shocked me with it. That was a wonderful surprise."

"You forgot the honey," she whispers back and I laugh out loud.

"Well, I didn't really forget," I confess. "I just didn't want to wait one more second to make love to you. The night's still young, though. Maybe I'll wake you up by eating honey off of you."

She snuggles in closer to me, lays her head on my shoulder, and sighs in deep contentment. "I love you, Dominic."

"I love you so much, Sophia–more than I can even describe with words. You're my heart, my love, and my world now. There's no going back, ever. You're mine. And I'm yours, always."

After several minutes, I take Sophia to the shower and thoroughly wash her beautiful body. Running my soapy hands over her stomach, I notice it's slightly bigger than it has been. I move my hands up to her breasts and back down her torso, rubbing them over the small bump again. I'm simply amazed and in awe at how her body is changing to incubate our baby.

"Did I hurt you?" I ask.

"No, not at all," she looks at me over her shoulder and smiles lovingly.

"The morning sickness seems to be getting better," I state, but I really want her to verify it.

"Yes, I'm just past my first trimester now and it hasn't bothered me as much this week. I hope it goes away and *stays* away," she laughs and covers my hand with hers, directly over her small baby bump.

We stay like this for several minutes, just relaxing in the hot water spray and protecting our baby with our embrace. So many scenes fly through my mind, imaging how it will be after the baby is born. There isn't a single scene that doesn't have Sophia front and center in my life. She's part of me now. I am her Dom, but she owns my heart.

When the water starts to turn cool, I turn it off and swiftly dry Sophia off before wrapping her in the large bath towel. I quickly run a towel over me and lead her to the bed. "Let's get some sleep, love. We have a big day tomorrow and you need your rest."

"What are we doing tomorrow?" she asks sweetly as she snuggles up to me in the bed.

I wrap my arm around her and spoon her from behind. I know she isn't going to like what I'm about to say, but I've given this a lot of thought and it has to happen. She needs to be there with me so that she can also have some kind of closure–whether the outcome is good or bad.

"We're going to have a talk with your parents."

# Chapter Seventeen

***Sophia***

"We really don't have to do this," I try to reason with Shadow as he puts our suitcases in the back of the SUV. "We can just go back to the airport instead."

He puts the last of our bags in and closes the vehicle door. With one hand still on the door and the other hand on his hip, he levels his gaze at me. "Sophia, you know I can't do that."

"This is a really bad idea, Shadow. I know what my dad was when I was younger and I know how it was when he finally showed back up. He could just as well be the one behind Dom's car wreck and his house burning down! How can you just let him walk right into this situation?"

Shadow doesn't respond verbally, but his lack of response coupled with the look he gives me tells me he already knows everything.

"What do you know, Shadow?"

"I know," he pauses, "better than to get in the middle of family drama unless I absolutely have to."

Dominic and Tucker walk out of the hotel and join us at the vehicle. Dom senses the tension in me, his eyes dart between Shadow and me. He gives me his best smirk before he addresses Shadow.

"Has she been trying to talk you out of going to her family's house, Shadow?"

Shadow's smile spreads across his face and I see the mischief dancing in his eyes. I have a feeling he's coming up with a response that will get me in just enough trouble so that Dom punishes me, but not enough trouble to make him mad over it. Narrowing my eyes at him, I respond with a challenge of my own.

He accepts it. Dammit.

"Well, you know Sophia, Dominic. She's playing the maternity card and her *'mother knows best'* routine. She says that the dad is clueless," Shadow replies in mock offense.

"Is that right?" One side of Dominic's mouth quirks up as he tries to hide his smile. "I will definitely have to correct that line of thinking," he replies, turning his seductive gaze to me, "Later."

Electricity shoots through my body, causing it to hum with excitement at what playful ideas he has in store for me. He knows Shadow is only joking but he's using it to set the stage for us. *Later.* He also knows that throughout the rest of the day that thought will be in the back of my mind, pulling me back to him right when I need it most.

The truth is, he knows how much I'm dreading this visit today. I fully expect my family to belittle me, try to shame me, or tell me I'm weak. They have no clue what weakness really is. Just because I'm Dom's submissive doesn't make me weak or spineless. If they push the wrong buttons, they will see first hand exactly how strong my spine is.

I roll my eyes as Dominic and Shadow walk off since I'm sure it's to talk about exactly what I said to Shadow. Tucker gives me a single nod and turns to walk off before I call his name.

"Tucker?"

He turns to look at me, "Yeah?"

"I haven't had a chance to really thank you for helping me that night. You even stayed with me in the hospital. You have no idea how much I appreciate that. You saved me from him and you didn't leave me to face it all alone. You're a good man, Tucker. There's a woman out there who will be so happy to find you one day."

Tucker wraps his arm around my neck and pulls me to him in a friendly hug. "For the record, you never have to thank me for helping you, Sophia. But, you're welcome and I'd do it all over again if you needed me." Releasing me, he continues, "Dominic is a different man with you. He loves you, Sophia."

Doubts about me still linger–in all of three of these men. I can't blame them but I can't help that it hurts, either.

"I love him more than anything, Tucker. I've meant every word I've said to him."

"He's very excited to be a father," Tucker says with a glance at my stomach. "You're going to be a great mother, too, Sophia. Congratulations." He flashes his rare smile at me and it makes me think that we'll be okay again.

"Thank you, Tucker," I say sincerely. "For everything."

Half an hour later, we turn into the drive at what I presume is my parent's house. It's a small, modest house on the outskirts of west Austin. The neighborhood is nice, quiet, and the streets are lined with well-kept older homes. It gives me a homey, cozy feeling as I look around, picturing the neighbors congregating for summer cookouts. Not that I'd ever experienced that with my parents growing up, but it's still a nice scene to picture here.

Dom squeezes my hand and draws me from the longings of my childhood. "Ready?" he asks, but we both know that question is asking so much more than the one word implies.

Giving a simple nod, we all exit the vehicle and walk up to the front door. The sidewalk is lined with well-manicured flowerbeds and the yard is dotted with ornamental trees. Everything looks so welcoming but I know that looks can be deceiving–because people are deceitful. Looking for the comfort that my Dom provides, I run my hand down the inside of his arm until our hands are once again locked. He simultaneously anchors me and sets me free.

Tucker knocks on the door and we all wait patiently. My heart is pounding in my chest as my confidence wanes and the trepidation sets in. Dom pulls me into his side, wrapping his arm protectively around me, and kisses me on my temple. If this visit stops the attacks on him, it's well worth the discomfort I feel now. Taking a deep, calming breath, I let go of the tension and see this for what it is. If they're not part of my life after today, it'll be no different than it was yesterday.

The door opens and a man who looks like the older version of my brother is standing before us. His eyes first dart to Tucker and Shadow, most likely because of their size, before moving to Dom and then to me. Recognition settles across his features and his mouth drops open in surprise. Several heartbeats pass before he breathes again, which is ironic since I am considering using my safe word, *heartbeat*, with Dom right now.

"Sophia? Is it really you?" he asks, his voice strained with emotion. His eyes glisten with moisture and I question if I'm just seeing things.

"Yes, Mr. Vasco, she is Sophia," Dominic answers for me. "We apologize for showing up unannounced like this. We have some things we need to discuss with you that can only be said in person."

He steps back to allow us room to enter and extends his arm into the house, "Come in, come in. Everyone have a seat. Make yourself at home."

As I walk by him, the thought occurs to me that I don't know what to call him. *Dad? Manuel?* Dom sits on the couch and I take the seat next to him. Tucker sits in a high-backed wing chair while Shadow walks around, making himself at home, and looking through all the pictures. He's the only one who doesn't seem to have a care in the world. I wonder if the real reason is because he has a faster reaction time to danger if he's standing rather than sitting.

My father takes a seat in his recliner and his eyes remain fixed on me. "Sophia, you are beautiful," he says emphatically but sincerely.

"Thank you," I reply. "We really should do introductions so you know who everyone is."

"Absolutely," Dominic says. "I'm Dominic Powers." Dominic rises and extends his arm to shake hands. "This is Nick Tucker, my head of security," Tucker and my father exchange nods, "And this is Shadow."

Everyone stops to look at Shadow, who is still roaming slowly around the room, examining every decoration as if he is committing it to memory. "How are you?" he asks, not missing a beat.

"Your name is Shadow?" Manuel asks.

"Yep," Shadow replies, not offering to elaborate or clarify.

"Mr. Vasco, I realize it's been a number of years since you've seen Sophia, but we have urgent matters to talk about. I don't want to be rude, but we need to focus on some questions we have for you," Dominic takes charge of the conversation. "It could be a matter of life or death for Sophia."

"Of course. If I can help her, I will," Manuel replies, concern laces his voice and fear sweeps across his eyes.

Dominic sits on the loveseat across from me and I feel the loss of his strength at my side. I trust him, though, so I know it was with a purpose in mind.

"Sir, do you have frequent contact with your son, Shawn?" Dominic asks.

"No, not for some time now," Manuel says solemnly. "No matter what I said, I couldn't keep him from the wrong people."

"So you didn't pay his bond to get him out of jail?" Dominic asks

"What? No, I didn't pay any bond for him. What was he in jail for?"

"He's in a lot of trouble, Mr. Vasco," Dominic starts.

"Call me Manuel, please."

Dominic smiles and nods in reply. "Do you know Harrison Dictman?"

Manuel's face contorts in disgust, "Yes, I know the bastard. Are you saying Shawn is in league with *Harrison*?"

"Shawn is in a lot of trouble, Manuel. He's facing serious prison time and Harrison has made sure the evidence temporarily disappeared until he gets what he wants. He's using it to control Shawn, and by extension, Sophia," Dominic pauses as Manuel's head jerks to me.

"What? How is he controlling Sophia?"

"He sent Sophia to work for me with an agenda to destroy me and my company, using the evidence against Shawn as leverage against her. He filed a fake sexual harassment lawsuit in Sophia's name and has had his lawyer demanding millions of dollars to keep it out of the media. When Sophia refused to help him, he beat her so badly she ended up in the hospital.

"He's after her again. Shawn called Sophia and asked her to meet him here in Austin for dinner last night so they could reconcile. When we arrived, Shawn was there, but he left Sophia alone with Harrison. Harrison's issues with me go way back. To be blunt, I need to know what your involvement with him is and if you play a part in any of this."

Manuel is shocked speechless for a moment. His mouth drops open and he prepares to speak a couple of times before anything actually comes out. "Hell, no, I'm not part of any of this! Why would I want to hurt my own daughter like that? If Shawn were here, I would kick his ass for being part of this! After everything we did to get Harrison out of Sophia's life and all the trouble he's caused our family, I can't believe Shawn would side with him!"

"What do you mean what you did to get Harrison out of my life?" I ask, dumbfounded at his statement.

Dominic must see the same haunted look that I see on Manuel's face. He urges, "Tell us, Manuel. Help us understand. We know you have ties to the drug cartel. There have already been two attempts on my life and one of them could've killed Sophia, too. We need to know everything."

Manuel scrubs his hand over his face, his hand rests over his mouth, and his eyes are downcast. It's obviously a painful memory and he's preparing himself for reliving it.

"I'd been laid off from my job and Sarah didn't work. Times were hard and I couldn't find work. A friend who'd been laid off with me called and offered me a job. He said I'd be a courier for a company, delivering packages back and forth, and I jumped at it.

"During one delivery, I was ambushed by a couple of guys demanding that I give them the packages. A scuffle ensued, and when it was over, both of those guys were out cold on the ground and I delivered my packages. I didn't know that was a test that I passed with flying colors. It earned me a promotion–in the cartel. I never even knew I was working for them.

"Anyway, they already had all the information on my family. If you know anything about them, Mr. Powers, you know you don't tell them '*no*' and live to tell about it. I accepted my promotion and for a while I was able to avoid doing anything more than roughing up some guys for money they owed.

"The night it all went bad, my partner executed a man for not paying what he owed the boss. Since I was there, I was an accomplice and I went to prison. I didn't realize it at the time, but after my 'promotion,' I became a different man. I had to so I could do the things I had to do.

"When I was released from prison, Sophia refused to have anything to do with me. That's when I realized how bad it had been for my family," he chokes up with emotion, then shakes his head and clears his throat. "The boss started calling me again and saying he had jobs for me to do. I felt trapped, and Sarah and I fought a lot about it.

"Sophia left one day and we searched for her everywhere but we couldn't find her. I was beside myself with worry. It was a few months later when I saw her with Harrison. I knew he was bad news and I didn't want her anywhere near him. So, I used my skills the cartel and prison taught me and threatened him within an inch of his life.

"What I didn't know was that he is the best friend of the boss's favorite son. The boss threatened Sophia's life if I didn't leave them alone. So, knowing how much Sophia loved Shawn, we arranged for Shawn to basically give her an ultimatum of picking between him and Harrison. I thought for sure she'd pick Shawn and come home," Manuel says sadly.

"That's not what Shawn said to me," I clarify. "Remember the whole scene at the market? When you and Harrison got into a fight and you told me I had dishonored you?" The rage is building up inside me as I remember the events of that day.

"That was all planned, Sophia. I had to make Harrison believe I had nothing to do with you so the cartel wouldn't hurt you. But when Shawn called you, he told you that," Manuel counters.

"No, he didn't tell me that at all. He told me basically the same thing you said to me that day. That I was an embarrassment to him and he didn't want anything to do with me again," I calmly explain, but I feel anything but calm inside. "He thought I was weak for choosing my lifestyle."

If this is even a fraction of how betrayed Dom felt by me, I still have a lot of making up to do with him. My eyes drift to Dom and he already knows what I'm thinking. I can see it in his eyes, feel it in his energy, and sense it in his presence. His love for me is a physical being that reaches out to comfort me. His eyes tell me to let him take my burdens.

My love for him is so overwhelming, I think it will bubble up and burst forth from me spontaneously. He is so strong and demanding, yet loving and giving. He commands me, owns me, and dominates me. But he cares for me, caresses me, and pampers me. Giving me more than I could ever ask for and taking so little in return, this man deserves every bit of submission I can give him. I can only say that because through his every action, he's shown that he's worthy of my trust.

"I can assure you, sir, Sophia is far from weak," Dominic says to my father but holds me captive with the adoration in his eyes. "She's weathered storms that would make some men crumble. She keeps me on my toes and she never ceases to amaze me."

My vision blurs from the happy tears in my eyes. The pregnancy hormones aside, this visit would be very emotional anyway, but my Dom knows what I need. He jerks his head to the side, indicating for me to move to the seat beside him and I quickly comply. Not because he ordered it, but because by his side is exactly where I want to be.

"You two look happy together," Manuel acknowledges.

"We are very happy together," I reply.

***Dominic***

It's obvious to me now how people have underestimated Sophia far too much in her life. She's far from weak–many people wouldn't have the guts to walk in her shoes. Watching her interact with her father has been hard for me with my need to protect and shelter her. But I know it's best for both of them to be able to say what's on their mind.

"So, you thought Shawn would help bring Sophia home and get her away from Harrison. What happened after that backfired?" I ask Manuel.

"Harrison called me one day and said he'd let her go, but he didn't want to just turn her out on the street again. Sophia had been accepted into college and needed help paying for it. So I paid all of her tuition, dorm room, books, and anything else she needed. That worked while she was in school but then she went back to him when she graduated."

"*What?*" Sophia exclaims, leaning forward in shock. "*You* paid for my college? Harrison told me he paid for my college and that I *had* to go back to him after I graduated."

"Sophia has already figured out that Harrison was grooming her in order to get to me. He blames me for his sister's death since I was seeing her at the time. We've never gotten along, but it's more than a coincidence that everything escalated when I started seeing your daughter. You and Harrison both have ties to the drug cartel, and the *Boston Brake Job* on my car is one of their tactics," I say and carefully watch his reaction.

"It's not a tactic of *this* group of cartel members. There are a couple of men in the area who know how to do it, and would have access to the equipment to do it. If you know for sure that's what it was, it wouldn't be either of those guys. They wouldn't leave any evidence," Manuel declares. "No, if there was proof of it, it's a newbie with access to some high-tech gadgets," he says distractedly, as if he's considering a preposterous idea.

"Any thoughts of who that may be?" I ask pointedly.

He closes his eyes and shakes his head, "Probably the same person who '*misplaced*' the evidence against Shawn to use against Sophia. He has a few aliases that he uses interchangeably, depending on what job he's handling at the time. The only person it could be–*Detective Ramon Cortez*."

My blood just turned to ice in my veins.

# Chapter Eighteen

"What did you just say?" I ask through clenched teeth.

I feel Shadow move to stand directly behind me when he heard my tone. Manuel looks at me then his eyes dart up to Shadow before he answers. "The boss's son is Ramon Cortez. He's a detective here in Austin and he's Harrison's best friend. Do you know him?"

"You could say that," I snarl in disgust. "I had no clue he was Harrison's best friend, though." Unable to remain seated with the amount of energy I have coursing through me right now, I launch myself off the loveseat and begin pacing. The scenarios are flying at me so fast I can barely keep up with them.

"Dominic," Tucker interrupts my thoughts, "where do you know him from?"

"He was the detective in charge of investigating Carol Ann's death."

Sophia gasps audibly and Tucker's face becomes hard, his eyes knowing, and his posture rigid. He's having the same thoughts and ideas that I am. My pacing resumes and the room is full of nervous energy, questioning eyes, and uncertainty as to how to proceed from here.

"That name isn't on the list of officers with the Austin Sheriff's Department," Shadow calmly interjects.

"You have the whole department memorized?" Manuel asks disbelievingly.

"Yes," comes Shadow's serious reply.

"That's because he doesn't use that name here. It's too easily recognized and associated with the boss, but most everyone knows who he is anyway," Manuel explains. "Besides, have you ever heard of a cop going straight from the academy to being a detective? He has friends and family in low places."

"That's how Harrison got the second page of Carol Ann's letter, isn't it?" Sophia asks, turning to me.

"That would be my guess," I reply. "This Cortez guy seems to have a penchant for making evidence disappear."

"What name does he use here?" Tucker asks.

"As a detective, he goes by his mother's family name-Nunez. But he also goes by Sebastian Montoya," Manuel says.

I freeze mid-step and my head jerks to look at Shadow. He's already looking at me with a knowing look. The pieces of this insane puzzle are finally coming together. Now we need to come up with a plan to put an end to it all.

"What is it?" Sophia glances between Shadow and me. "Who is that?" she asks.

Her innocence shines through her eyes. The concern for me that is prolific in her every action has just been verified and I have no doubts about my choice to give us another chance now. The odds were stacked against us, and I know there were plenty of people who thought I was a fool for letting her back into my life. But I listened to my gut and I'm so thankful for that now.

Before I can answer her, I hear the change in Shadow's tone toward Sophia as he answers her question. He's had the same internal struggle with trusting her. To be fair, I don't think the man really trusts anyone, but Sophia even less so. The warmth in his tone is unmistakable, almost apologetic, even.

"Sebastian Montoya is your lawyer, Sophia. For your sexual harassment lawsuit against Dominic and DPS," Shadow says with a smile.

Sophia swallows hard and nods in response. But she doesn't smile and that concerns me. She looks sad but she quickly tries to hide it. Standing, she addresses her father. "Can I use your restroom?"

"Of course, Sophia," Manuel says as he rises from his chair. "No matter what's happened, our home is your home."

I can't take my eyes off her as Manuel shows her to the hall bath. Her hand is covering her stomach again, shielding our baby and sending love through the warmth in her touch. But I know my girl, and I know something isn't quite right with her. I also know that she won't tell me until we're alone and she feels safe.

Shadow approaches me while Manuel is out of the room. "I think he's telling the truth. He's not involved in your wreck or the fire."

"Why was Sarah calling Sophia then?" I counter. I also believe Manuel is telling us the truth, but her mother's sudden calls during that exact time is concerning.

"We need to ask her that," Shadow replies. "Too bad she's not home."

Manuel steps back into the room and I think it may be time to let Sophia have a reprieve from all this drama. "Manuel, we've taken up enough of your time. Thank you for answering our questions and being honest with us. You've helped us tremendously."

"No need to rush off. Sarah will be home soon and she would love to see Sophia," he half pleads with us.

"Let me see how Sophia is feeling when she comes out. She's pregnant, just past the end of her first trimester, so I have to do what's best for her and our baby," I explain.

Manuel's shocked face tells me he didn't realize Sophia is sporting a baby bump. "I'm going to be a grandfather?" he asks incredulously.

"I imagine today has been a bit of a shock for you, Manuel," I reply with an understanding smile.

"Short time to wait, Dominic," Tucker says from the front window. "Looks like her mother is home now."

"She went to buy groceries. Let me help her get them in. We'd love for all of you to stay and eat with us," Manuel offers. "I'm not quite ready to let my baby girl leave yet."

She's *my* baby girl, but I won't correct him on that just yet. "Let me talk to Sophia and see how she's holding up."

Manuel walks out to the car and approaches Sarah, Sophia's mother. His animated gestures clearly explain that he's telling her what has transpired in her absence. The color drains from her face and she drops the bag in her hand as she runs to the door.

"Sophia!" she calls out as she bounds into the room. "Sophia!"

The bathroom door opens and Sophia cautiously walks back into the room. Stopping in the doorway, she and her mother stare at each other for several ticks of the clock before Sarah breaks the silence.

"Sophia," she sobs as the tears start flowing. "I'm so glad you're okay."

"Why wouldn't she be okay, Mrs. Vasco?" I ask, getting to the point.

"Who are you?" she asks in return and we all introduce ourselves.

"Shawn called me," she glances around nervously, now answering my question. "He told me that Harrison was obsessed with you, Mr. Powers, and that he would stop at nothing until he ruined you."

"Did he say why? Why is he so fixated on Mr. Powers?" Shadow asks.

"Shawn just said that Harrison is so jealous of everything Mr. Powers has. Harrison says he could've had it all, too, if Mr. Powers had just given him a job."

"Jealousy and greed are one of the most common motives of all crime," Manuel sighs.

"He kept saying that Harrison would send him to prison for a long time if Sophia didn't give back what was his. Shawn wouldn't ever tell me what it was the she supposedly took, so I called her to see if she could help Shawn," Sarah explained.

"She didn't take anything from him, Mrs. Vasco. She left him and he wanted her back. That's what he meant," I reply.

Realizing Sophia hasn't said a word yet, my concern for her wellbeing grows. She's leaning against the doorframe, all the color is drained from her face, and her hand is across her stomach. Crossing the room in two giant strides, I lean into her and wrap my arms around her.

"What's wrong, baby?" I ask quietly to avoid drawing attention as the others continue to talk.

"I don't feel well, Dominic," she whispers back.

"Too much stress on you?" I ask.

"No, I don't think that's it. I think I need to lie down."

Sarah notices something isn't right and hesitantly walks over to us. "Is everything alright? Can I get you anything?"

"We really should be going. Sophia's pregnant and she isn't feeling well. She needs to rest," I tell her.

"You can rest in here, Sophia," she says, pointing down the hallway. "The spare bedroom is quiet and comfortable. Manuel said he invited all of you to stay and eat with us, so you can take a nap while I cook. We'll take turns checking on you."

"I agree with her, Sophia. I don't want to put more stress on you by traveling if we don't have to."

"Okay," she says weakly, "I'll go rest now."

We get Sophia settled in the bed and Sarah asks if she can get her anything. "I remember saltine crackers and Sprite helped her morning sickness," I reply and sit on the bed.

She chuckles lightly, "I was the same way. I'll be right back."

"Should I be concerned that you so readily agreed to rest here? Are you feeling that badly?" I ask as I lovingly stroke Sophia's hand.

"I do feel pretty badly, Dominic. I hope a nap will help."

"You didn't eat enough at breakfast this morning," I gently chide her. "You have to eat more to keep your strength up."

Sarah returns with Sophia's crackers and Sprite. "Thank you," Sophia says as she sits up to take a drink.

Sarah watches her with concerned, motherly eyes before turning to leave the room. "I'll check on you in a little while."

"Do you need me to stay in here with you?" I ask.

"You don't have to, Dom. I'll be okay."

I lean over and kiss her softly on the forehead. My fingers skim across her skin as I push her hair away from her face. "I'll stay until you fall asleep. I love you, baby girl."

"I love you, Dominic," she replies in her sleepy voice before she yawns.

In a matter of minutes, Sophia is fast asleep and I silently leave the room to let her rest. Shadow and Tucker helped bring the groceries in and Sarah has set everything out to start cooking. "You don't have to rush on our account. I'd rather let Sophia get as much rest as she can before we wake her up," I say.

"Why don't we spend some time getting to know one another then?" Sarah asks and I heartily agree.

She makes drinks and snacks for everyone and we sit on the back porch and talk for about an hour. The minutes fly by but I learn a lot about them in our short chat. I believe they do love Sophia and want to be part of her life, and now their grandchild's life. Manuel wants to be rid of his association with the cartel but he knows he can't get away from them as long as he's in the area.

Sarah goes inside to start cooking and I walk off to check on Sophia. As I'm walking down the hall, Manuel softly calls my name.

"Dominic?"

Turning, I see him watching me like he's sizing me up and making his mind up about me. "You really do love her, don't you? She isn't just a plaything to you."

"She's my everything and the best thing that's ever happened to me. I love her more than anything and there's nothing I wouldn't do to make her happy." My answer seems to satisfy him as he gives me an understanding nod before he walks back into the kitchen.

Slowly turning the doorknob to open it as quietly as possible to keep from waking her. Sleeping soundly, she looks like an angel with her reddish-brown hair fanned out on the pillow behind her. Her eyebrows furrow, her eyes move behind her closed eyelids, and I wonder what she's dreaming about. She turns over and her eyes flutter open.

"Hey, baby," I call to her, "did you sleep well?"

She smiles her sleepy smile and stretches, "Mmmhmm, just what the doctor ordered."

Moving to the bed, I sit beside her and place my hand on her stomach. Pulling her shirt up to expose her stomach, I lean over and place kisses all along the small bump. "Are you hungry?"

"Oh, yes, I'm starving."

When my eyes meet hers, they are dark with desire and I don't think her answer has anything to do with food. I smirk at her, "I may have corrupted you, love."

"Spoiled me is more like it," she purrs. "But I'll let you spoil me some more."

"You have no idea how much I'd love to *spoil* you right now. But since I just met your parents, and you've just talked to them again for the first time in years, today may not be the best day to christen their spare bedroom."

"If you say so," she giggles. "Let's go eat if you're just going to be a killjoy. Your baby is hungry."

As we walk into the kitchen, Sarah and Manuel stop and just stare at us in awe. Sophia smiles shyly and addresses them.

"Thanks for letting me sleep. I feel so much better now," she smiles, but she still feels uncomfortable here. I can't imagine feeling uncomfortable in my parents' home, so I wrack my brain to think of a way to stop the awkwardness.

"Something smells good! Sophia was just telling me that she's hungry," I try to pick up the conversation. It seems to work, as Sarah takes Sophia's hand and says she's cooking all of Sophia's favorite foods.

Manuel tilts his head to the side, knowing I'm trying to help, and smiles at me in appreciation. Approaching me, he asks me to step outside alone with him. I know what talk is about to occur and I'm fine with it. Sophia is *My Angel* and that means she comes first in all things. But she is *mine* to have, to hold, to tie up, tie down, punish and reward.

"Dominic, it's obvious that you love Sophia and that she loves you. I don't really have a right to ask this after all these years, but she's still my daughter. Time apart doesn't make me love her any less," Manuel says.

"Of course. Ask away."

"Are you one of those Doms, too?"

Withholding my mirth at how he phrased it, I answer the real, underlying question that he didn't ask. "I am a Dom, yes, and Sophia is my submissive. But, you probably got the wrong impression from Harrison.

"We have a loving, committed and *monogamous* relationship. There is no physical abuse involved and whatever happens is only with her consent. She holds all the power to stop anything she's uncomfortable with doing. It's my job to protect her, love her, and continually earn her trust."

"Are you planning on marrying her?"

"I am. I'm never letting her go," I promise. "I hope I have your approval to ask her to marry me in the near future. But, I have to be honest with you. It will happen with or without your blessing. That's not a Dom thing. That's a man in love thing."

Manuel holds out his hand to me to shake, "You're a good man, Dominic. I'd be honored to have you in the family." We shake and he claps me on the back as we walk back in the kitchen.

Shadow and Tucker have both made themselves at home in the short time we've been here. Shadow is towering over Sarah at the stove while he helps her cook. "No, no, don't use regular salt and pepper to season that. Has no one taught you how to cook, woman?" he playfully scolds her as she laughs energetically.

"Shadow, if you don't get away from my stove!" She issues a mock threat but the smile on her face gives her away.

Tucker elbows Shadow out of the way, "Get away from her, man. She's busy cooking and you're interrupting her!" Turning to Sarah, Tucker says, "You'll have to excuse him. We don't let him out much but every once in a while he escapes."

Sophia is sitting at the bar, watching the interactions with a small smile on her face, but a little sadness still lingers. Walking up behind her, I wrap my arms around her and pull her close to me. "Penny for your thoughts?" I ask, my lips against her ear. I try to hold back my chuckle as I watch the cold chills crawl down her arm.

"I've missed this–the whole family get-together. Shawn and I used to joke around with Mom when she was cooking. I didn't realize how much I've missed it until now. We'll probably never have it again."

"Maybe not with him, but we will have our own family and our own memories," I assure her. "You've reconciled with your parents and we'll have my parents around."

She nods, "I know you're right. It's just a mixture of nostalgia and pregnancy hormones. Besides, I wouldn't let him near our baby after he just handed me over to Harrison last night."

I know she loved her brother and had hoped for a happy reunion. She must've been more heartbroken over it than she showed. Turning her chair around to face me, I hold her face in my hands and keep my voice low. "Love, I won't ever let him near *you* or our baby after he did that. You can put all the blame on me for why he's not invited to be a part of our lives."

She wraps her arms around my waist and hugs me tightly. "Thank you for taking such good care of me, Dom."

I kiss the top of her head, "That's something you never have to thank me for, Sophia. You're mine and I love taking care of what's mine."

Sarah, Tucker, and Shadow finish setting the table and Shadow pushes Tucker out of the way to claim his seat in front of the main course. "Move it, Tucker, or lose a limb. Your choice, man."

"Rude. That's just *rude*," Tucker shakes his head and takes the seat beside Shadow.

Sophia and I sit next to each other as Sarah and Manuel sit at either end of the table. Sarah went all out on the spread, but I have a feeling there won't be much left with the way Shadow and Tucker are eying everything. Manuel clears his throat and all eyes turn to him.

"I'd like to give special thanks for our daughter coming back to us. We've missed you so much, Sophia." Manuel says grace before we all dive into the food like we haven't eaten in months.

During dinner, Sophia relaxes and becomes more like her usual self again. She laughs and talks animatedly with her parents about our life in Dallas. An hour later, we've eaten all we can, except maybe Shadow and Tucker, and a quiet tension hangs in the air. The knowledge that Sophia is about to leave again is weighing heavily on Manuel and Sarah.

"We all appreciate your hospitality, Sarah and Manuel. The dinner was absolutely delicious. We should be going now but we'll stay in touch. It's less than an hour flight to Dallas–we can fly you up to visit with us soon," I offer.

Sarah stammers at my suggestion, unsure of how to answer. "That's much too generous, Dominic. We can drive to Dallas."

"It's okay, Mom. Really. Dominic is the best at taking care of me," Sophia says as her eyes float to me. "He knows this is important to me, so he wants to make it happen."

After the hugs, tears, declarations of love, and promises to see each other again soon, we leave for the airport. Tucker calls Mike, our pilot, and has the jet readied for our departure. Shadow has been on the phone with his security detail that has been following Harrison since he left the restaurant. He hangs up his phone and turns to look at me.

"Harrison is back at his house in Dallas. He called his friend Cortez and they're discussing how to handle the situation now. They aren't onto us, though."

"How does the security team know what Harrison and Ramon are discussing?" Sophia asks.

One side of Shadow's lip quirks upward, "Tucker may have dropped a bug or two in Harrison's house." Turning his gaze to me, he says, "They're planning their next move on you if you don't pay '*Sebastian Montoya'* soon."

"Let them plan. We'll be ready for them this time." My hands are clenched into tight fists, ready to pummel Harrison for everything he's done to Sophia and me.

"I have an idea," Tucker says. "It's not without risks, but it'll put an end to Harrison and Ramon's harassment. I can't guarantee Shawn won't be sent to prison afterward, though."

I turn to Sophia to gauge her reaction, silently questioning her with my eyes. She gives me an impassive look about her brother. After his betrayal knowing she is pregnant, I think she has accepted that the brother she once knew is long gone. Sophia cuddles up to me and lays her head on my shoulder. Her whisper is murmured so low, I know isn't meant for me to hear actually it.

"I can live without any other man but you."

# Chapter Nineteen

### *Sophia*

It's been two weeks since our visit to Austin and we have had Face Time chats with my parents nearly every day. It was awkward at first, but soon the conversations flowed naturally and it felt like old times again. I can tell that they already love Dom almost as much as I do. *Almost.*

"Dom, I'm almost four months pregnant now," I begin my argument.

Knowing me as well as he does, he quirks one eyebrow up and dares me, with the playful gleam in his eyes, to continue. "Yes, I'm well aware of your pregnancy status. Your protruding belly is one clue."

"I'm out of the danger zone now. The doctor gave me a clean bill of health," I continue making my case.

"That's not exactly what she said. She said to still be cautious about any changes. You were having cramps when we were at your parents and you didn't tell me about it until much later. Remember?"

*Oh, yes, I do remember that.* I was punished for my withholding of important information and it wasn't a good punishment. Until the doctor cleared me, Dom wouldn't take a chance on giving me a punishment fuck or even a spanking. What he did punish me with was actually worse. I wasn't allowed to touch him in any way for a full week - day or night. I couldn't even snuggle with him in the bed and he made sure I didn't by putting pillows between us.

"Dominic, I tried to explain that to you. I wasn't hiding it from you. It just felt like an upset stomach and it's embarrassing to discuss my gastrointestinal problems with you," I respectfully retort. "But, I'm okay now."

He crosses the room with his eyes fixed on mine. The flames in them have me rooted to the floor. His commanding presence has me in awe. He's only wearing his lounging pants and they hang low on his hips, showing off his perfectly sculpted abs and that damn sexy V that I licked repeatedly last night. He's already had his workout this morning before I ever woke, so he's fully awake and alert.

Bending so that his eyes are level with mine, he grabs my cheeks in his hand and holds my face as he speaks. "Sophia, we've discussed this. You are to tell me when you have any health problem, regardless of how small it is. It may start small but it can quickly escalate and I'm not taking any chances with your health. After everything we've done to each other, you shouldn't be embarrassed about anything with me."

Releasing my face, he kisses my lips and walks back to the closet. "Now, what is it you want to ask me?" he calls out.

"It's time for me to go back into the office and work. I've worked from home and kept my hours minimal. I'm able to go back to full time now until the baby is born."

He steps out of the closet slowly and pins me with his gaze. "Surely you're joking," he deadpans, but there's an icy undertone. "Two break-ins at my office and they haven't found out who is behind it yet. Harrison and Cortez are actively plotting against us and he has already hurt you once. There have been two attempts on my life. But you want to go into the office to work while you're pregnant."

"Dominic, I can't stay locked away inside the house forever. I love you and I love working. I'd be there with you, Shadow, Tucker, and the building security. The break-ins were at night after everyone had left. There are several other employees there, too. Plus, the office is an hour away from home, so if anything happened here, you wouldn't be able to get to me in time anyway."

Drawing his hand across his face, along his jawline until his fingers meet in the middle of his chin, he considers my argument. At least he listens to me and weighs all sides of the equation before making a decision. I can't very well go against his wishes about work because he will just fire me since Texas is an employment at-will state. My Dom will get his way with me regardless.

"Fine. You can come back to the office–with conditions. You'll ride with me to work and back home, *no exceptions*. If I have to go out of town and you can't go with me, you *will* work from home while I'm gone. You will not go *anywhere* alone except to the bathroom, and I am even considering having Dana escort you in there," he replies sternly.

Rushing to him, I wrap my arms around his neck and lift up on my tiptoes to kiss him. "Thank you! I'll hurry and get dressed so I can ride in with you today."

Dominic holds me tightly to him when I try to move away. His slow smile covers his face and his hand goes under my shirt. I roll my eyes, but I am sporting the biggest smile myself. It's become a daily practice for him to gently rub my stomach and feel our growing baby bump.

"I can't wait to feel the baby move," he murmurs to me. "You are so beautiful pregnant, I may have to keep you knocked up all the time. Maybe then you'd quit working."

I playfully swat his arm as I say, "Oh, stop it! I'm in the office with you! It's not like I'm looking for another job somewhere else!"

"Don't even joke about that," he replies with a serious tone.

I can't stop the laughter that bubbles up out of my chest. "Dominic, where would I go? And why would I go? I have all the perks I could ever ask for with you!"

"Speaking of perks," he wiggles his eyebrows suggestively, "I think it's time for our shower."

"We're going to be late for work," I try to object, backing away from him one step at a time. He begins moving slowly and deliberately toward me, stalking me like I'm his prey, and watching me through his brows. The feral look in his eyes is such a turn-on because I know it means he has wild things in mind for me.

"I'm sure your boss will understand," he quips.

In a split second, he takes off in a sprint toward me and I squeal in laughter as I turn to run from him. He's already caught me, though, and I'm swept off my feet into his arms. I love our playful times, especially in the midst of all the stress we've been under. The times when it's just Dominic and I are the best because he doesn't show this playful side to many people.

"You won't be able to carry me for too much longer."

"I'll just work out harder if I have to, babe."

"I love how you love me, Dominic," I lean up and kiss him. "But, I was talking about how my stomach will be too big!"

Setting me down, he starts the water before he undresses me, taking his time as he removes each article of clothing. "The house will be ready in a few weeks. Our playroom will be a separate room off our bedroom. It even has a secret door that only we will know about," he says looking up at me. "I can't wait to get you inside it."

"I'll melt into a puddle in the floor if you keep talking to me like that," I pant.

"Mmm, just the thought of having you strapped to the new play-furniture I bought makes me crazy," he continues and I moan softly. "All the things I can do to your beautiful body…"

"Whatever you want, Dominic. I'm yours."

Picking me up, he walks us into the hot water spray and to the tiled shower wall. I wrap my legs around his waist and he positions himself at my sex, ready to push into me. Instead of the fast, sudden thrust, he slowly lowers me onto him, letting me feel every glorious inch of him, pulling me down until we're eye to eye. Moving his hips, he rocks into me and I match his rhythm as I move up and down on him.

"That's my girl," he grunts when he feels me tightening around him. "Take it all, Sophia," and my body milks every last bit of him.

We're both breathing hard as we ride out the waves of our climax. While he's still inside me, Dominic leans in and covers my mouth with his. The slow, sensual kiss is just as erotic and mind-blowing as the heated, furious kisses. This is so much more personal and intimate. I feel the love and passion from the top of my head to the tips of my toes.

He slowly lowers my feet to the ground to allow me to get my bearings before he lets go. My hands rest on his chest and I watch him with rapt adoration. Everything that means anything to me is right here and I feel like the most fortunate woman alive.

What scares me the most is every other time I've felt this way, the carpet was yanked out from under my feet. The unknown dangers involving Harrison Dictman and Ramon Cortez still lurk around every corner and I'm waiting for them to make their move. I just hope that Shadow and Tucker are ready for them when they do.

By midweek, Dominic and I have settled into a normal routine of work and home life. With my office back on the top floor, I'm closer to him and he frequently checks on me. Between him and Dana, I can barely even go to the bathroom alone. I have to admit that having people around that really care about me feels great. Even if I do lose my privacy in the interim.

I'm back in Dom's office for another contract negotiation meeting when Darren enters. He smiles warmly at me and takes his seat. As the

Chief Financial Officer of DPS, his input is needed for the solvency of this agreement. Dominic is finishing up another call as Darren leans over toward me.

"I'm glad to see you two worked things out, Sophia," Darren says with a wink.

"Yeah, I know you just wanted to get rid of me," I kid with him.

"Oh, you know better than that!" he laughs. "I'm just an old man who's ready to retire. You're better off learning the ropes from Dominic."

"He is a great teacher, but you are great, too!" I assure him and he pats my arm in a grandfatherly way.

Dominic hangs up and joins our conversations. "Hey, Darren. We need your help on this one. The numbers look good on paper but something just isn't adding up right. I think they're hiding losses from us and I don't want to enter into this contract, do the work, and then have them file bankruptcy later."

"Let's have a look," Darren says, taking the file from Dominic.

Over the next hour, we dissect every part of their financials and the contract language before coming to a decision. At the end of our meeting, Darren gets up to leave just as I also stand. His eyes settle on my stomach and I know he wants to say something but is unsure of how to say it.

"You'll have to forgive an old man for asking, Sophia. But, are you pregnant?"

My hand instinctively covers my baby bump, not from embarrassment, but from pride. "Yes, I'm about four months now. We'll get to hear the baby's heartbeat at our doctor visit this Friday," I beam.

Darren's eyes cut to Dominic, flashing him a big smile, before turning back to me. "Congratulations, young lady. You look absolutely radiant and beautiful."

"Thank you, Darren," I reply sincerely. He kisses my cheek on the way out and we say our goodbyes.

"He thinks of you as one of his granddaughters," Dominic smiles as he leans back in his chair. "Speaking of grandparents, Mom called earlier and said she and Dad are coming up this weekend."

"Really? I can't wait to see them!" I reply enthusiastically.

Dominic's mother, Kayla, has called me weekly since Dominic and I got back together. She had already figured out I was pregnant and Dominic confirmed it during one of their conversations. Kayla has also been very supportive of me reestablishing the relationship with my parents and talking with her has helped me work through some of the issues they had with me being a sub.

Dana knocks on the door, drawing me from my thoughts, and walks in with Cheryl behind her. "Mr. Powers, Cheryl needs to speak with you. She said it's urgent."

"That's fine. Thank you, Dana," Dominic says. "Come on in, Cheryl."

Cheryl gives me a weary look, even after all this time and after she knows I'm not behind these allegations. When I greet her hard gaze with one of my own, she looks away and addresses Dominic. Something else I learned from Kayla–I submit to no one but Dominic. That includes our corporate lawyer.

"I spoke with Shadow's contact as he suggested. He backtracked the standard paper trail through the EEOC and we have verified that this is not a real case. Shadow's friend that helped me is very…unique. I gave him the limited information I had and he sent back most everything we need–the make and model of the printer, when it was available, and which stores carried it. I'm going to call the police and let them take it from here."

"No, don't call the police," Dominic replies emphatically. "There are Federal agents working on this case since it's bigger than just this piece. We can't involve our local law enforcement. You still owe the *'lawyer'* a return call, right?"

"Yes," Cheryl replies tentatively.

"Call *Mr. Montoya* and tell him we will meet with him here in my office a week from tomorrow. Tell him to bring several copies of his settlement request with him. We will discuss the terms of our settlement then."

"You're sure about this?" Cheryl asks.

"Yes. I'm positive."

Dominic's steely determination is obvious in his matter-of-fact tone, his narrowed eyes, and his rigid posture. He has met with Tucker and Shadow most every night since we returned from Austin. They've installed hidden cameras in Dominic's office and the stairwells after hours without letting anyone in the office know. If there's another break in, it will capture everything that happens.

"I'm worried about this, Dominic," I say when Cheryl leaves the room. "He's part of the cartel and he obviously still has ties to the police department here."

"I won't be here alone, my love," he says as he rounds his desk and sits beside me. Taking my hand in his, he kisses each of my knuckles, "It's time we put an end to all of this so we can move on with our lives, look forward to our baby being born, and not have to worry about our safety."

"I know you're right and I'm not questioning you. I just also know what Harrison is capable of, Dom. It scares me."

"My sub wants to protect her Dom?" He asks teasingly, just like he did before all this happened. His smile is warm and the love shines from his eyes. He is my Dom, he is my protector, and he is my lover. But if I can protect him, I will gladly do it.

"Always, Dom. Always," is my reply and will always be my reply.

Friday finally arrives and we're at my doctor's office for my monthly obstetrician appointment. After going through the standard checkup, we'll get to hear our baby's heartbeat for the first time. I am so excited and nervous at the same time. Dom is bouncing-off-the-walls excited about it. I asked for the earliest appointment available this morning since I knew I wouldn't be able to wait all day. Dom and I are looking through maternity magazines when the nurse calls my name from the doorway.

Finally, after what feels like an eternity, my belly is prepped with a big blob of the warmed ultrasound gel before the doctor presses the fetal Doppler against my skin. I watch Dr. Perry expectantly as the initial swishing sounds echo through the room. *Is that my baby's heartbeat?*

Then, I hear it and it's unmistakable. It sounds like horses galloping and it's beating so fast. A smile is permanently affixed to my face and tears spring to my eyes when I look up at Dominic.

"That's your baby's heartbeat, Mom and Dad," Dr. Perry informs us.

Dominic is at my side, holding my hand, but his eyes are glued to the Doppler in Dr. Perry's hand. The magical sounds emanating from the handheld machine are music to my ears. I don't want this visit to end because this makes it so much more real.

"Dominic," I choke out, "that's our baby. It's his *heartbeat*."

His eyes meet mine and he's in awe as much as I am. "This is incredible. I could listen to this all the time," he says before kissing me.

"Actually, you can get one and use it at home. They're safe and they even connect with your iPhone so you can track the heart rate over time," Dr. Perry explains.

"That's incredible," Dominic says. "We're getting one and we're using it every day."

Dr. Perry chuckles, "I wouldn't advise using it every day. It is considered safe, but I would still advise against overuse of it. It also doesn't replace your regular visits with me. Don't think you've become a doctor just because you have a Doppler and a search engine."

"Okay, a few times a week, then," Dominic agrees.

Dr. Perry pulls the fetal Doppler away from my belly way too soon. I'm not ready for it to be over just yet. She then measures my stomach to determine my uterus size and says everything is right on schedule. Dominic is already on the phone with a contact of his to have the top of the line fetal Doppler delivered to our house by the end of the day.

In this moment, my world is absolutely perfect.

# Chapter Twenty

### *Dominic*

My parents arrive at the lake house just before the high-end fetal Doppler arrives via special courier. When my mother realizes what's in the box, she grabs it from me and urgently calls for Sophia. The tone of her voice must have alarmed Sophia because she comes trotting through the house as fast as she can run.

"What? What's wrong, Kayla?" she asks as she bounds into the room.

"My grandbaby wants to talk to me," Mom replies with a huge smile.

Sophia exhales a relieved breath and laughs. "You scared the shit out of me!" But, she willingly moves to the couch, and following the instructions, we search until we find the heartbeat again.

Mom and Dad listen in amazement and we each take turns placing bets on whether she's carrying a girl or a boy. "It's a boy, I'm telling you," Mom says.

"Nope, definitely a girl," Dad declares. "Look at how radiant her skin is."

"Are you saying mine wasn't radiant when I was pregnant with Dominic?" Mom challenges.

"No, I would never say that," Dad placates her. "You were just *more* radiant when you were pregnant with the girls."

Tucker walks in with a manila envelope in his hand. Jerking his head to the side, he motions for me to join him in my study. Dad catches the subtle nod and his eyes meet mine. He knows everything that's happened so far and they've both been worried about us. If that envelope contains what I think it does, I'd rather talk to Tucker to get the news alone before involving the rest of my family.

"Excuse me for a minute," I say, kissing Sophia's head. "I need to talk to Tucker."

Sophia's worried eyes flit up to meet mine, questions swirl in them but she works hard to contain it. She knows it's obviously very important information. She also knows that Tucker wouldn't pull me away from this visit for anything other than information directly related to Harrison. "Don't take too long, okay?" she asks as she squeezes my hand.

"I will be back before you even know I'm gone," I assure her.

Walking swiftly into the study and closing the door behind me, I approach Tucker. "Tell me."

"The handwriting on the letter planted in your office is not Carol Anne's, exactly as we already knew. Shadow also took a sample of Harrison's handwriting, you know, from the file he accidently left in my hand. Anyway, it's not Harrison's handwriting either," Tucker smiles, before delivering the last part of the news. "But, it does match '*Sophia's lawyer's*' handwriting."

"So we know his has at least three aliases – Ramon Cortez, Ramon Nunez, and Sebastian Montoya. '*Cortez*' was the detective on Carol Ann's death and his real name that he keeps hidden,

*'Nunez'* is a detective in Austin, and *'Montoya'* is the lawyer on the fake sexual harassment lawsuit. He will be in my office Monday afternoon and he scheduled the latest meeting possible," I relay to Tucker.

"We'll be ready for him. Shadow is meeting with the FBI Special Agent in Charge now. Since this is cartel related, they will run the show, Dominic," Tucker says, his voice turning serious. "That means even Shadow won't have his usual way of circumventing the rules. They won't let us do anything that would jeopardize the case once it gets to court."

I stare at Tucker in disbelief, even though I know what he's saying is the truth and the right thing to do. The thought of not being in complete control of the situation doesn't sit well with me. "Then Sophia won't be there Monday," I assert. "If we can't guarantee her safety, she won't be anywhere near the office."

"Dominic, I can't stay here with her and neither can Shadow. We're both being pulled into this as backup because we're both state mandated. She'd be safer there with us and the FBI agents than she would be here alone," Tucker reasons.

"I'll send her home with my parents," I decide on the spur of the moment. "I can't take the risk, Tucker."

Tucker doesn't respond immediately and I know...in my gut, I know what he's about to say. "They want her here, Dominic. After they arrest him and put the printer, the IP address of his computer, his ties to the cartel, and of course, all the aliases he uses, they will question her to build the case against him and Harrison."

"That doesn't mean she has to be here!" I roar. "They can question her later!"

Tucker keeps his eyes trained on mine. "Dominic," he pauses, and I wait on baited breath. "They think he's coming for her. They think he's been watching her come and go from the office. He'll know if she's not there. That's most likely why he scheduled the meeting at the end of the day, when there are fewer people around."

"*What the fuck, Tucker?*"

"Dominic, it's the best way to end it quickly. We will all be in the office next to yours watching on the video feed."

"And if someone gets to her while you're watching *my meeting*?" I shout as I point in the direction of Sophia. I am about to pick up my desk and throw it through the fucking window. *Are these fucking idiots not fucking thinking?*

"You have to let us do our jobs, Dominic."

"I need to think about it, Tucker. I'm not just going along with letting my pregnant lover be put in a dangerous situation because some asshole agent I've never even met says it's best. Who is it best for–him and his career? Certainly not Sophia, not our baby, and not me!"

Tucker's chuckle rumbles through the room, "I told them you'd say that."

"So you haven't agreed to this shitty plan?"

"Hell, no," Tucker smiles, "but they are adamant about it. They say he won't show if she's not there, man. You know I'd never let anything happen to Sophia if there's anything I can do about it."

"What if there isn't anything you can do, Tucker? What if there isn't anything any of us can do?" I ask solemnly.

He simply nods, knowing there's no answer that'll satisfy me, pacify me, or ease my tension about Sophia's presence in the office with that bastard there.

"Is there anything else I should know?" I ask, much calmer now.

"Shawn's bail money was also traced back to Cortez. So, he hid the evidence and paid to get him out of jail. Dominic, Shawn is missing now. Our guys have been working the case in Austin and they haven't seen him in several days. It doesn't look good," Tucker warns.

"Keep me posted," I say and scrub my hand over my face. "I don't want to worry Sophia unnecessarily. We'll cross that bridge when we have to and not a second before. She's been through too much already and her cramping before was exacerbated by stress."

"Are Sophia and the baby okay?" Tucker asks, his concern evident on his face and in the inflection in his voice.

"Yeah, but there are things we need to keep an eye on to make sure they stay that way. If she knew her brother was missing, she'd insist on going Monday because she'd see the two events as being connected."

"They may be connected, Dominic. They could very well be holding her brother as collateral to make sure she's there. Shadow said he told you that Sophia is their primary target now. They've used her love for her brother against her all along."

"That's what worries me, Tucker. Either way–if they have her brother or if they get to her, she can't win," I sigh. "And I can't let her lose."

Rejoining the others, they instantly sense the tension rolling off both Tucker and me. They may have even heard my raised voice behind the thick, wooden door. But no one comes right out and asks us about our conversation even though the giant, crimson elephant is sitting in the middle of the room.

"Who's hungry?" I ask, changing the subject before it's even brought up.

"I know I am," Tucker replies enthusiastically. "What's on the menu?"

Mom rises from her seat and gives me her *I-already-know-everything-and-you're-in-a-shitload-of-trouble* look. "Your father and I already planned our meal for tonight. Since I didn't get to cook breakfast for everyone," she says with a smile, "I'm cooking dinner."

"Let me help you with that, Kayla," Sophia says as she stands.

Mom wraps her arm around Sophia's and the two of them walk off to the kitchen. Once they're out of earshot, Dad wastes no time in jumping in. "That was some conversation the two of you had in there."

"How much did you hear?" I ask, concerned that Sophia heard the part about her brother.

"We couldn't make out any words, actually. It mostly sounded like muffled shouting when we could hear anything. But, it was enough that your mother and I would start talking to draw Sophia's attention and try to mask it more. She knows something bad is up. So, why don't you fill your old man in?"

Over the next thirty minutes, Tucker, Dad and I rehash the details of what was just shared with me. When the smell of the food cooking starts wafting through the room, I know dinner is almost finished and they'll be back for us at any minute. Surprisingly, Dad agrees that Sophia needs to go to work Monday, just like she does any other day, to avoid sending up a red flag.

"Let's go find them before they come find us," I say as I head toward the kitchen.

Sophia's setting the table and Mom is putting the finishing touches on the food. My feet seem have a mind of their own as they carry me straight to Sophia. Wrapping my arms around her waist, I pull her in as close to me as possible. Her arms find their place around my neck as her body molds to perfectly fit mine. I know there are others in the room with us and they probably feel somewhat uncomfortable. I know they're waiting for our public display of affection to end so we can enjoy our meal together. I also know that I'm not ready to let her go yet and she feels it, too.

Leaning my head down, I whisper softly into her ear. "Your Dom has a confession to make."

Her muscles stiffen for a fraction of a second as a bolt of worry rushes through her before she relaxes in my embrace again. *She trusts me.*

"You can tell me, Dom."

"I'm your Dom, but you own me, *My Angel*. My heart, my love, and my life all revolve around you now and that'll never change. You can never leave me, Sophia."

I can't shake this ominous feeling that something terrible is coming. Like a barometer senses when a thunderstorm is gaining strength, the strong foreboding feeling can't be ignored. It whispers to me, taunts me, and tells me that regardless of what I do, Sophia will be mercilessly snatched from my hands. No matter how much sense it makes to allow her to go to work as usual, my gut tells me to run away with her and let them figure this out without us. I understand we can't tip off Cortez or *Harry Dick-man* to our plan, but no one else is being asked to put the love of his life in a dangerous situation. Knowing Sophia, she'll insist on being there Monday, if for no other reason than she thinks *she* has to protect *me*.

Squeezing me harder, she whispers back, "You'll never lose me, Dom, I'm yours forever. I could never love anyone else after being loved by you. Why would you think that's even possible?"

Pulling away, her confusion at my statement is obvious on her beautiful face. She searches my eyes before leaning up on her toes to pour all of her love for me into her kiss. I don't have it in me to tell her that's not how I meant *'leave me'* and I'm breaking inside just thinking about this. Holding her face in my hands, I let her see deep into my soul through my eyes as I say the next words to her.

"I believe you, I trust you, I forgive you, and I love you. I never want to see the regret over anything that happened in your eyes again."

Tears pool in her eyes before she blinks them back. Nodding, she swallows the feelings trying to overtake her. "I love you, too, Dom. So much."

"Let's eat," I say, breaking the moment. Placing my hand on Sophia's stomach, I gently rub it. "My baby girl and my baby are hungry."

Mom smiles but I see the same worry in her eyes that's in me. She's always been able to read me like a book and she knows this conversation was much more important than it appeared. She looks at Sophia's stomach where my hand still rests and quickly averts her eyes. Dad walks up behind her and wraps his arms around her, whispers something in her ear, and she nods in agreement.

"Your mom had a fabulous idea," Sophia compliments her. "I can't wait to try this! I've never had fondue before."

Taking our seats, we enjoy our time together as if the devil isn't lurking just around the corner. We talk while our skewers rest in the coq au vin mixture, slow cooking our food. The scene of us sitting around the table looks like so much like a perfect family portrait it hurts. Stretching my arm out, my hand rests on our baby and Sophia doesn't even blink, as if it's just a normal, everyday gesture. Just when I think she hasn't even noticed, her hand finds mine and her fingertip draws lazy circles around my knuckles. She doesn't look at me at all–she doesn't even miss a beat in talking with my parents.

But she feels me, she knows she's mine, and I don't give up what's mine.

***Sophia***

"Do you want a boy or a girl?" Kayla asks me in between bites.

"I would love to have a boy first," I answer honestly. "One who looks just like his daddy. But honestly, either is fine with me. I really only want a happy, healthy baby to love and spoil."

Dominic's hand is resting on my belly and has been for some time now. Using his thumb, he absently rubs up and down over my protruding stomach. The rest of his hand stays splayed out across me, like he's shielding us from something unknown. His comment about leaving him caught me off guard. As much as I love being around our friends and family, I can't wait until we're alone so I can ask him what's really going on.

"I think a little girl, with her mom's reddish-brown hair and beautiful brown eyes, would be best," Dominic chimes in.

"How about one of each?" Shadow asks from the doorway, surprising us all.

"Don't even joke about that!" I narrow my eyes at him and try to give him my meanest look. It only succeeds in making him laugh. When I move to get up, Dominic's arm becomes stiff and he holds me in place. Kayla quickly jumps up and grabs a plate for Shadow.

"Thank you, ma'am," Shadow says as he kisses her cheek and takes his plate. "Whose has been cooking the longest? I'm calling dibs on that one."

"The hell you say!" Tucker retorts, his Southern drawl is more pronounced when he jokes with Shadow.

He blocks Shadow's attempts at getting to the fondue pot, wrapping his arms around the fondue cooker and guarding his skewer like it's Fort Knox. Grabbing an empty skewer, Shadow jabs the sharp, pointy ends at Tucker's arms. Tucker jumps with each stab and Shadow's determination increases. When Tucker is least suspecting it, Shadow jerks his arm downward and jabs Tucker in the ribs, making his arms fly away from the fondue cooker and opening it up for fair game.

Shadow grabs Tucker's skewer and quickly pops the chunk of steak into his mouth. He can't hide his satisfied grin as he exaggeratedly chews, moaning in appreciation, and rubbing his stomach. He is really hamming it up, rubbing it in Tucker's face, and drawing out his own brand of torture. For such a big, serious guy, he can be so funny and down to earth when he's relaxed.

Kayla and Rick are both smiling from ear to ear, waiting to see what these two clowns do next. I noticed, though, that Rick quickly withdrew two of his skewers from the cooker and put them on his plate. Probably just in case Shadow gets any more ideas.

"This is the best steak I've ever eaten. Tucker, you must tell me your secret recipe," Shadow heckles. "Do you marinate it first? How do you tenderize it?"

Tucker glares at Shadow and the entire table erupts in uncontrollable laughter. Shadow leans back in his chair as far away as he can get from Tucker while still sitting beside him. His shit-eating grin is still fully intact and he's not even trying to hide it in the least. My shoulders are shaking, I can't breathe, and every time I look at Tucker's sour face, it makes it even worse. Tears are streaming freely down my face when I grab my napkin to wipe my eyes. Turning my head toward Dominic, I expect to find him in the same fits of laughter.

But he's not laughing at all. He's just staring at his empty plate, oblivious to the comedic scene around him, and he has the saddest look I've ever seen on anyone. His eyes are downcast as he twirls and empty skewer between his thumb and index finger. There's no hint of a smile or any indication that he's even heard a word that's been said. My heart instantly drops to my stomach and I fight back the painful tears that are threatening to fall. I don't know what's suddenly so wrong, what's on his mind, or how I can help him.

He looks like he just lost his best friend.

# Chapter Twenty-One

“So, Dominic, I understand you have some reservations about our plan for Monday,” Shadow nonchalantly says as he scoops up another bite.

Dominic’s eyes fly up to meet his, the fire has returned, and his lips are drawn into a tight, straight line. His pissed off look is much more convincing than mine, but since Shadow isn’t one to back down, either, there’s a silent war of wills happening. Everyone keeps eating in silence and blatantly avoids looking at either of them.

It appears I’m the only one who’s been left out of this tidbit of information.

“What’s the plan for Monday?” I ask, my eyes darting between Dominic and Shadow to see which one will answer me first. Shadow smiles at Dominic but their staring contest is still ongoing.

Abruptly standing up, my chair slides across the floor, causing all eyes to turn to me. "Someone needs to tell me about *'the plan'* for Monday, NOW," I demand, making air quotes with my fingers to show my disgust with being left out.

"Sit down, Sophia," Dominic replies, trying unsuccessfully to hide the anger in his voice.

"No," I use my assertive voice. "Something's up and you're intentionally leaving me out of it. I'm not a child and I'm not going to break. I deserve to know what's obviously got you so upset tonight."

"You haven't told her?" Shadow asks, but this time there's no hint of joking. His face changes to something lethal and scary. "Why haven't you told her?"

"Told. Me. What?" I stress each word as I slam my hands down on the table.

"Sophia," Dominic says, all traces of anger in his face and voice have been carefully hidden, "let's go upstairs and talk."

As I straighten to stand upright, I see a slight shake of Shadow's head as he continues to show his disapproval. Dominic stands and extends his hand to me. The lost, sad look has returned to his eyes and I know this is what he was thinking about before Shadow said anything. "Come with me," he urges.

Taking his hand, he firmly grips mine and wordlessly leads me up to the bedroom. After closing and locking the door, he leads me to the bed and has me sit on the edge of the mattress. Then he completely stuns me when he drops to his knees on the floor in front of me and lays his head in my lap. His arms wrap around my hips and he just holds me for several, quiet minutes.

Lovingly stroking his head, running my fingers through it, and rubbing his shoulders, I wait for him to collect his thoughts. "I wasn't keeping it from you, Sophia. I just wanted to talk to you about it alone," he finally speaks but keeps his head in my lap.

"About what?" I ask quietly, still running my fingers through his hair.

"I'm meeting with Ramon Cortez late Monday afternoon. The FBI will be there, watching from another room. They have information that he is after you–to kidnap you or…" his voice drops off and I can't seem to find mine.

"They say you have to be there, Sophia. He's had someone watching you come and go from the office. So, if you don't show up for work like you normally do, he will know something is up. They want me to willingly put your life in danger so they can get information on him, maybe make an arrest.

"How can I do that? My job is to love you, protect you, and earn your trust. If I knowingly put you in a dangerous situation that I can't control, I'm not holding up my end of the relationship. But more than that," he sighs heavily, not wanting to say the next part.

Pulling up from my embrace, his eyes find mine and that sad, haunted look breaks my heart. His big hand wraps around the back of my neck and he pulls my face close to his. "More than that, I have a *really* bad feeling, Sophia. I can't lose you."

Now his comments from just after his meeting with Tucker make sense. He doesn't think I'd leave him for another man. He thinks I'm going to be taken or maybe even killed. My Dom doesn't worry without a reason and he isn't scared of any man.

"Why do you think you'll lose me, Dominic?"

Leaning his forehead against mine, he tells me. "They were after me at first, with the car wreck and the house fire. But, now it seems that *you* are their primary target."

"Is this because of Harrison?"

Dominic springs to his feet and paces the floor. His hands are in his hair, running through it over and over, until it's standing on end in wild, sexy spikes. I remain still, watching his agitation grow.

"That's what I've been going over and over in my mind. It doesn't make sense to me. Why would Cortez go to such great lengths to get to you as a favor to Harrison? He can't do anything to help Cortez in return. A man like Cortez doesn't do something for nothing.

"I think there's something we've missed and it's the unknown factor that I'm having a hard time dealing with. I don't even know where to begin to look for answers. I don't know how to keep you safe when I can't see which direction the threat is coming from."

He stops pacing, his back is to me, and his hands are drawn into tight fists. I expect him to punch the door and run his hand through it at any moment now. He feels out of control and the old doubts about his worthiness to be a Dom are trying to resurface. He is my Dom, though. He commands my body with just a glance. His voice thrills me beyond measure. He owns my body, my mind, and my heart with a single touch.

There's no man who could ever compare to Dominic Powers.

I quietly remove my clothes and slide up the bed. The soft clicking of the buckles on the wrist restraints draws his attention to me. When he sees me lying on the bed completely naked, partially restrained, and totally his, the Dom I know and love comes out to play.

With a slightly amused quirk of his mouth, he stalks toward me. "It appears that my sub has started without me. Since when has this become acceptable?"

"My apologies, Dom. I deserve to be punished for that," I reply submissively.

"You do realize that it isn't *actually* punishment when you ask for it like that," he deadpans, but still sheds his clothes in the process.

"How should I ask for it then, Dom?"

"You just did, little girl."

He finishes latching the buckles on the wrist restraints before moving to my ankles. "One more month and we'll be in our new house, with our new playroom. So many different possibilities and combinations I can employ in there. For now, you'll have to take the punishment I have handy."

I bite my bottom lip, pulling it between my teeth. The expectant tone of his voice tells me it isn't quite as mundane as he wants me to think it is. He opens the second drawer of the nightstand and removes a small, stainless steel U-shaped device. On the open end, the two sides touch and curl up on the sides. Small, clear jewels hang off of the curled ends.

After coating it with a dab of flavored lubricant, his smile is completely devious as he crawls up on the bed. "Clit clip," he says by way of explanation and I gasp. This brings an even bigger smile to his face. "You've heard of them, then."

*Oh, yes, I've heard of them!*

His fingers find my already wet pussy and he takes his time as he runs his fingers all around and in me. Using his thumb and index finger to completely spread me open, he slides the closed end of the clip over and just behind my clit. The open end pushes my inner labia together and the closed end pushes away from me, resulting in a fully exposed clit. The added weight of the jewels adds to the stimulation.

His tongue flicks across my sex, warm and wet, and with my bundle of pleasure nerves completely exposed, streaks of electricity shoot through my entire body. "Umm, my cupcake," he says in jest before his mouth devours me and his tongue licks around the outside, then the inside, before finding my nub again. When he sucks on it and then pulls it through his teeth, I feel like I'm about to break the restraints and come up off the bed.

"You're squirming, Sophia," he chastises me. "You know how I feel about squirming while you're restrained." Leaning over, he picks another device from the second drawer. When he holds it up, my eyes open wide and my jaw drops open.

"You wouldn't," I whisper in disbelief.

"Oh, but I would. And I will," he says with a wicked grin as he attaches the two nipple clamps before he picks up the third clamp, meant to clamp my clit in a different way.

The mixture of the two types of clamps is the best painful pleasure I've ever experienced. Until I feel his cock poised at my entrance, the tip just barely moving against me. Opening my eyes, I find Dominic watching me with intense eyes. He's waiting for me to look at him so he can see what I'm thinking and feeling. "That's my girl," he says a split second before he plunges as far into me as he can.

The sudden invasion fills me, stretches me, and I instantly come. Without permission. He notices but he keeps going, because part of my punishment is his constant rubbing against my fully exposed clit. The intense build up of pressure low in my pelvis begins quickly and escalates just as fast. There's no way I can stop the flood of my climax with all the stimulation he has provided.

When he unexpectedly removes the second clit clamp, allowing the blood flow to rush back into the fully exposed area, my arms and legs involuntarily jerk, pulling violently on the restraints. They don't give, though, and I'm helpless to fight against the barrage of ecstasy he's giving me.

"Fuck, baby, you're so wet. I feel your come running out of you," he growls at me. His voice does things to me that are just unbelievable and I feel the release of the glorious pressure again as I scream his name.

"Ahhh," he groans as he pumps into me a final time before he joins me in our post-coital bliss. He removes the nipple clamps and the initial clit clamp, sending a whole new sensation flowing through me. His body covers mine, but he's careful to not put pressure on my pregnant belly.

Pulling his knees up between my legs, he leans over and lays his head against my baby bump. He kisses my stomach where the baby is protected, and whispers, "I love your mommy so much, little one. Just wait until you meet her. You'll fall in love with her, too."

Dominic quickly unbuckles the restraints and massages both of my wrists and ankles. As always, he leans against the headboard and pulls me into his lap. With loving kisses and soft strokes against my hair, he tells me over and over how much he loves me, how proud he is of me, and how beautiful I am. The contact of skin on skin, without making love, but being this intimate, is my favorite part. It's so much more than sex and it's so much more than the words. It's the real feelings behind everything we do with no barriers, nowhere to hide, and nothing else in the world exists.

"Are you okay?" he murmurs against my skin.

"I'm perfect, Dominic. Are you pleased?" I ask, genuinely interested.

"You always please me, Sophia. You were made for me and only me."

That's the last thing I remember before sleep takes me. Wrapped in my love's arms, sheltered by his protectiveness, and warmed in his embrace, I fall into a deep sleep and don't wake until the next morning. When I open my eyes, Dominic has placed me on my side of the bed and he is spooning me from behind. His arms are wrapped possessively around me and his leg is in between mine.

I love waking up this way.

"Thank you for last night, *My Angel*," he says in his sleepy voice.

"For what?"

"For your way of reminding me that I'm still your Dom," he clarifies. "You knew exactly what I needed." He pauses for a few seconds, but I can feel he has more to say, so I stay silent until he's ready.

"You need to go into the office Monday, love. This is the only way I can think of to draw out the truth. I won't let him hurt you. He will not take you from me. I'm putting an end to him once and for all, Sophia, no matter what it takes. By threatening what's mine, he has invoked my fury…and maybe a little madness.

"I will protect you with my life, baby, but it'll be *his* life first."

Chills cover my body, but this time they're not the good ones that emanate from the sexy timbre of his voice. The hard, iciness of his voice says he's made up his mind, he has a plan in place, and he won't be deterred no matter what the outcome may hold. Dread fills me, knowing the outcome is inevitable–someone will have to die.

*Dear God, please protect Dominic. I can't do this without him.*

With the turmoil in Dominic's mind settled, we're now able to enjoy the rest of the weekend with his parents. As we're dressing Saturday morning, we're talking about everything and nothing when I feel a sudden fluttering in my lower abdomen. I stop talking in the middle of a sentence and my hand flies to my belly. Dominic is instantaneously at my side.

"What's wrong? Did I hurt you last night?"

I smile brightly at him, "No, Dom, you didn't hurt me at all. I just felt the baby move for the first time!"

"What? Really?" he asks excitedly as he places his hands on my stomach. "Make her move again."

"I can't make him move. He just did it on his own," I laugh. "There! Did you feel that?"

"No, I didn't feel anything," he says, his brow furrowed and his eyes boring holes into my stomach as he wills the baby to do it again.

"He must be too little for you to feel him move yet. I barely feel it, but it kind of tickles, like a hummingbird flapping its wings inside me," I try to explain so he can experience everything with me.

"That's amazing," he replies in awe. "I can't wait to feel her kick."

"I'm sure he'll be kicking all the time before we know it."

"Do you realize that we are going to become parents in a few months?" He asks this as if he's only just realized that my pregnancy will eventually end with the delivery of a small human.

"Yeah. Scary, huh?"

"No. It's not scary at all. It's incredible. If I had a choice before it happened, I would've waited a few years to give us more time together alone first," he wraps his arms around my waist, "but I wouldn't change it now for anything."

Leaning into him, I deeply inhale the mixture of his intoxicating scent and his manly cologne. He knows I need this so he doesn't rush me. After a few minutes of selfishly keeping him to myself, we walk downstairs to start breakfast for our guests. Dominic's chuckle rumbles through his muscular chest when we hear noises coming from the kitchen and smell bacon frying.

"Mom's cooking breakfast for us. You know it's her thing."

"Kayla! You're out guest! You're not supposed to do all the cooking when you come to visit," I laughingly scold her.

"Honey, this is part of who I am now after thirty-something years of cooking breakfast for Rick. Besides, you and Dominic needed the extra time together. It's almost ready so pull up a seat," she says as she inclines her head toward the table. "Let's have a family breakfast."

Tucker and Shadow join us just in time. Shadow walks straight to the coffee maker and pours a cup while Tucker claims his usual place at the table. Shadow and Tucker's eyes meet and they lock onto each other. Tucker's narrow to mere slits as he glares at Shadow, while the amusement dances in Shadow's eyes.

"What's going on with you two this morning?" I ask, unable to withhold my smile. They're like two brothers who constantly pick on each other–but wouldn't allow anyone else to do the things they do to each other.

"Last night, I walked in on Tucker – " Shadow begins but Tucker quickly cuts him off.

"Shut it, man. I don't care what the CIA taught you. I will flat kick your ass right here in the kitchen."

Shadow's laugh reverberates off the walls and echoes throughout the house. Tucker's face is bright red with embarrassment and anger. Shadow is fully bent over at the waist, his head almost to his feet, as he holds his stomach from laughing pains. "Oh my god, I can't breathe!" he pants as he tries to regain his composure.

"You should fucking *knock first*, man," he swears under his breath as Shadow takes his seat beside Tucker. This only makes it harder for Shadow to quit laughing. He quickly covers his mouth and turns his head away from Tucker, burying his face in his own muscular shoulder as his body continues to shake.

Holding up my hands in surrender, I say, "Just forget I asked, okay? I really don't want to know now." I can't withhold my own snicker, which comes out as a very unladylike snort. This is apparently the worst thing I could've done because Shadow launches from his chair just as he bursts out in laughter again.

Kayla, Rick, Dominic, and I all exchange humorous glances before we all erupt in laughter, at Tucker's expense. Tucker covers his face with his big hands, but soon he's shaking from laughter and joins us in openly laughing at himself. This is apparently something we all needed because everyone is wiping away happy tears before we begin breakfast.

Shadow retakes his seat and Tucker elbows him in the ribs, just for good measure. "For the record," Tucker starts, "I'd like to clarify something."

"Tucker, we really don't need to hear about your nocturnal activities at the breakfast table. Just leave it at that," Dominic says with a smirk.

The past two days have flown by way too quickly. We just dropped Kayla and Rick off at the airport for their flight back home. It's strange how quickly I became attached to them, having them around, and spending time with them. It's much like the way I fell in love with Dominic–it only took a short time around him to know he is a wonderful man. He's strong, confident, and loving.

I couldn't ask for a better partner for the rest of my life. My love for him is so strong I can't help but just watch him as he drives us home. Tucker and Shadow have both been working nonstop since all of this began so he gave them the day off today. He said they needed to rest up and be ready for tomorrow.

Dominic's eyes constantly roam from the road ahead, to the rearview mirror, and each side. He's intently watching for anything even remotely dangerous in our vicinity. Needing to feel him, I slide my hand over his and lace our fingers together. He picks them up and kisses the back of my hand before giving me his mega-watt, melt-me-where-I-sit smile.

"I love that smile," I tell him.

"Good. You'll be seeing it for the next seventy years or so."

"If anything happens to me tomorrow, I want you to know something," I say softly.

His face takes on a look of fierce determination. "*Nothing* will happen to you."

"I still want you to know."

"Okay."

"If anything *ever* happens to me, I want you to be happy again. I want you to find someone who sees how perfect you are, who feels how loving you are, and who knows that no other man compares to you."

# Chapter Twenty-Two

***Dominic***

We're quiet on the hour drive to the office this Monday morning. Shadow is driving us, as usual, and Tucker is following several car lengths behind us. Sophia is snuggled up to me, her head in the crook of my shoulder, and my arm is wrapped protectively around her.

Shadow and Tucker didn't take the day off yesterday like I instructed. They met with the FBI team and covertly got everything set up for today. Part of me is glad the meeting isn't until the end of the day so we have time for any last minute preparations. Or time to change my mind and get Sophia as far away from here as possible.

Another part of me wants to get it over with as soon as possible so that this fucking black cloud isn't hanging over our lives. We should be enjoying every moment of Sophia's pregnancy. Our only concern should be what color to paint the nursery and what decorations Sophia wants to buy. My every thought should revolve around my promise to make her the happiest woman in the world.

I should *not* have to worry that she'll die today. That shouldn't even be a remote possibility. I just got her back in my life, in my arms, and in my bed. Leaning my face down, I place soft kisses on her forehead, nose, and then on her lips.

"Are you scared?" I ask her.

"I'm scared something will happen to you."

"I'll be fine, *My Angel*. Don't worry about me. I'll crush him with my bare hands if I need to," I assure her. She doesn't look pleased with my response.

"He won't fight fair, Dominic. Promise me you'll be careful."

"Promise me you'll stay in your office and won't come out until I come get you."

"I promise," she says and then raises her eyebrows at me.

"I promise I will be careful, baby," I concede. "Hey, remember last night? I'm looking forward to doing that again tonight."

Her cheeks fill with the beautiful shade of blush pink I love to see on her. There were no whips, restraints, or clamps last night–it was slow, intimate, and full of love. We were in sync, insatiable, and connected on more than a physical level. The thoughts of losing her plagued my dreams again, of not getting to her in time, of seeing her being stripped from my arms, so I woke many times during the night. Each time, she awoke to find me ready to make love to her one more time, and she accepted me with open arms.

Once inside the office, I find it harder to let her go than I anticipated. "Sophia, we're bringing your laptop to my office. You can work in there with me today until it's time. It'll make me feel better."

"Sounds good to me, Dom," she replies with a relieved smile.

The day goes by too quickly and before I know it, five o'clock is approaching. Everyone is set up in the next room, the video cameras are rolling, and Sophia is safely tucked away in her office. After a lengthy fight with the FBI SAC, I finally had to relent on my demand that Tucker stay in Sophia's office with her. There are too few here, and because of legalities, we can't supplement them with more Steele Security personnel. Tucker has been deputized by Shadow so he's under their command for this operation.

Our guest of the hour, *Sebastian Montoya* shows up right on time and Dana shows him into my office. Standing, I refuse to move out from behind my desk to greet him. I'm sure if I do, I will rip him limb from limb. He extends his hand to me and I glare at it for several seconds before returning the gesture.

"Mr. Powers. Thank you for seeing me today," his Latino accent is thick, but it's his demeanor that makes him sleazy. His fake smile doesn't reach his cold, black eyes. He's close to my height but he's not nearly as thick and muscular as I am. His black hair is slicked straight back off his face. "Is your lawyer joining us?"

"No, she's not. I prefer we settle this like men." *In more ways that one.*

"Ah, you are much like me, no?"

*No, I'm nothing like you.* His insulting question doesn't deserve an answer. "Have a seat," I gesture toward the chair.

"Mr. Powers, I will get straight to the point. As you know, this case would be best settled out of court. The damage to your reputation, and by extension, your company's reputation, if the embarrassing details of your…proclivities…were to reach the newspapers, would be catastrophic.

"My client is wiling to accept a settlement of fifty million dollars as compensation for pain, mental anguish, lost wages, and her extensive post traumatic stress disorder. Surely you can understand that the abuse you inflicted upon her has caused long-term psychological issues. She will require therapy for many years to come."

It is taking every ounce of my considerable self-control to not launch myself across the desk and choke him out where he sits. As he drones on and on about the abuse I've inflicted upon Sophia, he has no idea that she sits in the office down the hall, working directly with me again. He has no clue that she's pregnant with my baby, living in my house, and sleeping in my bed. His surveillance team has simply kept tabs on her coming and going from the building to make sure they can pull off this scam on me. *Idiots.*

That gives me hope that he's not after Sophia at all. With Cortez as the head of this scheme, the others will likely disappear when he's taken down. Cut the head off, the rest scatter into the wind.

"*Fifty million dollars* for pain and suffering? You can't be serious," the sarcasm and disdain is not hidden in my voice at all. "There's no way anyone has suffered mental anguish to the tune of fifty million dollars."

He sneers, "Part of that amount is to avoid your own mental anguish over the downfall of your company. Imagine how your investors will react to the news and bad press you'll receive over this lawsuit."

What an idiot. DPS is a privately owned company. I don't *have* investors.

"You do have a point there," I stall. I'm supposed to keep him talking and get him to admit to extortion. The amount he's thrown out there is astronomical and he's already hinting at hurting my business if I don't pay, but he needs to be more direct with his threat. "I think I'll have a drink. Bourbon?"

"Sure. Neat, please," he replies with a smirk I'd like to bitch slap off his face.

As I'm walking to the bar at the other end of my office, I turn to him and say, "What makes you think that my sex life, outside of work, would hurt my business?"

Cortez stands and moves toward me. "Mr. Powers, if your bedroom antics were cast in such a light that showed your desire to harm and demean women, it would definitely hurt your business."

"I don't harm or demean women."

"But that's what the world will see when this gets leaked to the press. They'll see videos of you abusing women, belittling them, calling them awful, dirty names," he replies in a chastising manner.

"There are no such videos of me doing any of that."

"Maybe not of you, per se, but it'll look and sound like you. It'll do enough damage and cause enough suspicion. I'd even be willing to be that more sexual harassment lawsuits against you would spring up."

"With you as the attorney, no doubt," I say as I pin him with my glare.

"Yes, as a matter of fact, I would be the attorney representing them," he smiles widely at me, thinking he's won this game of chess. What he doesn't realize is he just admitted to practicing law without a license to the FBI on top of the extortion.

Cortez walks past me and straight to the liquor cabinet. "You seem to have forgotten my drink," he maintains eye contact, *tsks* at me as he opens the cabinet door, and retrieves a glass.

The whole scene unfolds in slow motion before my eyes. My thoughts are running rampant through my mind and my blood is beginning to boil as the only logical conclusion becomes clear. He knew where the glasses were kept without asking, without seeing me open the cabinet, and without even looking.

He's been in here before now. He is the one who broke into my office.

"You don't think I know who you are, do you?" My voice is low and threatening. The anger inside me has been replaced with pure, unadulterated rage, and I'm about to unleash it all on him. "Sebastian Montoya. Ramon Nunez. *Detective Ramon Cortez*."

His arm stops in midair as he's retrieving the tumbler. His back is as straight as a rod and just as stiff as one, too. He wasn't expecting this–he didn't expect me to remember him from a few years back. Even though he had a different name and a different look back then, it's not nearly enough to throw me off. All the time spent protected by his cartel boss father has made him too cocky and careless.

"How do you know those names?" he finally asks.

"Surely you don't think I would forget the detective who investigated my girlfriend's death."

His head whirls around to face me. "That was you? I never even really knew your name," he says nonchalantly, his face holds a mixture of surprise and amusement. "You see, I was only there to help Harrison. I couldn't let my friend go to prison for murdering his whore sister.

"And now, I'm afraid you must also die. If you'd just signed the papers without running your mouth, I wouldn't have to do this. But since you obviously know who I am, I'm afraid I have no other choice. Not to worry, I will still have your money since I'm very good at what I do. Your death won't be questioned."

"You mean you'll just forge my signature and make my death look like a suicide. Like you've done before."

He laughs, an evil, maniacal laugh, "Exactly like I've done before!"

When his hand reaches inside his jacket, I know he's reaching for his gun so I rush at him and body slam him on the floor. He is no match for my muscular build and he's instantly lying flat on his back with the breath knocked out of him. Jutting my hand out, I grope for his gun but he quickly blocks my hand with his arm and tries to knee me in the groin.

This only serves to piss me off more and I punch him repeatedly in the face. While he's disoriented, I grab the gun from his holster and move to stand. As I do, the FBI team rushes into my office, with Tucker and Shadow bringing up the rear. Their guns are drawn and they're all yelling instructions at both Montoya and me. The scene is utter chaos as the team, minus Tucker and Shadow, begins to surround us.

"Hands up in the air where we can see them!" one agent yells.

"Put the gun down, sir!" another yells at me.

With my hands held up, I slowly lower the gun to the counter in front of me.

"Now step away!"

I take two steps away from the gun just as Tucker and Shadow reach my side. Tucker is more pissed off than I've ever seen him. "He's not the one you should be focused on right now, dumbass!" he yells at the agent while pointing at me. "The fucker on the floor is the one you should have your guns trained on!"

"Standard safety protocol, Tucker," the agent retorts. "Anyone can be a threat at any time."

Two agents are picking a dazed and bloodied Montoya up off the floor while Tucker and Shadow walk away to help the other agent secure the cameras and other evidence from my office. In a flash, Montoya jerks free from the agents, grabs the gun from the counter, and begins to lower his arm toward me. Bending at my waist, I rush to grab him around the waist, tackle him like I'm a linebacker, and we both fall back to the floor.

Agents are grabbing and yelling at us as we roll on the floor, but we both keep wrestling for control of the gun. His knee jerks up and this time he makes contact with my crotch, causing me to flinch. He takes advantage of the moment to roll us over. When we're in mid-roll, an agent trying to stop us tears Cortez's arm free from my grasp and he has complete control of the gun. His hand with the gun is now wedged between our conjoined bodies and the barrel is pressed firmly against my chest. Instantly grabbing his gun hand with mine, our eyes connect and I instinctively know one of us will not walk away from this fight.

Grunting, groping, and wrestling with all of our might, we are locked in a battle of wills and strength. Mere seconds tick by but they feel more like hours as neither of us is willing to give in to the other. I'm much stronger than he is but the hold I have on him is compromised by his bodyweight. There's no way I can let go to get a better grip, but I know I have to do something right now. Without warning, the blast from the gun booms through my office, ricocheting off the walls. There's complete stunned silence from everyone in the room for a nanosecond before the yelling resumes, this time with a different intensity.

"Dominic! Dominic, talk to me! Are you hurt? Are you shot?" Tucker yells at me as he closes in on me, tossing agents out of his path as if they weigh no more than a feather. Shadow is immediately behind him. *"DOMINIC! SAY SOMETHING! ANSWER ME, DAMMIT!"*

"Get this motherfucker off me," I respond, pushing Montoya's lifeless body off to the side. Dominic and Shadow lift me up off the floor and another FBI agent takes the gun from my hand to bag it for evidence.

"You scared the shit out of me, man," Tucker says between heavy breaths.

"You and me both, brother," I say as Tucker cups my shoulder with his hand. "Cortez was about to shoot me. I saw it in his eyes. When he realized this was a set up, I guess he figured he had nothing to lose. I bent his hand back away from me a split second before he squeezed the trigger. He ended up shooting himself, stupid son of a bitch."

"Sophia is going to freak out when she sees you," Shadow says as his eyes drop to my blood soaked shirt.

Jerking the shirt off me, the buttons fly across the room and I drop it in an evidence bag, too. "I'll grab a spare shirt from the closet behind Dana's desk."

"Do you want me to go get Sophia?" Tucker asks.

"No, not until they get the body out of here. It'll be bad enough when I tell her about it. I don't want her to see it and have a visual to go with the story. I'll text her from my phone and tell her I'm okay."

After sending the text, I walk into the closet and grab a white button down shirt. Looking around, I'm glad to see that the top floor is vacated so only those of us who were involved in this sting operation are still here. Taking a seat in my chair, I drop my head into my hands and try to calm my heart that's still beating out of control.

"I heard what he said about Harrison," Tucker says quietly.

"All this time, Tucker, that bastard has blamed me for Carol Ann's death. All this time, I thought she killed herself and I've lived with the guilt of asking what I could've done to prevent it. Only to find out from this bastard that Harrison killed her. I really can't even process it all right now."

"We'll take Harrison down. Maybe it's time for you and Sophia to take a vacation together. Get away for a while and just relax," Tucker offers.

"Maybe you're right."

An hour later, Cortez's body is gone but the bloodstains in the carpet serve as a reminder. I've been asked to leave my office while the FBI takes the cameras and all the over evidence they need for their case. Since the shooting and subsequent death happened during an official investigation, and in front of a handful of federal officers, I won't be questioned further. I can't help but think Shadow played some part in that.

As the agents leave, I thank them personally for their help today. One loose end to tie up and this is all over and done with. Shadow and Tucker walk out with them to help carry the equipment and boxes to the vans waiting in the parking garage. I'm mentally drained but physically I think I could raze a building on my own. The adrenaline from the day has built up so much in my body, that's probably all that's running through my veins right now. Once that dissipates, I know I will crash.

*Harry Dick-man* has his penance coming to him and he will pay dearly for what he's done. With the flurry of activity after the agents crashed through my office door, I haven't had much time to think everything through. My only rational thought about it is I need to know the whole story of what happened that day. My preference is to hear it from Harrison himself–to make him recount it, watch him squirm when he has to admit to his actions, and then punch him square in the mouth. For starters.

But that's not my priority at the moment. I need to check on my love and get her out of here as soon as possible. I know she's been worried about me for the last few hours and I don't like the stress that puts on her. It's been a long day and I can't wait to get her into bed and just hold her close to me all night. The quiet hallway and deserted offices make my gloomy attitude worse as I walk toward her office.

An errant thought seizes my heart and constricts my breathing. The hall seems to be a thousand yards long. I'm only getting farther and farther away from her office door no matter how hard I try to reach it. My nightmares are becoming a reality and it's one that I know I can't handle. This can't be happening.

Sophia never texted me back.

# Chapter Twenty-Three

***Sophia***

It's been a long time since I've felt a full-fledged panic attack threaten to overtake me, but it's here now. As I pace back and forth in my office, I am picturing what's happening in Dominic's office while he meets with Cortez. None of the scenes I create in my mind have a good ending and I'm making myself sick with worry. The morning sickness has passed, so I know this nausea is simply from a severe case of nerves.

I put my hand on the doorknob at least a dozen times–ready to run to the ladies room as my lunch threatens to make a reappearance. My promise to Dominic is the only thing that's stopping me. Turning away from the door, I walk the same path across the floor toward the windows. One hand is on our baby and the other hand is on my forehead, shielding my eyes, as I say another silent prayer to keep my Dom safe.

A gunshot suddenly rings out across the office, causing me to jump and shriek from surprise. Tears instantly spring to my eyes and both hands are steepled over my mouth. My body starts shaking, my knees give out from under me, and I crumble to the floor. *No, please God, no–not Dominic!*

Uncontrollable sobs wrack my body, making it impossible to take a full breath. My tears pour from my eyes, blurring my vision as I collapse into a fetal position. Dominic had a bad feeling something would happen to me, but I've had a bad feeling something terrible would happen to him. I'm afraid to leave my office–I'm afraid I'll find that Cortez has killed him. Grasping my chest in pain, I have no doubt that someone could die of a broken heart. It was bad enough when we were apart, but this feeling is even worse. Helplessness. Despair. Afraid to hope. Afraid to know the truth. One question swirls in my mind, stuck on repeat and tormenting me. *How can I go on with my life without him?*

I don't know how much time has passed with me in the floor repeatedly begging God for a miracle when the door to my office swings open and a man rushes toward me. Excitement overcomes me because I know it has to be Dominic. He's fine and has come to take me home where it's safe, where we'll be together, and where we'll raise our family. My heart swells, and the tears of pain that still blur my vision turn to tears of gratitude. Wiping my eyes and struggling to bring my breathing back under control, I raise my eyes to meet his sexy blue ones.

"Awww, what's the matter, you little bitch? Your boyfriend get shot?" Harrison taunts me. "He should've died a long time ago."

Terror has robbed me of the ability to move and has rendered me mute. How can Harrison be here? Why is he here? What is he going to do to me–and my baby? My muscles are locked down and refuse to cooperate with the voice screaming in my head, telling me to get out of here and run as fast as I can. I should be screaming for Dominic, or

Tucker, or Shadow, for *anyone* who can get me away from this deranged man. But I'm suddenly a lifeless mute–because if he's here, it must mean that my Dom is gone.

Carrying his duffle bag, Harrison moves behind my desk and sits in my chair where he's hidden from the line of sight of my office door. Removing his gun from his waistband, he places it on my desk while glaring at me with the most menacing eyes I've ever seen. Moving slowly in my attempt to avoid alarming him, I push up from the floor and stand, leaning against the window. Thankfully, my high-heels came off my feet while I was crouched in the floor. If I get a chance to run for it, I can run much faster in my bare feet.

One disadvantage of standing is that my pregnant belly is much more prominently visible. I know the very second that Harrison realizes my condition. "*Fucking hell*, you're pregnant with his fucking baby, ain't you?"

My arms unconsciously cover our baby and I take a step backward. Harrison continues his tirade without waiting for my confirmation. "That's just fucking great," he scoffs.

Then his face changes, lightens, and he looks almost happy. "Actually, it may be great after all. Daddy Dom-Big-Bucks would pay through the fucking nose for his baby and his bitch. We're going to wait right here for him to come for you."

"He's okay?" I manage to squeak out.

Harrison scoffs, mocking me with his absurd jealousy of Dominic, "Yes, your pathetic excuse of a Sir is okay, Sophia. I heard him say he shot Cortez. His security team was way too busy with the dead body cleanup to notice that I slipped in through the back stairwell."

Relief washes over me after hearing that my Dom is alive and well. When that shot rang out, and with Harrison's cruelness, I just knew I'd lost him. Hearing that he's okay, even from this dickhead, is the best news I've ever heard in my life. I know he'll come for me as soon as he can, but now I can calm myself, even with *Harry Dick-man* here.

"What do you want from me, Harrison?"

"I want you to sit down in that chair right there," he points to the chair in front of my desk, "and don't speak until your boyfriend comes looking for you."

Moving toward me, he removes a rope from his duffle bag and smiles his twisted, sadistic grin. I try to run but he easily grabs me by my hair and drags me back, forcing me into the chair. After tying my wrists and ankles to the chair, he pulls something else out of the bag and I can't see what it is at first. When he holds it up to taunt and harass me, I feel all the air being sucked out of my lungs.

It's the ball-gag.

"Now hold your pretty little head still or I'll have to fuck it up again," he warns. Knowing he'll do that and much worse, I don't struggle against him too much. If it weren't for my baby, I'd fight him until I passed out, but I have to try to keep my wits about me for the baby's sake. For the next hour, we sit in complete silence and wait for Dom to walk into this trap. I'm silent because of the gag and I'm also unable to swallow very well. The humiliation of slobbering on myself is part of what gets Harrison off. But this time, he doesn't even seem to notice, so I think it has more to do with Dom's reaction to seeing me like this than anything else.

Harrison picks up his gun and moves over to the floor to ceiling windows. His arm is bent at an angle and his forehead is resting on his forearm as he stares off into the Dallas city streets. The soft clicking of the door opening catches his attention and he quickly moves behind my chair. He turns it so that we're both facing the door and he's behind me with the gun pressed against my temple. I can't stop the tears that flow because I know he's capable of pulling the trigger as soon as Dom walks in.

When the door fully opens, my Dom is standing there, filling up the open space and looking larger than life. His eyes are hard and the muscles in his jaw are ticking. Mad, angry, livid, furious, enraged–none of these can describe the intensity of the fire building inside my Dom's eyes. He's staring Harrison down, daring him to make the wrong move, and challenging him to look him in the eye like a man.

"We have some business to finish, *Dick-man*," Dom's voice is hard, cold, and dangerous.

"That we do, Mr. Powers," Harrison replies, his voice holds a different tone. "I've had enough of playing the fool in this whole charade. In fact, I've had enough of our entire game, and I'm going to finish what Ramon couldn't."

Harrison's uneducated, unsophisticated drawl is obviously missing. His speech is more refined but his demeanor is even more calculating. I don't know who this man is or where he came from. The rules of engagement have suddenly shifted on me and I'm struggling to keep up.

"You killed your own sister, *Harry Dick-man*," Dominic spits his words out at him in disgust. "Why? What did Carol Ann ever do to you?"

I involuntarily gasp, but with the ball-gag still restricting my verbal abilities, it doesn't draw either man's attention. My head is reeling from Dominic's statement. If Harrison killed his own sister, he'd have no qualms about killing Dominic or me. Not that he ever really cared about me, but it speaks volumes to what the man is capable of doing.

Harrison removes the gun from my head as he moves to my side. Sitting on my credenza, he smiles at Dominic. "So Ramon told you, huh? It was unfortunate, actually. I went over to try to talk some sense into her. It was *embarrassing* to be part of the toughest criminal organization ever, at my level, and have to admit that my sister was some rich-boy's whore-toy.

"She was setting up the romantic dinner she had planned for you two on the balcony when I got there. I tried to talk some sense into her, but she walked away from me, saying everything had to be ready for you when you got home. We got into an argument over her 'choice' and it turned physical. I grabbed her arm and told her I was dragging her out of the condo to take back home where she belonged. But she panicked and pulled away from me. When I reached for her again, she jerked backward away from me, lost her balance, and fell over the rail."

"You fucking bastard! All this time, you blamed me for her death when you knew you were the cause of it. You let me believe she killed herself when she was nowhere near being suicidal," Dominic answers, pure hatred pouring through his words. "She was pregnant and you killed your own sister!"

"It was *your* fault, Dominic. You never should've brain washed Carol Ann and led her into that lifestyle. It's embarrassing," Harrison shakes his head. "Much like you did this one here," he gestures toward me. "If you hadn't pulled her even more into your sick life, she wouldn't have to die today.

"It's really too bad that I hate you so much, Powers. You know how to make a woman self-destruct better than any man I know. We could've been friends if you'd stayed the hell away from my sister. Now, you'll be responsible for the death of two pregnant women," Harrison taunts, pressing the buttons that he knows will provoke Dom the most.

Turning his gaze to me, Harrison continues trying to push Dominic to make a move. "Look what a mess you're making, Sophia! You're drooling all over that pretty shirt. You'll have to be punished for that," he says mockingly.

"The only man who punishes Sophia is *me*. I already owe you a major ass kicking for what you've done to her in the past. You've just earned an extended hospital stay for even touching her.

For binding and gagging her, you'll eat through a straw for the rest of your fucking life," Dominic threatens.

Harrison's bravado waivers for a moment after Dominic so calmly issued his promise and dismissed his jabs. His eyes widen and his lips slightly part as he inhales sharply. His body tenses and stills completely, waiting for Dominic to pounce on him. Harrison seems to have forgotten he has a gun in his hand because he *looks* scared. If I were on the receiving end of the look that Dominic is giving Harrison right now, I would be scared, too.

"You think you scare me, Powers? I've been in the cartel for years now, taking care of deadbeats so the boss can keep his hands clean. After all I've been through, I know I can take care of a pussy like you."

Dominic smirks, his eyes alight with amusement. He's actually glad that Harrison is challenging him. "By all means, put that gun down and face me like a man then. Unless you *are* scared?"

Harrison puts the gun down on the credenza as he moves to meet Dominic face to face. "You won't get a chance to sucker punch me this time. I'm ready for you."

"I wish that were true, *Harry Dick-man*," Dominic laughs as he emphasizes the insulting nickname, "but you could never be ready to take me on."

Harrison begins to respond, no doubt with yet another sarcastic remark, but he doesn't get the chance to finish his verbal assault. When he opens his mouth, Dominic's hand is lightning fast as it flies through the air and makes immediate contact with Harrison's throat. Harrison's hands wrap around the front of his neck as his face turns bright red. His eyes are open wide, confusion churns in them, and he makes strange wheezing noise when he tries to breathe.

Dominic wastes no time in throwing another punch that connects with Harrison's eye. He stumbles backward, already unsteady from the first unexpected hit, and lands on his ass. Dom keeps advancing on him, intent on inflicting as much bodily harm as he can. Dom swings his leg around in a low roundhouse kick and his foot connects with the side of Harrison's head, knocking him over on his side. Dom jumps on top of him with his full body and continues to pummel Harrison's face with his fists until both are battered and bloody.

When Harrison stops fighting back at all, Dom pushes against him, adding insult to injury, as he stands. His big shoulders heave with his heavy breathing as he stands over Harrison for several seconds before walking away from him. Dominic picks up the gun from the filing cabinet and puts it in the waistband of his pants at the small of his back.

He then rushes to me and removes the ball-gag first, then begins working on freeing my hands and feet. I've been tied for so long, and so tightly, my hands and feet were already asleep. The sudden rush of blood back into them is extremely painful and my Dom takes a minute to massage me, even with his hands injured and his knuckles bloody.

Throwing my arms around his neck once I'm free, I smother him with kisses mixed with my tears. He's kneeling on the floor in front of me in the perfect position for me to hold onto during my mini-meltdown. "Thank God you're not hurt. I heard the gunshot and I wanted to die with you. Oh my god, Dominic, I was so scared and distraught. Are you hurt? What can I do?"

I'm rambling like a lunatic, asking him a million questions at once, but not giving him time to answer any of them. Especially between the kisses I can't seem to stop giving him. His amused chuckle makes me smile as he says, "Slow down, *My Angel*. I'm fine and no, I wasn't the one who was shot. I sent you a text to let you know I was okay and to stay put, but I see you were a little preoccupied in here." He holds up the ball-gag, joking with me to lighten the mood, and gives me his full-wattage smile.

"Don't think I'm wearing that thing ever again, Dominic. I'm adding a new hard limit," I reply with a smile of my own.

"Nah, babe," he says casually. "I'm not really into ball-gags. I can think of better uses for your mouth than that." Dominic sits back on his heels and we both laugh, but I can't deny that he really does have the best ideas.

The hairs on the back of my neck suddenly stand at attention and my smile falters. "What is it, babe?" Dominic asks.

"She feels the barrel of a Glock .40 in her back," Harrison hisses from behind me.

Dominic meets my terrified gaze, and despite his best attempts to cover it up, I see the fear in his. Harrison has nothing to lose and everything to gain by taking me away from Dom. No challenge of being a lesser man or being scared will sway his vengeance this time. By allowing him to live, Dominic knows he just gave Harrison another chance to kill me.

"Did you really think I wouldn't have another weapon on me? I'm a professional killer by trade, Powers," Harrison says as he stands up behind me. "Now move back – away from her."

Dominic puts his hand behind his back, pretending to use it as leverage to move. His eyes meet mine and I know what he's planning to do. Using all my body weight, I jerk to the side, toppling my chair over and giving Dominic a clean shot. Simultaneously, Dominic withdraws the gun from the back of his pants and rapidly fires five rounds toward Harrison. The sound of glass shattering and rushing wind immediately fill the office and I crawl across the floor to Dom's side.

Turning my eyes toward Harrison, I watch in horror as the front of his shirt fills with blood from the gun shot wounds. His gun is still in his hand, but he doesn't have the strength to use it. His entire body sways back and forth, his gait extremely unsteady. Rooted to the floor, I watch with my eyes transfixed on him. It's like driving by the scene of a bad car wreck. I'm unable to look away but at the same time I'm afraid to see the aftermath. He finally stumbles backward and tumbles out of the broken window from twenty stories up.

Dominic drops the gun and pulls me into his lap, his arms wrapped protectively and possessively around me. "Are my girls okay? Do we need to go to the hospital and have you checked out?" he asks with one hand on my stomach and deep concern in his every syllable.

Unable to speak, I just shake my head from side to side and bury my face in his neck. He pulls me close and lets me cry until I have no more tears or energy to cry anymore. I hear others moving around in my office, but somewhere in the back of my mind, I absently wonder if I'm going into shock. I don't care who else is here, I don't care what they're doing, and I don't care what they want.

No one else matters except the three of us– my Dom, our baby, and me –in our very own cocooned world right here in the floor of my office.

# Chapter Twenty-Four

### *Dominic*

Vengeance is an odd thing. In the first few days after the clusterfuck at my office, I felt nothing but relief that the nightmare was finally all over. Cortez, also known as Montoya, and *Dick-man* were both out of our lives forever. The black cloud that hung over us had dissipated and we only had blue skies and silver linings to look forward to.

My immediate thoughts after leaving the office building that day was to get Sophia to the hospital, have her thoroughly checked out, and make sure our baby was safe. She shut down completely while she clung to me like I was her only lifeline in the turbulent seas. Tucker, Shadow, and the FBI agents rushed back to the top floor after I called

Tucker when Sophia didn't answer my text. They fitted me with a recording device before I opened her office door, so everything Harrison said and did corroborated my version of what happened.

When they tried to question Sophia, she didn't even hear them. When one agent touched her, the daggers thrown from my eyes made him retract his hand before he lost it permanently. She only responded when I asked her questions, but only with a nod or a shake of her head. As I carried her in my arms the twenty stories to the lobby, I whispered reassuring words to her, promising her that it was over and we're all healthy.

We spent the night in the hospital that night and I slept in the small, uncomfortable bed with her. The next morning, I awoke to find her staring at me. Her small hand caressed my scruffy five o'clock shadow as her eyes darted back and forth while she studied my eyes. When I started to speak, she put her finger over my lips to gently silence me.

"I never dreamed I'd be lucky enough to find a man like you. You give all of yourself– your love, your thoughts, and your loyalty –without expecting anything in return. You're the only one who really knows me, understands me, and has stood by me. You've saved me so many times and in so many ways. I don't deserve you, Dominic, but I will never let you go."

Cradling her face in my hand, I assured her, "You're couldn't be more wrong, my love. You deserve every bit of love I can give you and more. I promise you'll never be without me again, because I can never be without you again."

The fetal monitor and ultrasound showed the baby was fine and not in any kind of distress. Sophia was well hydrated and the doctor discharged her with orders to take it easy for a few days. Taking care of her over the next two weeks gave me something to focus on, an important duty I had to perform, and a sense of accomplishment from helping her. It gave my mind something else to think about other than the faces of the two men I was forced to kill.

As of this morning, Sophia lovingly informed me that the doctor said to take it easy for a few *days*, not a few *weeks*, so my continued hovering over her is unnecessary. Neither of us has been back to the office yet and this former workaholic is in no hurry to return. Sitting in my study at home, I've reread the same paragraph of this request for proposal four times and I still have no idea what it says.

"Dominic?" Sophia calls from the doorway. My welcome reprieve, she looks stunning in her new silky nightgown. It hugs her pregnancy curves beautifully. My temperature rises just from raking my eyes up and down her delectable body.

"Yes, my love?" I answer, holding out my hand for her to come to me.

When she takes it, I pull her into my lap. Caressing her bare leg with my hand, I lean into her neck and lick it from the hollow spot above her collarbone straight up to her earlobe. "What can I do for you?" I murmur suggestively against her ear and enjoy watching the cold chills instantly roll across her skin.

"I've been thinking," she says breathlessly as I continue licking her neck.

"Mmmhmm," I hum against her skin, "go on."

"I've decided you're right," her declaration stuns me.

Pulling back, I can't help the half-smile I give her, "Can we just leave it at that for the rest of our lives? No further explanation is needed."

"Dominic!" she laughs. "I'm serious!"

"I'm listening," I stroke her cheek with my fingertips.

"I don't want to go back to work," she rushes to say. "I want stay home to take care of you and our baby."

"Did I force this on you? Am I turning you into a recluse?" The old accusations that I was responsible for Carol Ann's agoraphobia flood my mind. Sophia's revelation makes me question if there's something I'm unintentionally doing wrong.

"No! Not at all! I won't stay in the house all the time. There's plenty of shopping, parks, and other things to do outside. I just don't want my time divided between my family and my career," her explanation soothes my thoughts. Then her face falls, "Unless you've changed your mind? Do you want me to keep working?"

Pulling her face to mine, I claim her mouth as my territory. My tongue stakes its claim and she willingly submits. Rearranging her so that she's straddling me, I deepen the kiss as I thread my hands through her hair. Taking a breath, I give her my word.

"You never have to work again if that's what you want, *My Angel*. I'll just work at home more often so I can sexually harass you whenever I want."

"I'll take you up on that," she says with a wicked smile on her face as she quickly frees my cock from my pants. "Right now."

Lifting her hips, she positions me at the entrance of her pussy. She moves her hips back and forth, teasing us both before she lowers herself onto me. When she's taken all of me inside her, she moans and throws her head back. Pushing her flimsy gown up and over her head, I expose the fullness of her breasts. Her nipples are pebbled and ready for some attention, so I take one into my mouth while rolling the other between my thumb and finger.

She begins rocking on me, riding me, and her face displays her pure bliss. Standing with my cock still inside her, I lay her on her back on the top of my desk. Hooking my arms behind her knees, my hips surge in and out of her as I watch her breasts bounce from the intense pounding. She reaches her first orgasm and I have to bite my lip to hold back when the rush of her warmth flows over me.

"That's my girl," I say as I pull out and help her stand. She looks at me curiously until I turn her around to face the desk and bend her over. Her sexy, welcoming smile thrown over her shoulder is the sexiest fucking thing. "Are you ready?"

"Yes," she pants and presents herself even more by spreading her legs farther. Pushing into her, she gasps as my girth stretches her to accept my size. Moving slowly to let her acclimate, she becomes frustrated and reaches her hand around to grab my ass cheek. Chuckling to myself, I gladly comply with her wishes and bury myself balls deep in her over and over.

When we're both panting and barely able to hold onto our control, I lean over close to her. "Come for me now, my girl," I command and she obeys. Grunting, I follow her into our consummated pleasure, allowing her inner muscles to squeeze every last drop out of me.

"On second thought, I may not get any work done with you sexually harassing me like this," I tease her as I pull her gown back over her head.

"Why don't we both quit work and hire a CEO to run the company then?" she laughs, but I inwardly wonder if she's onto something.

"Sophia Vasco," the nurse calls from the doorway.

Over the past month since "the incident," I've worked in the office a grand total of three days. We're here today for Sophia's five month checkup and the ultrasound that'll hopefully tell us whether we're having a boy or a girl. We have a little wager on which one it'll be. I say it's a girl, and if I'm right, I get to name her. Sophia says it's a boy, and if she's right, she gets to name him.

"Ugh, let's go. I have to pee so badly I'm sure my bladder will burst any second now!" Sophia complains as she rises.

The baby seems to have grown overnight and her stomach is expanding. I love it. I love how beautiful she looks while she's pregnant with my baby. Following her and the nurse, her vitals are recorded and we're escorted into the ultrasound room. After Sophia changes into the hospital gown, she lies back in the chaise lounge chair and gets comfortable.

The ultrasound technician comes in and prepares to begin with the warmed gel. "Hi, Sophia. I'm Mandy. So, do you want to find out the sex of your baby?"

"Yes, we both anxious to know what we're having!" Sophia says excitedly.

"Let's see if the baby wants to cooperate today," Mandy says with a warm smile.

She places the wand on Sophia's abdomen and we're both anxiously watching the monitor. When Mandy presses down harder to get a better image, Sophia whimpers. "Oh my god, I have to pee!"

We all laugh at her candor. "That's the bad thing about this. We really need your bladder full to get the best picture. It's not that way with a 3D ultrasound if you decide to have one later," Mandy says. "Just drink plenty of water for at least the two weeks before your appointment."

"I definitely want to have one later on when we can see the face better," I reply.

Once Mandy has the baby on the screen, she points out all the features to us and we stare at the black and white grainy images like it's the Holy Grail. When she gets the image that we're looking for in the middle of the screen, she stops moving the wand and smiles brightly.

"You're sure you to know the sex, right?" she clarifies.

We both reply with an excited, "Yes!"

"Congratulations, Mom and Dad. You're having a baby boy! And he's proud–he's showing off really well for us!"

I squeeze Sophia's hand, conveying my love and excitement in a simple touch, and she squeezes back. Tears of joy glisten in her eyes and I feel like my heart may explode inside my chest. Every step of this pregnancy has been a new experience and a new feeling for me, but seeing my baby today has been a monumental occasion. I can't wait to hold my son for the first time and that's all it takes for any lingering guilt to disappear over the choices I had to make. It was them or my family–and there's no question who I would choose every time.

On the ride home, Sophia animatedly talks about everything she has planned for the nursery, the playground, and the activities. The crews have finished building the main house and we're moving in this weekend. Sophia wanted to wait until we knew for sure what we were having before she picked out a paint color for the nursery. Now that we know, our family home will be a reality.

"I'm taking you home and then I have to go into the office for a little while. I have some work that has to be done there. I'll be home this evening," I say before I kiss her hand.

"Don't be too long. I'm picking out names tonight. Without you, there's no telling what I'll choose!" she cautions.

"Don't you even start without me!"

"Then you'd better hurry home!" she beams at me.

Over the past month, I've hired a headhunter to conduct a private search for someone to replace me on a daily basis so I can step back from the frequent traveling and long days. During that time, I also hired an external auditor to comb through our financial data to make sure we're positioned to hire the best.

Cheryl left me an urgent voicemail to double check the data she highlighted from the completed audit. My expected "few hours" in the office has turned into another late night here as I check and recheck every fact and figure. I had only planned to pack up my personal belongings and the files I need over the next week or so, but so much for the best-laid plans.

The setting sun draws my attention to the scenic view outside and it reminds me of Sophia's comment about just enjoying spending time outside. Mentally chastising myself to reign my thoughts back into the task at hand so I can get home, I don't hear anyone in the hallway until he's already in my office.

"Dominic, my boy, what are you doing here so late?" Darren asks jovially.

"Hey Darren, I thought everyone was already gone. I'm just finishing up some things here before going home. What are you doing here so late?" I answer absently.

Darren walks to the other side of my office and pours two tumblers of bourbon. He places mine on my desk and takes a seat across from me. "You look like you could use a drink," Darren says.

"Yeah, I think you're right," I say as I pick up my glass.

"It's funny how things happen, isn't it? One day, you have everything figured out, then life throws a monkey wrench in all your plans and you think you're fucked again. But then, it just seems to all come together again in the end," he says cryptically.

Furrowing my brow and narrowing my eyes in confusion, I ask, "What do you mean, Darren? I'm not following you."

"Let me tell you a story. Humor an old man," Darren says as he gets up and closes my office door. I lean back in my chair, sensing I'm not going to like where this story ends.

"My youngest sister, Lex, was one of those *'oops'* babies. She was born the year I graduated from high school. She was a complete surprise to my parents, you see, but she quickly became our favorite. As my only sibling, I was more than protective of her–she was more like my own child rather than my sister.

"She got married young and had a baby. My niece, Hope, was more like one of my granddaughters. I doted on her all the time. She was so much like her mom. Full of life, big heart, beautiful soul, and she was gorgeous. She graduated high school at the top of her class and had a bright future ahead of her," he pauses, overcome with emotion.

*Was? Had?* I can't voice the question stuck in my head. *Why is everything in the past tense?*

"When I first met Sophia, I felt like the breath had been knocked out of me. She reminds me so much of my Hope that it hurts to even be around her. Honestly, that's the main reason why I sent her back to work with you. It was just more than I could bear.

"Anyway, I digress. Hope went off to college and got mixed up with the wrong boy. You know teenagers, they think they know everything and anyone older than them is just *'out of touch,'* so of course she wouldn't listen to reason when I tried to tell her. He was all hyped up on drugs and into things he shouldn't be into, but she was in love and defended him.

"She got in the car with him one night and he was too drunk and high to drive. When he wrecked the car that night, he killed our Hope," he pauses as he reflects on what he just said. "You know, saying that out loud, it resonates even more with me. He killed our *hope* in more ways than one."

"Darren, I had no idea. I'm so sorry. Why didn't you tell me when this happened? If I'd known that it was so hard on you, I would've never agreed to have Sophia report to you. I feel like I added to your grief." I never knew any of this and now I feel like an ass for not realizing he wasn't acting the same sooner.

"Don't blame yourself for that, Dominic," he replies. "I've helped support Lex financially for the last seven years since her husband passed, but she always worked and contributed. But, she just hasn't been able to go back to work after losing Hope going on two years ago. Money has been tight for my own family, and in some rash decisions, I made a few bad investments that has really cost me. My wife, my sister, and I are all about to lose everything we have.

"I came across something interesting while I was researching ways to make my money back. You authorized a life insurance policy on yourself, payable to DPS, upon your death to ensure the company keeps going. Having that money would solve all of my problems at once."

*No, surely not.*

"When I realized exactly who Sophia was, the stars just seemed to magically align right over my head. Her brother was involved with the drug cartel in Austin and his best friend was the cartel boss's son. Her crazy ex-boyfriend had started all kinds of trouble for both of you. Those connections were perfect to take any suspicion off of me," he says ominously, but his eyes have glassed over and I'm not sure if he's talking to me or to himself now.

"Suspicions of what, Darren?"

"Your death, Dominic," he replies, his tone holds a hint of astonishment that I haven't already figured this out. "Shawn and Ramon tried more than once to make it look like a tragic accident, but you just wouldn't cooperate. When you survived the car wreck, I wasn't too surprised. Those two idiots couldn't pull off something that sophisticated.

"But, when you got out of the burning house after being drugged, I just couldn't believe it. I thought I'd lose everything I've worked my whole life to obtain. Shawn outlived his usefulness when he figured out who I was. He wasn't going to live anyway. His fate was sealed the day he killed my Hope, he just didn't know it.

"Imagine my surprise when I found out that *Harrison* was also part of that same group, but he was a hit man for the cartel. I thought I'd been given another chance at redemption! Harrison and

Ramon together would surely be able to take you and Sophia out, right? There was already a clearly documented case between you, Sophia, Shawn, Harrison, and Ramon.

"It was the perfect scenario. All of you would die, the insurance policy would be paid to the company, and I would convince your grieving parents to give me control of DPS. Rich Daltry made an offhand remark about wishing he could acquire a company like DPS during one of our calls, and that gave me the idea of selling DPS for hundreds of millions, and walk away with more than I ever imagined.

"But you killed them both, despite the odds. You and Sophia both lived through it all! How can that be? A lowlife thug took Hope from us. My sister can barely function now. My wife and I are about to lose everything. But, you and your little pregnant whore have it all–even after she betrayed you!

"So, I have to take this into my own hands," he says calmly. Too calmly. "Your death will look like a cartel retaliation for you killing three of their own, most importantly the boss's son."

"Three?" I ask.

"Harrison, Ramon, and Shawn."

"You killed Shawn?"

"Of course. I just told you–he outlived his usefulness." He removes a gun from inside his jacket and levels it at me. "Let's go to the parking garage. I don't want to answer more questions about how someone got past security here."

"You helped Ramon get in here," I say, realization setting in.

"Yes, that was all part of Harrison's agreement. He wanted you to be publicly shamed for his sister's death when your office was packed up after your death. He really wasn't that bright, but he was intent on destroying you in every way possible. Now, move."

Slowly walking to the door, I ask him, "Why didn't you just tell me you needed help, Darren? You know I'd help you."

"I was going to, Dominic, until I realized that you were sleeping with the enemy's sister. I've really been conflicted over Sophia's fate because her personality reminds me so much of Hope. But, at the end of the day, it all comes down to family. Hope is my family. Besides, if Sophia's left alive, your parents will want to give the company to her and your baby. That means the cartel will retaliate against her, too."

"You mean you will kill a defenseless, pregnant woman, who reminds you of your loved one," I clarify, hoping the bluntness will shake his resolve.

"Family, Dominic. It's all about family."

*Yes, it is.*

When I open my office door, I know we're not alone.

# Chapter Twenty-Five

### *Sophia*

"Something is wrong, I can feel it. Please go check on him," I beg Shadow. "Dominic told Tucker to stay with me in case of an emergency while I'm pregnant, so he won't leave me. I'm about to drive into downtown Dallas and check on him myself!"

"All right, little one. Let me see what I can do. You're just lucky I'm back in the area this week," he playfully chides me. "Where are you anyway?"

"I'm at the main house looking at color swatches for the nursery. Do you want me to meet you at the office?"

"No, ma'am. You stay put. Dominic would have my head if something is wrong and I put you in danger," Shadow laughs. "Leave it to me."

"Thank you, Shadow. Call me as soon as you can. Dominic isn't answering his phone. He wouldn't ignore repeated calls from me."

"No, he definitely wouldn't do that. Give me a few minutes. I'm not far from his office now."

We hang up and I pace the floor, not knowing what else to do. Over the past month, Shadow has called and checked on us a couple of times a week. We really became attached to him when he was here all the time and missed him when he left after *'the incident.'* I knew we couldn't keep him, but the big guy is really great to have around.

It's killing me to wait and do absolutely nothing. Pacing back and forth, wringing my hands, and looking at the clock every sixty seconds is not helping at all. "Tucker!" I yell as I jog down the hall.

He steps out from the kitchen doorway. "Are you okay?"

"No, something's wrong. I'm doing to Dominic's office. You can follow me if you can keep up or you can drive me."

"That's not a good idea, Sophia," Tucker says, but even he can't hide his concern for Dominic.

"Good idea or not, I'm going." I grab the keys and briskly walk to the garage door.

"Hang on," he says with resignation. "I'll drive."

I toss him the keys and we jump into the car. Tucker floors it when we turn on the main road. Time seems to stand still as we fly by the other cars. The miles are longer and longer the closer we get. The usual forty-minute drive might as well be a three-day cross-country excursion. Dominic still hasn't called me back and my imagination is running away with terrifying scenarios. This hasn't happened since the day I thought he'd been shot. I've had nothing but good thoughts and good feelings. But this just isn't like him, at all.

"Hurry, Tucker," I plead. "I'm sorry. I know you're doing all you can do. I'm just scared."

"I understand, Sophia. You don't need to apologize. We're almost there."

When the building is finally is sight, my heart is beating even faster than Tucker was driving. When we pull into the parking garage twenty minutes after we left the house, my pounding heart comes to a halt and tears spring to my eyes. I can't believe what I'm seeing. *No, God, please!*

An ambulance and several police cars are in the parking garage and their emergency lights are still going. The paramedics are rolling the stretcher toward the open door in the back and Dominic is lying motionless on the stretcher. Shadow is following closely behind them, his ear glued to his cell phone, and a cop is putting Darren Hardy in handcuffs. Tucker screeches to a stop and I jump out of the car in a mad dash to my Dom.

"Dominic!" My scream echoes through the empty parking garage.

Dominic's head jerks up off the stretcher in search of my voice. "Stop! Let me off this thing!" he demands.

He sits up and swings his legs over the side and that's when I see his blood-soaked shirt. I finally reach his side and all I want to do is wrap my arms around him, but I don't want to hurt him. "You're bleeding! What happened? Where are you hurt?"

"Calm down, love. You're scaring my son," he smiles. "I'm okay, thanks to Shadow."

"I knew something was wrong! What happened? Tell me," I demand, not feeling the whole submissive thing right now.

"Seems our friend Darren was behind most everything," he says and my mouth literally drops open. "Anyway, he came to my office tonight to finish what he started but he wanted to do it here in the garage to look like a cartel retaliation. He said he was coming after you, too, so he could get my company and the money. When I opened my office door, I saw Shadow hiding in Dana's closet."

"He only saw me because I *wanted* him to see me," Shadow clarifies.

"Anyway," Dominic grins and cuts his eyes to Shadow, "*when Shadow let me see him in the closet*, I made a break for it to get away from Darren. He fired his gun and it grazed my shoulder. Shadow's scared of you, Sophia, so he called an ambulance to take me to the hospital."

"She's scary as shit, man. You should've heard her on the phone earlier," Shadow replies and shivers exaggeratedly.

"Why do you think I insisted on driving here? Her driving is even more terrifying," Tucker chimes in.

I know what the guys are trying to do. They're trying to make the moment much less scary by being light-hearted and funny about it. And I love them for it.

"Very funny, guys," I say with a smile as I wipe the tears from my eyes. Looking at Shadow and Tucker, I add, "And thank you, both, so much."

Sitting on the stretcher beside Dominic, I peek inside his shirt to see the wound. "You should go on to the hospital and let them check that. At least let them clean it so it doesn't get infected."

"Okay, but I'm riding with you and Tucker. No need for an ambulance."

"I need just a minute, Dominic," I say as I make eye contact with Darren.

"Sophia, don't," Dominic says softly, his eyes silently asking me to comply.

"I need to say something to him, Dominic." Waiting for his nod out of respect, I lean over and kiss him before I get up. "Thank you."

Slowly walking over to the police car where Darren's just been frisked, I stop when I get directly in front of him but stay out of his reach, just in case. "You knew I didn't have much of a family life, how I lost my parents and my brother when I was younger, and how that hurt me. You told me once that I reminded you of your niece and you talked about how much you loved and missed her. How could you disgrace her memory like this? How could she be proud of the man you've become?"

His face falls as my words take root in his mind. I turn my back to him and walk away before he has a chance to respond. There's nothing he can say that would make up for this now. He tried to kill the love of my life– the man who is my whole life –and then he was going to kill our baby and me. And for what? Money?

Dom is standing now, watching Darren with an alarming intensity as I put him behind me and set my eyes on my future. There's a veiled warning in

Dom's eyes that I think Darren completely understands.

"What is it, Dom?" I ask, knowing there's always more to the story than what he told me.

Dom looks over the top of head and locks eyes with Darren again. When I turn around and look at Darren, he opens and closes his mouth a few times as if he wants to say something, but he's too ashamed. Dom wraps his arm around me protectively and possessively.

"Sophia," Dom says softly as he leans his mouth to my ear. "This won't be easy for you to hear."

I brace myself, tightly gripping Dom's arm that's around me, covering our baby, but I can't tear my eyes from Darren's. Whatever Dom is about to say, I have a feeling it involves what Darren said to him. The cop stands behind Darren, holding his handcuffed hands to make him listen. Holding my breath, I wait for Dom to continue.

"The girl that died in the wreck Shawn had was Darren's niece, Hope. Sophia," he pauses, his voice full of dread and pain, "Darren murdered Shawn."

The screams and tears come simultaneously as I'm overcome with sorrow. I know I'm shouting *'NO!'* over and over, but no other words come to me. NO–he can't be dead. NO–he can't be gone. NO–we never reconciled. NO–he is only nineteen.

Just. NO.

Dominic is holding me up, as he's always done and as he will always do. He is my rock, my shelter, and my white knight in a cold, black world. He cradles me in his arms and comforts me, letting me feel everything and deal with it in my own way. Darren watches with tears streaming down his face. He took my brother's life in revenge for his niece, thinking only of the suffering his family has endured. It's only now that, as he watches the grief consume me, he realizes Shawn also had a family who loves and misses him, regardless of his mistakes.

"Get him out of here, Officer Jordan." Shadow says with a cup to the officer's shoulder, showing his gratitude.

"You got it, big guy," the officer responds and pushes Darren's head down as he gets in the backseat of the cruiser.

Shadow walks over to me, his eyes full of compassion. "I'm so sorry, little one," he says as he wraps his big arms around me. I squeeze him hard, conveying my gratitude for everything he's done for us and step back into Dom's arms. "Let's get Dominic to the hospital to be checked out now."

Hours later, we're back home after Dominic's shoulder injury has been thoroughly X-rayed, cleansed, stitched, and bandaged. They said he will be sore for a while, especially the next few days, but it really was "only" a flesh wound. Now I have the horrendous task of calling my parents to tell them their son is gone.

*Gone.* I overheard a couple of paramedics talking with the nurses in the emergency room while Dominic and I waited. One of the paramedics said they were trained to never use the words *gone, passed away, passed on*, or anything like that when delivering the worst news a family can hear. They're trained to say *dead* so that there's no confusion, no misunderstanding, and no hope.

*He's dead.*

"Do you want me to help you?" Dominic asks. There's no need for elaborating, we both know what he means.

"Just be there with me?" I ask as my voice breaks.

"Of course, baby."

Opening FaceTime on my MacBook, I call my Dad's cellphone. It's late, way too late for them to be up, but I can't hold this news until morning. After a few rings, Dad's sleepy face fills the window. "Sophia? Dominic? Are you two okay? What's going on?"

When the phone rings at nearly three in the morning, it's never with good news. "Hi Dad," I say, now comfortable with calling him that again. "I hate to wake you but this can't wait until morning. Is Mom up?"

"I'm here, honey. What's wrong, Sophia?" Mom replies as Dad extends his arm so I can see them both now.

Taking a deep breath, the tears streaming down my face, and Dominic's arms wrapped around me from behind, I look into my parents' eyes and tell them that Shawn is dead. We cry together as I recount the details of the evening and Dominic fills in the blank spots for us. After talking and crying for the last thirty minutes, we disconnect with promises to try to get some rest and talk again later.

We all need time to process this.

Dominic made sure that Shawn's funeral was beautiful. No expense was spared as he tried to help us find closure and come to terms with the gaping hole left in our lives. Mom and Dad wanted him buried in Dallas, close to Dominic and me, because they plan to move here with us soon.

Dominic's parents and his sisters, Emma and Stephanie, also came in a show of emotional support. Kayla and Rick hugged Dominic and me a little longer than usual after the funeral ended.

Tucker was with us, too. He told Dominic that the cartel would probably try to retaliate against him for killing the boss's son and two other members. Shadow's contacts are staying close to the situation and keeping him updated on what's happening. Dominic and I talked about it and made a decision that life is too short and too precious to live scared all the time. Whatever happens, we'll deal with when we have to. For now, we're focusing on the good.

Darren has been charged with pre-meditated murder for killing Shawn and attempted murder for shooting Dominic. There are other charges for the conspiracy to commit murder and arson. He's currently in the county jail awaiting trial. Dominic was concerned about his wife and his sister, so he set up trust funds for them both to live comfortably. If only Darren had just told Dominic to begin with, none of this would've happened.

We all made a trip to Shawn's apartment and packed up the few belongings he had left. In his room, on the nightstand next to his bed, was a note he'd written to me. It must have been written right after our meeting at the restaurant. He told me how much he loved me, missed me, and how sorry he was for how he'd treated me. The letter said that he was trying to find another way out of it, even if he had to kill Harrison himself to protect me. I consider that letter our reconciliation now and it's in a box with my most precious belongings.

The box is now at my new home with Dominic. My life. My love. My family. The weather has turned cooler and Thanksgiving will be here in another month. The best birthday present I could ever ask for is happening tonight–we've moved the last of our belongings to the newly built house. *We're home.*

"Are you ready to officially move in our new home, *My Angel*?" Dominic murmurs in my ear as we climb the front steps to the door.

I can't help but laugh at him. "Dominic, we've been here every day for the last two weeks, arranging furniture, decorating, and getting all the finishing touches done. What makes you think we haven't *officially* moved in yet?"

"Because now it's all completed and this is the first time we've unlocked the door to our new, completed home!" he explains, as if that makes all the sense in the world.

"Okay, if you say so, Dom," I concede in mock surrender.

"Oh, your Dom says so," he replies with that wonderfully wicked gleam in his eye.

Dominic sticks the key in the front door, turns the lock, and opens the door for me to enter first. When I walk into the great room, my breath is taken away. I can't believe my eyes and I'm shocked at the lengths that even Dominic has gone to this time just to surprise me.

The room is pitch black except for the blanket of stars across the ceiling. The tiny, white lights are suspended from the ceiling, casting a soft candlelight glow onto everything. Slow music is playing softly from the surround sound speakers. As I step fully into the room, I notice the red carpet that creates a path from the great room to the kitchen. On either side of the path is a row of staggered luminaries that have been suspended from the ceiling. Each one has a different letter cut out that's illuminated by the candle inside.

Adorning every open space the room and along the lighted path are vases upon vases full of the most gorgeous red long-stem roses I've ever seen. The fragrance in this room alone smells finer than the most extravagant florist. All of my senses are on overload– sight, sound, smell, touch, -and if the aroma wafting on the air from the kitchen is any indication, taste is next.

"Oh, Dominic, it's beautiful! I can't believe you went to all this trouble! You really didn't have to do this for me," I ramble, but I love that he did this for me.

One side of his mouth lifts as he tries to contain his smile. "*My Angel*, take a few steps back and tell me what the luminaries say."

Doing as he asks, I take a couple of steps back. I start at the beginning and call out the letters. "M- A –R –R – Y – M – E."

My head is spinning and my heart is pounding out of my chest. Surely I misread that. Staring at the candlelit lettering, I go over them once, twice, three more times in my mind. *He's asking me to marry him?*

Whirling around to face him, I find him knelt down on one knee with a small, velvet box in his outstretched hand. "Sophia Michelle Vasco, you've been the master of my heart from the moment I met you. If you say yes, I will gladly surrender it to you for the rest of our lives. Will you marry me?"

Gripped by shock, I can only stare at him for a few seconds. He takes the opportunity to open the box and display my engagement ring. The candlelight reflects off the diamond solitaire, showing off its brilliance and sparkle. Even as big and beautiful as it is, the diamond ring doesn't hold a candle to the man holding it.

"Yes," I say softly, "yes, Dominic. I will marry you." The full weight of the moment finally sinks it and I shriek, *"YES! I WILL MARRY YOU!"*

My heart is already so full of love and happiness that only my Dom can give me, and then he does something like this and completely lifts me up to a whole new level. I can't live without this man, who is more than I could've ever dreamed up. He slips the ring on my finger and stands up to kiss me. His kiss is never just a simple kiss, though, and soon we're on the thick, throw rug in front of the fireplace. He makes sweet love to me and repeatedly refers to me as the "future Mrs. Powers."

When we finally make it to the kitchen, I am famished and we enjoy an intimate, candlelit dinner. Feeding each other and enjoying our time alone, this is a moment I want to hold onto forever.

"One more thing," he says with a smile. "Happy Birthday, *My Angel*." He pulls a beautifully wrapped box from underneath the table.

When I open the box, I'm floored again at his thoughtfulness. Pulling out the gift certificate and artwork pamphlet, I unfold it on the table between us and gasp. "It's beautiful, Dominic! I love it! Where?"

"Come with me," he says with an excited smile. He leads me to the main staircase and points to the bare wall. "Right here."

The gift certificate is from a local, well-known artist who will come to our home and paint a large family tree on our staircase. Every member of our family has a place on the tree and in our home. Standing with our arms wrapped around the other, we envision and plan for the tree, how many children will adorn the limbs, and where our parents and siblings will go.

"Dominic," I say hesitantly. There's something I feel I should do, but I don't want my request to douse his excitement. "I have an idea. Don't say no right away–take as much time as you need to think about it first. Promise?"

Tilting his head to the side, he studies me for a few seconds, "Promise, love. Let's hear it."

"I think you should give your baby with Carol Ann a name and memorialize it here."

He wraps his arms around me, fully embracing me and pulling me tightly to him. Kissing the side of my hair, he whispers softly into my ear, "You are the most amazing woman. I love your idea, Sophia, and I love you more than life itself." His quiet sniffle is the only clue I have to how much it affects him.

# Epilogue

## *Sophia*

Today's the big day! I'm so nervous, and excited, and nervous, and thrilled, and nervous.

"I can't do this," I say, letting my nerves get the best of me.

"It's a little too late to back out now, babe," Dominic chuckles in response.

"No, I think I want to stay like this. I'm good. We're good, right?"

"Nope. Time to move forward with our lives together. There's no going back, remember?"

His words take me back to our wedding night when we christened our new playroom. The whole day was absolute perfection. We had a small, intimate wedding with only our closest family and friends in attendance. Kayla and Rick brought Dominic's sisters, Emma and Stephanie, with them. They are both beautiful and fun to be around. We instantly clicked and I have two new best friends now.

My parents have moved to Dallas to get away from the cartel. Shadow helped them severe the ties by changing their names and helping them disappear. Dominic gave my dad a job in his security department at DPS, so they've both been around a lot more. Of course, Dana, Christine, Tucker, and Shadow were also there to celebrate our lifetime commitment with us.

Our nighttime Christmas wedding was held inside our new home, in the very room where Dominic proposed to me. My Dad gave me away to Dominic, Emma was my maid of honor and Tucker was Dominic's best man. The enormous Christmas tree, that Dominic insisted we buy since it was our first together, stood proudly beside the fireplace as we exchanged our vows.

Dominic's vows to me brought tears to my eyes. "Every day, you'll feel my love for you. It lives, breathes, and grows stronger every day. I freely give all of myself to you forever. I'll go to the ends of the earth and back to give you what you need, what you want, and whatever makes you happy."

"Dominic, all the best memories I have are with you. I promise to give you all my best for the rest of my life. My love, my heart, my thoughts, and my dreams start and end with you. From this day forward, my world revolves around you. I am yours forever."

We exchanged matching wedding bands that we picked out together but each had secret inscriptions made. His ring read, "I am Her Dom." My ring read, "I am His Angel." We both laughed when we read them, knowing that we're so connected now there really is no going back.

Then we posed for pictures in front to the lit tree and in front of the family tree that has been beautifully venerated in our home. The words we spoke to each other in our vows have been added to the family wall, at the roots of the tree. They are a constant, visual reminder of the promises we made to each other and how those promises ground us, bind us, and make us stronger.

The family tree Dominic gave me for my birthday has become sacred to us both, so it was important that it was included in our wedding photographs. The symbolism of family it represents strengthens us every day. All of our family holds a special place on it and in our lives. Dominic chose to name his unborn baby Cameron Powers, since it can be for either a girl or a boy, though he says he feels like it was a girl. Cameron's place is lovingly displayed on our family tree and I think Dominic is at peace with what we now consider her final resting place. But here, she will always be with her family. She will always be next to her brother, Hunter Devan Powers.

After our family dinner, we retreated to the playroom for the first time. Even though we've lived in the house since the night he proposed, he wanted our first night with the new toys to be our first night as man and wife. Even with my seven-month pregnant protruding belly, his eyes told me I was the most beautiful woman he'd ever seen. His touch said that even after a lifetime together, he'd still never get enough of me.

His flogger, bullwhip, restraints, and clamps each had their own story to tell. Each of their stories all ended the same, though–with me screaming his name in pleasure, over and over again. Since some positions are just too uncomfortable, and even somewhat dangerous for the baby, Dominic and I have made good use of the new love swing he installed many, many times. It gives him complete control of my body–and he loves that.

He promised me, in a somewhat Dominant/threatening way, that once I've healed from the delivery, every piece of equipment in the playroom will be utilized to its fullest potential. That promise gave me tingles!

Which brings me back to the present moment in late February and the excruciating pain in my lower back as another labor pain hits me. Gripping Dominic's hand in mine as I wait for the contraction to subside, he winces in pain along with me.

"That bad?" he asks, obviously concerned for me.

"Yeah, that bad," I reply on an exhaled breath. "It's stopped for now. Let's time it until the next one."

Dominic is driving us to the hospital in the dark of the early morning hours. I woke him up around one o'clock this morning when the pains started and they've progressively gotten stronger. We're approaching the hospital now and Dominic is still as calm, cool, and in control as he always is.

Me? Not so much. Back to my original argument. "I can't do this, Dominic! I'm scared! I can just stay pregnant."

"I'm all for doing what it takes to keep you pregnant, Sophia. Just not always with this baby. He's coming out to meet us. Today," Dominic replies, way too happy and excited for my current condition.

"Here comes another one!" I strain to say, as the contractions get stronger.

"That one was closer–three minutes apart," he says as he pulls into the hospital parking garage. Thankfully, there are parking spots close to the door since I've already told him he's not dropping me off at the door and leaving me alone.

Walking in through the emergency room entrance since it's still really early, and really dark, and the main entrance is locked. When the triage nurse looks up at me, she smiles and calls for a wheelchair to take me to the labor and delivery floor.

*Oh my god, this is really happening! I'm about to have a baby!*

The labor and delivery staff know what they're doing, I have to give them that. I'm changed into a hospital gown, have a fetal monitor strapped around me, and my charge nurse even twisted my doctor's arm to let me have an epidural early so I don't have to wait around in pain all day.

***Dominic***

My family members, Sophia's parents, Tucker and Shadow are waiting outside our room. It may be selfish, but after all we've been through together, Sophia and I wanted this time, this special moment, to be only the two of us. We will invite the rest of the family in after we've had time alone with our son. The nurse walks in to make her standard round and check on Sophia's progress. Before I know what's happening, the hospital bed is transformed into a birthing bed, and everything is moving so quickly.

"What's happening?" I ask, confused as to how I can help.

"She's dilated to ten centimeters and the head is crowning. You're about to meet your baby," the nurse says with a smile.

I'm more excited than a kid on Christmas morning. The love of my life is about to share the best gift she could possibly give me.

"But everything I read said the first baby would take longer, even more than day, before the actual delivery!" Sophia exclaims and the fear overtakes her beautiful face.

Moving beside her, I take her hand and softly kiss each knuckle. The nurse replies, "Everyone is different, sweetie. Some women can be in active labor for several days. As long as her water hasn't broken and the baby isn't in distress, we'll try to let her have it naturally. Other women only have a few hours notice once labor starts."

Sophia looks up at me, her eyes wide, but then she realizes the date. "Oh, Dominic! He'll be born on *your* birthday!"

I give her my full-on smile in return. "I was actually just thinking about how you're trying to one-up the birthday gift I gave you."

She laughs, noticeably relaxing now. "I love you, Dominic. I'm scared but I'm more excited than anything."

"Ready to meet our son?" I ask her before leaning in to kiss her.

"I'm ready."

After the nurse has everything in the room prepped and ready to go, the doctor strolls in and takes her seat at the end of the transformed bed. Sophia's legs are up in the stirrups as she checks her and confirms that she's ready to push. Taking my place at her side, I coach, encourage, and help her in every way I know how. When she has to lean forward to push, I help hold her up. When she lies back again, I wipe the sweat from her brow and tell her how amazing she is.

"Here we go, Sophia," Dr. Perry says. "Last push before you get to meet your baby boy. Give me all you've got."

Leaning forward, Sophia bears down, holds her breath, and pushes with all her might. Her face is strained and red, her breathing nonexistent at the moment, and her eyes are determined. This is it. This is the last one. We're about to hold our baby in our arms for the very first time.

I don't know how to hold a baby. Shit. I don't know how to hold a baby!

"Here he is!" Dr. Perry exclaims as our baby makes his entrance into this world. The nurse rushes over to wipe him off and the doctor looks up at me. "Dad, do you want to cut the cord?"

"Yes," I stumble over a simple, one-syllable answer.

Taking the scissors from the doctor after she clamps off the cord, I cut the cord in the center, severing the physical tie to Sophia. The nurse whisks him away to quickly wash him off, weigh him, and wrap him in a baby blanket. Within ninety seconds flat, he is swaddled in the blanket and being placed into my arms.

It is the most natural thing I've never done before–holding my son, cradling him close to my chest, talking to him as I take the few steps back to Sophia. I inhale his sweet baby scent, rub my nose over his soft baby skin, and place my lips on his plump baby cheek.

"Sophia, are you ready to meet our son?" I say as I place him in her arms.

She looks down at him and tears of elation flow down her beautiful cheeks. "Hunter Devan Powers, welcome to our little family. Your Daddy and Mommy love you so much," she whispers.

Wrapping my arms around Sophia and Hunter, I'm overwhelmed with love and pride. Of all the accomplishments I've had in my life, this is by far my greatest. The nurse takes my phone and takes several pictures of us together as a family for the first time. This is my life. This is my world. This is my love. It's all about family. I'm all about my family.

She is *My Angel*. I am Her Dom. This will never be over.

*The End*

# About the Author

A.D. Justice is happily married to her husband of 25 years. They have two sons together and enjoy a wide variety of outdoor activities. A.D. has a full-time job by day, with a BS degree in Organizational Management and an MBA in Health Care Administration. Writing gives her the outlet she needs to live in the fantasy world that is a constant in her mind.

Thank you for reading and supporting A.D.'s books! Please take a moment to leave a review of this work. You can find her online at:

Facebook: https://www.facebook.com/adjusticeauthor

Twitter: https://twitter.com/ADJustice1

Web: www.adjusticebooks.com

Email: adjustice@outlook.com

Made in the USA
Charleston, SC
25 March 2015